The Winterkeeper

by

Anna Schmidt

Do what you can, with what you have,
where you are...Theodore Roosevelt

BUCKET LINE BOOKS LLC

Printed in the United States of
America

First Printing, 2019

ISBN 978-1-7337227-1-1

Bucket Line Books LLC

www.booksbyanna.com

For

Larry

Acknowledgments

Kathryn McKee, Special Collections Curator,

Yellowstone Historic Center [& Research Lifesaver]

Marsha Zinberg, Editor Extraordinaire

Natasha Kern, Agent and Dear Friend

He was a winterkeeper in the vast untamed land known as Yellowstone. The first time Millie saw him he was wearing baggy wool pants, a heavy canvas jacket frayed at the cuffs and collar and a faded plaid wool hat with earflaps. He was average in height and built solid, like the densely packed snow he dealt with day after day over the long Yellowstone winter. His hair and beard were sprinkled with gray but were mostly the brown of black coffee. His eyes were the cerulean blue of a clear summer sky, and his face was tanned and furrowed by the weather. But the thing she remembered most about him was that he listened more than he talked, and in 1933, when she was fourteen, that was exactly what she needed most.

Millie

-1-

Gardiner, Montana--March 1933

At her mother's funeral, fourteen-year-old Millie Chase stood shivering in the snow-covered graveyard and watched as workmen lowered the casket into the hole they'd managed to carve out of the frozen earth. A furry frost had already formed on the dirt walls. The minister said some words about dust to dust, but Momma wasn't dust.

She was a woman who strangers turned around to stare wherever she went. Looking at her made other people smile, and she always smiled back. She might even stop and talk to the person—ask what kind of work they did or give them some compliment about how the outfit they were wearing was bringing out the color of their eyes. People always seemed to feel better after they'd been with Millie's mother--even for just a couple of minutes.

"Millie, just because our family has been blessed to enjoy the finer things in life," Momma used to say, "that doesn't mean any person you meet is any less valuable. Never forget that."

At the church service, Millie had seen her laid out on the white satin lining of the casket. She wore a lavender dress better suited for summer and somebody had put too much lipstick on her. Millie had resisted the urge to use the handkerchief she carried to blot it away. Nobody had asked for her opinion on what her mother might want to wear, but Millie knew she never would have chosen that dress.

Now as the minister took a step closer to the open grave and bowed his head, an icy wind whipped strands of straight brown hair against her cheeks, which had turned raw with the cold. Others followed his lead, but Millie just stared at that hole in the ground and the polished wood box with gilded handles that held the mother she would never see again.

Her father had been killed in battle during the war right before she was born. "The Great War," she'd heard it called, although she never understood what could possibly be great about any war. He was buried somewhere in Europe. Momma had always promised that one day the two of them would travel there and say a proper goodbye.

But then three years earlier—when Millie was eleven--Momma had married Roger Fitzgerald and pretty much seemed to forget about traveling to say goodbye to Millie's father. At first, she was okay, figuring Momma seemed so happy. Of course, that didn't last. She glanced up at Roger as he made a show of dabbing his eyes and then blowing his nose with a clean white handkerchief. She was not fooled, although it sure looked like others were. These last months while Momma got sicker and sicker, Roger had barely stopped by her room once a day. Now a woman Millie had seen at parties and suppers given by her mother and Roger touched his shoulder and then looped her hand through the crook of his elbow like she was staking her claim or something. Millie couldn't resist smirking and hiding a smile when Roger pulled free of the woman's grasp before stepping forward and dropping three red roses on Momma's casket.

He nodded to Millie, indicating she should do the same, then stood next to her while the other mourners tossed in small sprigs of juniper and sage. How come Roger didn't know Momma never liked red roses, she wondered. Never really cared for roses at all. But he'd ordered them special.

The cemetery sat on a hill that overlooked the town. Beyond the small cluster of buildings that were the shops and other businesses of Gardiner, Millie could see the Roosevelt arch that marked the entrance to Yellowstone National Park. She could see the railroad station as well. She wondered if Roger would send her back to Chicago, where she and Momma had lived before they met him. But she had no relatives there any more—and as far as she knew, neither did he, so probably not.

They stayed until the cemetery workers started to fill the hole, the dirt pelting Momma's casket like last night's icy snowstorm had tapped at Millie's bedroom window. Afterwards, she had little choice but to go back to Roger's house. As far as she was concerned, he wasn't even her stepfather—just a man Momma had married, so what was she supposed to do now?

As they walked away from the grave, Roger placed his large hand on her back and steered her toward the shiny black car that reminded her of pictures of tanks she'd seen. Gus, his chauffeur, saw them coming and opened the rear door. After they entered, he closed it with a firm click. Nobody else in Gardiner had a chauffeur, but apparently Roger felt he needed somebody to drive him around because he was this bigshot businessman.

Millie wasn't sure what he did exactly, just that Momma had said he was going to get a government contract and make a lot of money. That's why they'd moved to Gardiner. He had an office where he went every day, and Momma had told Millie he bought businesses that were struggling, brought them back to life and then sold them for a lot of money. Back in Chicago after they were first married, Momma had been real proud of Roger, making him out to be some kind of hero. But Millie realized she hadn't heard her talk much about that since they'd moved to Montana.

As Gus drove away, Millie twisted around and craned her neck to see the grave and the few mourners still gathered there, talking to each other like they would if they were in a shop downtown. Nobody was watching as the cemetery workers continued shoveling dirt to fill the grave. *Couldn't anybody even wait to see her fully buried?*

"Sit still," Roger snapped. He lit a cigar and blew out a stream of foul smoke before picking up the folded afternoon edition of the newspaper left for him on the seat. Millie scooted as close as possible to the door, making herself small so he might forget she was even there.

It didn't take long to make the trip from the cemetery to the three-story house on the hill, the largest house in Gardiner. It was the kind of house Millie had seen pictured in books about fairy tales—the house where the evil witch resided—the house to avoid passing by crossing to the other side of the street. It was late in the afternoon and every window glowed with light, the way Roger liked it. He'd bought the place right after moving the family to Gardiner from Chicago. Millie remembered asking Momma how come just about everything was changing. How come Roger's business was all of a sudden in Montana instead of in Chicago? Had he run out of failing businesses to buy back there? It sure seemed to her like, with all the closed and boarded up shops all over the city, there were still places that could use some help.

But they moved to Gardiner, and Millie remembered him telling Momma how he hated coming home to a dark house. She'd gotten the message and always made sure every lamp in every room on every floor was on as the sun set.

Of course, now Momma wasn't there, so it must have been the housekeeper, Clara, who had made sure the lamps were all lit. The people who had been at Momma's funeral were supposed to come back to the house after. Millie had seen Clara and a couple of other women hired to help her preparing a lot of food, setting up chairs and polishing glasses and silver serving dishes before she and Roger left for the church. Clara didn't even get to come to the service to say a proper goodbye.

"What's that?" Roger rattled his newspaper and leaned toward Millie as he stared out the window on her side. He spoke in that voice he used when he was about to explode. It had fooled Millie and Momma early on—that voice. It wasn't loud or even mad. No, it sounded like he was just asking. But now Millie knew, so she sat as still as possible. She followed his gaze and saw a single candle burning in the upstairs tower window that had been Momma's room. No other light in that room—just a flickering flame.

Gus pulled the car to the curb and got out. He glanced up at the window before coming around to open the door for Roger and followed him up the walk, leaving the car door open. "I guess Clara thought maybe…"

"Clara is fired," Roger said. "Now get somebody up there to get rid of that damned candle and turn on a proper light."

They both seemed to have forgotten all about Millie, so she stayed where she was, trying to figure out her next move. She hadn't lived in Gardiner long enough to make many friends, and once Momma started getting sick, she always rushed home from school to see if she was any better and keep her company. For her whole life up to now, it was just Momma and her—even after Roger came along, and truth be told, Millie liked that fine. She just wished they could go back to how things used to be.

Before Momma married Roger, they had lived in Chicago where they had a nice house, plenty of money, and lots of friends. Momma's parents owned a bunch of hotels and when they died, the hotels were sold, and Millie heard

Momma's friend and lawyer tell Momma that she'd never have to worry about money ever again. But then right around the time she met Roger, stuff started to happen. Millie didn't really understand it but knew there was something to do with banks and the stock markets and such. She also knew that Momma was worried. Then one night while they were still in Chicago, Momma went to a party. Roger was there. Millie sometimes thought theirs was what the movie magazines called a whirlwind romance because not six weeks later, Momma and Roger were married.

At first Roger moved into the house with them. Then one day, Momma told Millie the house was going to be sold and they would be moving to their "new life" in Montana. She seemed happier than she'd been in some time, so Millie was okay with it—at first. She wasn't crazy about Roger, but then he didn't seem all that fond of her either. Momma assured them both that in time they would be "head over heels" for each other.

Well, that sure never happened.

Things went along all right for a while, but then just a couple of months after they moved, Momma and Roger started arguing--shouting at each other. Best Millie could figure out, Roger had taken some of the money left by her grandparents and lost it.

"That's not your money," she heard Momma tell him one night. She had taken to sitting at the top of the curved stairway that wound itself up from the fancy first floor to the second, where their bedrooms were, and on to the third, where her room was.

"We're married, in case you've forgotten," she heard Roger respond.

"That money belongs to Millie," Momma shouted. Millie had never heard her so upset. "It's for her education—her future. We've already lost so much, Roger, and who knows how long this recession will last? You had no right…"

And then Millie heard something that sounded like a crack, followed by a silence so scary, she was all the way down to the second-floor landing when she saw her mother leave the front room, holding her cheek. She didn't make it three steps before Roger grabbed her arm, twisted it hard behind her back and pulled her close, so his face was right next to hers. "Don't ever walk out on me," he said.

That was the first time Millie had heard that voice. And although it was not the last time she saw bruises on Momma's arm or neck, she never saw or heard Momma stand up to Roger again. Of course, it was just a few months after that night that she started to get sick. And once she did, at least Roger didn't hurt her any more.

Now Millie watched from the back seat of the car as Roger and Gus entered the house, leaving the front door wide open in spite of the cold. She heard Roger giving out orders and saw people rushing around. A few seconds later, the candle went dark and lights came on in Momma's room.

With Momma gone, along with both sets of grandparents and her Dad, it would be just her and Roger and the servants. But he'd fired Clara and she was the one Momma had told Millie she could lean on. She was just about to get out of the car and go around to the back door to go inside so she could avoid Roger when she saw Clara hurry down the driveway, clutching her purse and a paper shopping bag.

Millie scrambled from the car and chased after her, the patent leather shoes Roger had insisted Clara buy as part of her outfit for the funeral slipping and sliding on the skim of ice that had formed on the recently shoveled sidewalk. "Clara!"

Clara looked back at Millie, then up at the house and hurried on. "Wait!" Millie tried to catch up, but Clara waved her off and quickened her step. Her boots gave her traction and she was able to put distance between them before Millie could catch up to her.

Millie stood there watching the housekeeper hurry away. She had no idea where Clara lived.

"Millie, he wants you inside." She hadn't heard Gus come after her, but now he put his arm around her shoulders and guided her back toward the house. "People will be coming soon," he added, and the way he said it, Millie thought he meant it to make her feel better.

It didn't.

An hour later, the house was full of Roger's friends--people Millie didn't really know. Since they'd moved to Montana, Momma had lost touch with pretty much everybody they used to know back in Chicago. They never came to visit, and Millie and her mother had only gone back once, the Christmas just after they had moved away. Now with Momma's dying a few days ago, everything was happening so fast Millie wasn't even sure if anybody had told her Chicago friends.

Once inside, she stood with Roger while a line of strangers touched her face or stroked her hair and told her how beautiful Momma was—as if she didn't know that. After a while, nobody was paying her any mind, so she climbed the stairs. The door to Momma's room was half-open, and she went in, closing it behind her. The first thing she did was turn off the overhead light, leaving only the small bedside lamp lit. Momma hated that ceiling light— said it hurt her eyes. She sat down at the dressing table and lined up the bottles of perfume, lotions and rouge pots. In the mirror, she saw the closet door ajar, Momma's clothes hanging in perfect alignment—the way Roger liked. Roger had his own room down the hall, but Millie knew he came to Momma's room several nights a week before she got sick to have what Clara had told her were "relations."

Clara had blushed beet red and drawn her lips into a tight line as if she had just eaten a sour pickle, before adding, "And that, young lady is all you need to know."

Millie walked to the closet and sat on the floor, scooting back until she was surrounded by the scent of Momma that clung to her clothes. She unbuckled the patent leather shoes and kicked them off, then pulled Momma's favorite fur coat from its satin hanger and made a sort of nest for herself. Downstairs, she could hear her stepfather laughing, and someone was playing Momma's grand piano—the only thing Roger had agreed to let her bring from the house in Chicago. Whoever was playing it wasn't nearly as good as Momma was.

2

Next thing Millie knew, it was morning, and with Clara gone and Momma dead, she understood no one had come looking for her because there really was no one left to care.

Crawling out from the closet, she saw by the clock on the bedside table that it was nearly nine. Hopefully Roger would have left for his office and she'd have the whole day to figure out what came next. The one thing she had decided before falling asleep was that she would not live with Roger. She'd rather go to an orphanage.

I am an orphan, she thought. *Mildred—Millie— Chase has no parents, grandparents, aunts, uncles--family.*

The thought hit her like the punch Jeremy Turner, the class rebel, liked to deliver to her upper arm. Momma said Jeremy picked on her because he liked her. She wondered if Momma thought Roger hit her because he liked her, but she'd never asked.

She checked the hall outside Momma's room to be sure nobody was there, then ran up the stairs to her own room. At least no one was expecting her to be in school that day. After she'd changed out of her Sunday clothes into heavy socks, flannel-lined corduroy pants and a thick wool turtleneck sweater, she crept down the back stairs to the kitchen. Nan, the maid who came in twice a week, was drying and putting away the last of the dishes from the night before—a large punch bowl, glass platters and sterling serving spoons. Normally that would be Clara's job, but Clara was gone.

"You want some help?" Millie offered.

Nan glanced nervously toward the swinging door that led to the dining room. "Shhh. Your father is in there with his lawyer."

He's not my father, Millie wanted to say, but stayed silent as she edged closer to the door.

"Lavinia's will is ironclad, Roger," the lawyer was saying. "The estate goes to her daughter-- period."

"But the child is only what? Thirteen? Twelve?"

Fourteen, she was tempted to shout.

"She'll need guidance—a guardian to manage her investments," Roger continued, in that voice that promised an explosion was coming.

"Some time ago your wife appointed a Chicago woman—Virginia Baker—to serve in that capacity. The woman's brother-in-law was Lavinia's attorney— everything goes through his office."

"Never heard of her," Roger groused. Millie could hear him drumming his fat fingers on the table. After a minute he asked, "What happens to Lavinia's will if I adopt the kid?"

"That really won't change the terms of the will."

She jumped away from the door when she heard a crash and the breaking of glass and china. She didn't have to be in the room to know Roger had swept the dishes from the table with his forearm. It wasn't the first time. "Well, figure out something to make this happen, Alvin. What am I paying you for?"

"Look, Roger…"

"Nan! Get in here and clean up this mess," Roger bellowed. "And tell Gus to bring the car around."

Millie shrank back as Nan pressed a button that would signal Gus, then grabbed a broom and dustpan from the pantry and hurried past her. A minute later she heard the front door slam and shortly after that heard the growl of the car rolling down the driveway.

She assumed the lawyer had left as well, although there was nothing to really say that he had. She realized she hadn't eaten since lunch the day before, so she scrounged around the pantry. As she grabbed a handful of sugar cookies Clara had made and stored in a large glass container, she noticed the backpack, poncho and floppy canvas hat Momma wore the one time they'd visited nearby Yellowstone National Park. The garments were hanging on an old wooden coatrack in the corner of the pantry.

"Did I ever tell you I have a friend who lives right here in this park?" Momma had asked that summer day, as the two of them shared a picnic. She'd finally given up on getting Roger to go with them anywhere. Gus ate his lunch in the car, the motor idling. Roger didn't let Momma go anywhere unless Gus took her and stayed until she was ready to come home.

"Maybe we should go see her," Millie remembered suggesting. She knew Momma missed her friends and she was thrilled to hear one might live so close.

But Momma had just smiled. "Maybe. I really don't know if she's even here anymore. We sort of lost touch after..."

"But if she *is* still here..."

Momma had cupped Millie's cheek. "There were some hard feelings. Best let sleeping dogs lie," she'd said. Millie had no idea what that meant but she did know Momma didn't want to talk about her friend anymore.

She also knew Momma's friend had sent her a Christmas card with a return address of a post office box in the park. The card was addressed to their old Chicago address in the most beautiful handwriting Millie had ever seen. Momma read the message, clutched the card to her chest and cried. "Come summer," she told Millie, "we really have to go see Ginny."

But they never would—not now that Momma had died.

After she'd read the card, Momma had told Millie to put it in the drawer of the bedside table so she could answer it when she felt better. Like so many things she'd planned on doing that also never happened.

Stuffing another cookie in her mouth, Millie ran up the back stairs.

The card was still there. It was signed "Ginny" and wasn't that short for Virginia? And hadn't the lawyer said Momma had appointed Virginia Baker to take care of Millie? She stared at the return address—*Mrs. Nathan Baker*--and a post office box number. Maybe she could write to Ginny, let her know Momma had died, and maybe she might write back and say, "Come live with us." Clearly Ginny was married. Millie wondered if she had kids.

But sending a letter and getting an answer would take days—maybe a week or more. Even if the calendar said it was nearly April, the ground was still covered with several feet of snow, and Millie didn't even know if Ginny and her husband stayed in the park through the winter. From what Clara had told her, most everybody left. But the more she thought about it, the more it seemed like the best idea to go there—go to the park and try to find Ginny. And if not her, then some kindly ranger and his family who would take her in until Ginny could be told she was there.

I have a choice—not just staying with Roger, but maybe...

Millie folded the card, still in its envelope, and stuffed it into her pocket. Then she shoved the drawer to shut it, but it stuck. If she left it half-open and Roger saw it, he'd know somebody had been snooping. She pushed harder. But the drawer refused to budge, so she pulled it all the way out. A piece of dried yellowed tape trailed from the bottom.

Taking care not to disturb the contents, she raised the drawer above her head so she could see well enough to press down the tape. That's when she noticed the inside edges of the tape were fuzzy, as if they'd been holding something in place.

When she first got sick, Momma had asked her to read Nancy Drew mysteries aloud to her. Now she felt just like the amateur sleuth as she examined the drawer more carefully. Something had been taped to the bottom of that drawer and was now missing. What had it been and where was it now? And who had taken it?

Carefully, she removed the tape, so the drawer would fit. She remembered all the times during Momma's illness that her mother had assured her that despite the hardships others were living, Millie would never have to worry. Then she thought about the way Roger had been pushing his lawyer to find a way past Momma's will.

He wants the money—my money.

She turned and saw her reflection in the gold-framed full-length mirror where Momma used to stand when she was getting ready to go out. Stepping closer, she looked for any hint that one day she might become the beauty her mother had been. Throughout her life Momma had told Millie how much she looked like her father—a man Millie knew only through the photographs she'd been shown. He had a kind, smiling face with eyes that seemed to twinkle as they stared back at her. He had thick, brown hair and ears that stuck out a little like hers did, but he was still a stranger.

Millie wondered where that photograph was now. For that matter, she wondered what had happened to the albums Momma had shown her while telling stories of how her parents had met and fallen in love. Millie hadn't seen those albums since Momma got sick, and she recalled the day Clara had taken several boxes of things from Momma's room and carried them up to the attic. "To make room," had been her answer when Millie asked why.

Room for what? she remembered thinking, but she'd been more concerned about Momma. She'd gotten real sick real fast, forcing her to spend most of her time in bed. A doctor came and went. Millie heard him tell Roger he could find nothing to explain her weakness and need to sleep. *Malaise,* he'd called it, and later that day after Roger went to work Millie looked it up in the big dictionary in Roger's study. That was of little help. Words like sickness, unhappiness and melancholy did not explain why her sunny, laughing mother was not getting any better. But she assured herself that at least a person couldn't die of unhappiness. Although as it turned out, apparently Momma did.

The girl in the mirror stared back at her. She was gangly, skinny—all legs and arms that often seemed at odds with each other when it came to moving with anything like the grace Momma had. Momma's hair was a fairy-tale princess gold while hers was the mousy brown of the ugly step-sisters. Momma's short hair framed her face with ringlets and curls, while Millie's hung straight to the bottoms of her earlobes and had to be constantly hooked behind her ears to keep it out of her eyes. A *Buster Brown,* the lady in the beauty shop called it. Millie hated it. Who wanted to look like some character out of the funny papers?

She imagined Momma standing where she was now—recalling the way she'd studied every detail of her hair, make-up and whatever she had chosen to wear. Millie would sit on her bed, giving her opinion when Momma asked if Millie thought her lipstick was too dark or the seams of her silk stockings were crooked. Before she married Roger, she was never so nervous about her looks. Before Roger, she would dress quickly, with barely a glance at herself in the mirror.

In those days back in Chicago, no matter the occasion—a luncheon, a meeting of the hospital auxiliary, or a charity ball—she would send Millie into her closet for some detail she felt was needed to complete the outfit. "Millie, bring me that rose-colored silk scarf, please." And Millie would scurry to do her bidding. Those were her favorite times with Momma, because even after Roger came into the picture, those were times when she had Momma all to herself.

Millie stretched the hem of the turtleneck over her bony frame and turned the way Momma used to do to catch a glimpse of her backside. "Roger says satin makes me look fat," she'd heard her mother mutter one night before she started getting sick. "What do you think, Millie?"

She'd wanted to tell her she thought Roger was a turd and he was the one who was fat, but instead she pretended to consider the question.

Motioning for Momma to turn, Millie walked slowly around her. Then she asked her mother to spin around so the gown flared out around her legs. Millie took hold of her hands and twirled with her, and Momma laughed. She was so beautiful.

Tears leaked from the corners of Millie's eyes as the memory of Momma's reflection faded, replaced by the image of an ordinary fourteen-year-old girl staring out from the mirror. For a minute, Momma had been there—full of life. But she was gone. Millie was alone and she was so scared it felt like her insides were jumping around like those Mexican jumping beans Momma once brought back from a trip she took. What would Momma do if she were here now? After all, she'd been pretty much alone after Millie's father and grandparents died.

She squared her shoulders, remembering how Momma would gently remind her to stand tall. The previous summer Millie had shot up several inches and was suddenly taller than many of the boys in her class—including Jeremy Turner. "Be proud of your height, my darling," Momma would whisper as she stood behind her, hands resting lightly on Millie's shoulders. "The boys will grow." Then she would pull Millie back against her, wrap her arms around her and kiss her hair.

That would never happen again.

So much would never happen again.

Outside the bedroom door, Millie heard Nan coming up the stairs. She hurried back to the closet, not wanting Nan to discover her in Momma's room, but the maid passed by and went to Roger's bedroom at the far end of the hall.

What if I leave this house today and go somewhere Roger can't find me?

When she heard Nan switch on the vacuum cleaner, she saw her chance. She looked around the closet, choosing small mementoes to take—a scarf, a pair of wool mittens, and Momma's hiking boots that she hoped would fit since her own were too small. On her way to the door, she passed the dressing table and picked up a small atomizer filled with Momma's favorite perfume, and a picture of the two of them taken when Millie was just a little kid. Momma had always said it was her favorite photograph of Millie, no matter how much Millie argued for something more recent.

She listened at the door to be sure Nan was still vacuuming, then slipped out and up the stairs to her room on the third floor. There, she gathered essentials like underwear, socks, her toothbrush, and the pea coat she'd been told was like the one her father might have worn in the Navy. Finally, she dug deep between the mattress and bed springs and pulled out Momma's old black satin evening purse with the rhinestone clasp. This was where she'd hidden the money she'd been saving from her allowance. The plan had been to buy a portable Victrola she'd seen advertised in one of Momma's magazines. She'd saved four dollars and seventy-two cents. She stuffed the money in the front pocket of her corduroy pants, put the atomizer and picture inside the purse and wrapped it in the clothes she'd collected. Bundling everything together, she ran two flights down the back stairs to the kitchen.

The vacuum cleaner had gone silent, but she could hear Nan moving around in the upstairs hall, singing some song she must have heard on the radio.

In the kitchen, Millie grabbed a flashlight along with Momma's backpack, poncho and hat from the pantry and stuffed the poncho along with her own clothes inside the backpack. Then she started loading whatever food she thought she'd need for the long walk to the park and then further on to find Momma's friend. Finally, she put on her coat and Momma's gloves, hat, and the boots—which fit perfectly. After hooking the straps of the backpack over her shoulders, she checked to be sure Gus hadn't returned.

And she left.

In geography class they'd been studying weather and she was surprised to learn that while Gardiner averaged a good deal less than fifty inches of snow a year, in the park that figure could be doubled or even quadrupled. There was still a lot of snow on the ground in Gardiner. So, she had to wonder how much there would be in the park. Surely Mammoth, at the north end of the park couldn't have that much more, could it?

Beneath the light layer of fresh snow that covered the sidewalks, there was ice, but the soles of the boots held as she hurried down the street. She figured with Momma's funeral just yesterday, nobody would question her not being in class, even though it was Friday and a school day. On top of that, the streets were deserted because of the ice and the deep ruts created by the thawing and re-freezing of that ice. She hitched the backpack more securely on her shoulders and pulled her scarf over her nose and mouth as she walked as fast as she could away from that house.

In the distance just behind the railway station, she could see the arch named for President Roosevelt—the first one. In school she'd learned that Teddy Roosevelt had been mainly responsible for making sure there were national parks. She headed toward the arch.

The one time Gus had driven Momma and her to the park, it hadn't seemed like it was all that far from that entrance to a bunch of buildings—park headquarters, according to Gus. There had even been a hotel. In summer, there was a bus that went between town and the park, but Millie was pretty sure it hadn't started to run yet, with the park still shut down for the winter. Besides, the last thing she needed was for somebody to question why she would head for the park on such a day, not that she thought Roger would care. On the other hand, from what she'd overheard the lawyer telling him, maybe he would care. It sounded to her like he needed her before he could get his hands on whatever money Momma had left.

Fat chance.

It wasn't long at all before Millie concluded that just getting to the arch was going to be a lot harder than she'd thought. First of all, the sidewalk that ran in front of Roger's house ended after just two blocks. Then, because piles of snow had narrowed the road, she had to stop often to let trucks pass, all the while trying not to fall in a ditch or get splashed by stuff flying out from the wheels.

Once she reached the railroad station, she stopped to rest, understanding how little she really knew of the area surrounding Gardiner beyond Roger's house, the school and the stores where she sometimes went with Clara to buy supplies. Even then, they were usually in the back seat of the car, with Gus driving them wherever they needed to be.

The first time she and Momma had stepped off the train in Gardiner, Millie thought the place looked like towns she'd seen in cowboy pictures she used to go watch on Saturday afternoons. She and her friends would wonder if towns in the West really looked like that. Turns out they did—at least this one did. There was a main street that ran from one end of town to the other, lined with buildings made of stone or wood, none of them over three stories tall. That was a lot different from the skyscrapers she used to pass as she walked home in Chicago. In fact, the house there was four floors tall, not even counting the basement or attic. So, Gardiner was quite a change. Momma thought of it as an adventure. Momma saw most things as adventures, and not ones to be scared about.

At first, Millie hadn't minded living in a place so different from Chicago that it was almost like a foreign country. She'd made a few friends at school, and although Roger didn't like having them come to the house, a couple of times right after they moved in, Millie had gone to theirs. Still, it was hard to make real friends in a place where most people had known each other their whole lives. Everybody was polite and even friendly but stuck to themselves and what Roger called "their kind," so making friends was hard. Momma kept telling her it would take time, and even though Millie thought more than a year was long enough, she'd followed Momma's advice and just kept trying. The main thing was that Momma was so happy—at least at first. Millie would have moved to the moon to keep her that way.

3

When finally, she reached the arch, Millie stopped to get her bearings and catch her breath. She looked up at the inscription: *For the Benefit and Enjoyment of the People.*

She sure hoped that message would be true for her. Hitching her backpack higher, she pressed on. Once she passed under the big stone arch behind the station, she let out a long breath and squinted at the way ahead. There was a road of sorts, but as far as she could see the land was rugged with high hills that turned into mountains and lots of snow everywhere. She hesitated, but then thought about Momma. She could even imagine her saying, "Come on, Millie. It's an adventure."

Millie saw a long stick someone had left propped against the stone arch, and using that, took a step forward. She found the snow packed enough to keep going, and after a while she was aware of the town disappearing behind her.

I'm really doing this!

But that first burst of excitement didn't last long. The road into the park was even narrower than the one she'd left, and the winds were strong, blowing the snow in her face. Each step felt as if she were climbing a mountain. More than once she lost her balance, and breathing was difficult. After what seemed like forever, she looked back and could still see the town in the distance, so she walked faster, figuring she still had a long way to go. Darkness came on suddenly in this part of the country, especially on days like this, when the clouds were gray and so low it felt as if they might fall out of the sky. The temperatures were dropping, and with all the times she'd fallen or gotten splashed, her clothes were wet. She hoped a ranger might be on duty in one of the buildings Gus had pointed out that day, but at the very least she would need to find shelter for the night.

Every few yards it seemed she kept having to stop to catch her breath. In school they'd learned all about the difference altitude could make in the amount of oxygen available—thin air, Clara called it-- and told Millie she would adjust in time. Seemed to Millie, though, like the higher she climbed the more effort it took to breathe.

Just past the arch, she'd seen a sign that it was five miles to Mammoth—the address on Virginia Baker's Christmas card. Millie figured she could easily walk five miles. But she hadn't counted on the snow or the steep climbs or the slippery downhills. Every step felt as if she were lifting a heavy box or pulling a loaded wagon when it was really just her.

After a while she noticed she was following the river and remembered Gus telling her and Momma it was called the "boiling" river because there was a part of it that was hot springs and people went there to swim, even when it started to get cold, or in spring before the weather turned nice. Millie didn't think anybody would be foolish enough to be swimming on a day like this, no matter how hot those springs were.

Her stomach growled and she felt a little weak, like her legs just wouldn't support her. Pausing, she leaned on the stick she was using as a cane. She had brought food but no water. On the other hand, there was water all around her—snow piled up everywhere she looked. She made a small snowball and licked it. Then she started eating it like she might eat one of the Italian ices she and Momma used to buy back in Chicago on hot summer days. With her back against a cluster of rocks, she opened her knapsack and pulled out the box of raisins she'd taken from the pantry, along with a package of saltines.

The snow melting in her mouth and the raisins and crackers she was chewing made her feel better and she set off again. Along the way she kept scooping up little balls of snow and sucking on them, wanting to save what food she had in case she couldn't find anybody once she reached Mammoth.

Finally, just as what light there was had started to fade, Millie topped a hill and saw spread out below her a whole bunch of buildings. There was a line of red roofs— the cluster of buildings called Fort Yellowstone that Gus had said were built during the years the army lived there. There were a couple of gray stone buildings and the hotel where they had used the bathroom that day. Millie pulled back the sleeve of her coat and checked her watch. It was going on four o'clock. It had been just past eleven when she'd left the house.

She hurried as fast as she could down the road. It didn't take long to figure out that the place was deserted. Shadows spread across the snow-covered lawn where Gus had said the soldiers had once drilled when the place was a fort. Millie listened for any sound that might signal somebody was around. It was so quiet, it felt downright spooky. Although the road from the gate to the cluster of buildings had offered her a trail of ski tracks to follow, as she hurried from one building to the next, she stepped twice into what she thought was packed snow and sank into it up to her knees. She recalled Clara had said she couldn't remember a winter when they'd already seen so much snow. "It just keeps coming," she'd commented one day when the two of them were looking out the kitchen window.

Millie climbed the steps to a building marked *Administration* and tried the door, even though there was a hand-lettered sign posted that read *Closed for the Season*. Locked. The steps had been shoveled, which made her hope that someone might be inside, but after peering through a window, she realized she was too late. It dawned on her then that, it being Friday and all, probably nobody was likely to be there before Monday morning. Millie felt her chest tighten and knew this time her trouble breathing was because she was really scared. It was starting to look like she had maybe made a big mistake. She should have written to Momma's friend, asked her to come to Gardiner, and toughed it out in the meantime at Roger's.

But she couldn't risk going back now with dusk coming on, so she started looking for a place she might at least stay out of the cold for the night. Coming back down the steps, she stopped dead. Not ten feet away from her stood a huge moose with enormous and scary-looking antlers. Hurrying back up the steps, she hid behind a pillar to wait for the beast to move on. Never in her life had she felt more alone.

She tried one other door with no luck. No use trying to go around to the side or back because the snow had drifted so much that she knew she was bound to get soaked, and she was already shivering. Besides that, big moose and his friends might be there. Her heart pounding, Millie decided she would just keep trying until she found something open—or somebody home in one of the houses down the way—although, given the fact she didn't see a single light, that seemed like a long shot. She headed for the hotel. On the way to the front entrance, a side door caught her eye. She skittered down the steps leading to the entrance and her spirits rose when she saw that because snow had drifted and ice had formed around the base, the door had not closed all the way. No footprints or ski tracks, so she figured it had been a while since anyone had been there.

Millie pushed the snow away with both hands, soaking her mittens in the process. By now her whole body shook with the cold. Under a loose top layer, the snow was frozen solid, so she took a small log from a pile of wood under one of the overhangs and used that to chop away the ice. Finally, she was able to pry the door open enough to step inside and pull it shut. It took a moment for her eyes to adjust to the shadows and to feel relief at being out of the wind, but she was still colder than she could ever remember being.

She found herself in a dark narrow hallway, but up ahead there was still some light coming through a window, so she moved toward it. Along the way she passed a lot of doors and realized these were rooms where people stayed. The doors were all open and she could see the beds had been stripped and the mattresses propped against the wall or covered. It was a little creepy passing all those empty rooms, so she hurried on, calling out—just in case anybody was there.

"Hello?"

Somewhere water dripped, sounding like the clock that sat at the foot of the stairs in Roger's house. Millie shuddered both from the cold and from wanting no reminders of him or that house. She did wonder if he'd returned from work and noticed she was gone.

"Anybody here?"

At the end of the hall of empty guest rooms, she came to an area where a stairway led up to the second floor and beyond, and a doorway that was marked *Lobby This Way*. In the lobby was a large fireplace and some furniture that had been covered the way Momma used to do at their summer cottage on Lake Geneva when the season ended. Millie walked past the desk and on through the double doors that led into the dining room, where all the chairs and tables had been pushed to the sides and covered with canvas sheets. The room smelled musty, and outside the large windows she noticed that it had started to snow again. She also saw the streetlamps had come on and the sun had fully set. Surely if there were streetlamps, somebody was living here. She thought about going back outside and walking from one building to the next until she found that person.

But then she remembered the moose and decided she'd best wait for daylight. In the meantime, she needed to eat something and make a place she could sleep for the night without freezing to death.

The hotel was what Momma used to call bone-chilling cold, but at least she was inside, protected from the wind—not to mention any critters. Her hiking boots, socks and pants were soaked, and she was having trouble feeling her toes and fingers. As her eyes adjusted to the shadows and gloom, she made her way from the dining room back to the main lobby. There, she turned her attention to the fireplace she and Momma had admired that day they'd stopped to use the restroom. She tried a couple of wall switches, but no lights came on, and because the only light came from the streetlamps, she pulled out the flashlight she'd added to the backpack at the last minute and flicked it on. She needed to get a small fire going, but first she really had to pee.

Who knew running away could get so complicated?

Nate

-4-

Once the snows came, Nate Baker got to and from work on skis or snowshoes. The cabin he shared with his wife, Ginny, was high in the hills that rose up behind the town of Mammoth, and he had at least half an hour's journey each way, depending on the weather. Still, Nate relished the trip no matter how many times he made it, or what he might face going to and from the only job he'd ever known. There was a different kind of peace that came with the start of a new winter day in Yellowstone—a kind of promise, it seemed to him. The way the light and shadows played over the snow-covered landscape, the silence interrupted only by the song of a bird—this morning a mountain bluebird, a sure sign of spring coming. In summer he drove one of the company trucks to wherever he might be needed that day, and the growl of the motor broke the silence and drowned out any sounds of tourists and their chatter. But in winter it was just him and the wild, sparkling stillness that was Yellowstone after the tourists had left and before they returned.

After a weekend of bad weather, he was relieved to see blue skies with no threat of more snow. An unusually strong storm that started late Friday night had brought winds of forty miles per hour whipping the snow into eddies and drifts twice his size and making travel impossible—at least from his cabin. He'd spent the entire weekend digging out a narrow path he could follow now to the trail that took him to Mammoth.

In the distance, steam rose from the thermal springs that gave that area of the park its name. He saw a half-dozen bison huddled on the terraces. The bulky, thick-coated animals tended to wander there toward winter's end, seeking not only warmth, but the first green shoots of spring. Winter in the park was all about survival and finding enough to eat was key. These days it seemed as if making it from one day to the next was a struggle for man or beast. A few weeks earlier Nate had gone into Gardiner and seen people standing in long lines outside churches. Soup kitchens and bread lines were common now that the economic depression was entering its fourth year and hunger stalked the country. Nate was grateful for a lot, but still being able to earn a living topped the list.

As he approached the administration building in Mammoth, he noticed a couple of deep divots in the snow near the foot of the steps. At first, he thought the imprints might be from a fox diving for food beneath the cover of snow—a mouse perhaps. He bent down to get a closer look, because normally a fox would make three or four bounds and landings before catching its prey. Maybe this fox had gotten lucky.

Even though this north end of the park never got as much snow as other areas due to its proximity to geothermal features like the hot springs, the combination of wind and snow had been unusual for this time of year. By early January, several feet of packed snow capped the roofs of the hotel and other buildings. Now the stuff hung off the edges in sweeping cornices that could bury a man like an avalanche if they broke loose. Nate retrieved his tools—a crosscut saw and a square-tipped shovel--from a storage shed at the back of the hotel, his mind still puzzling on the unusual shape of the divots.

Human—had to be, he thought.

He looked around. There was no sign of tracks from snowshoes or skis other than his own, so whoever had made these divots must have worn boots. Could be a lone hiker—a stupid hiker. The snow cover on top of several feet of densely packed ice to either side of the trail that led between the buildings could be up to a six-foot man's mid-calf. A woman or kid would be knee-deep in the stuff. Even as well as Nate knew the area, he still used his ski pole to test the depth of snow or the thickness of ice before taking his next step. Of course, there was the possibility the person had come by car, maybe stopped to see if anybody was at the headquarters. The road from Gardiner to Mammoth was kept cleared enough even in winter for traveling to and from, but he saw no tire tracks. Besides, with the weekend's storm, the road hadn't yet been cleared. A vehicle would need chains to make the trip and he saw no such tracks.

More worrisome was the idea that the footprints belonged to a poacher. Over the last few seasons, illegal hunting had become a huge problem, as thieves took advantage of the fact that the park was almost deserted over the winter and staffing was skeletal. Some sought trophies to sell—antlers, whole heads, skins--while others wanted to add to their private collections. But more recently, his friend, Park Ranger Dan Atwood, had talked of a new breed of poacher. With the hard times continuing, more often than not these thieves were after food.

Banks had closed, businesses shut down, farms had failed and there was little work. Protecting the wildlife was the domain of the rangers, but Nate's employers—the men who held the concessions contract for running the hotels and shops that served tourists--worried those poachers might also break into the buildings seeking food, shelter or both. In some ways Nate had not only the ice and snow, but also these interlopers to thank for still having a job when so many others were out of work.

As one of the park's winterkeepers, a fancy title for those maintenance men who stayed on once Yellowstone shut down in early November, Nate's main responsibility was to take care of the commercial buildings at the northern end of the park in the area known as Mammoth Hot Springs. He had spent the last twenty-five years of his life here, working his way up to supervisor and managing a crew of two to four men, depending on the season. But in October, as the tourist season was winding down, Nate had received the news that his employers could not afford to post more than one winterkeeper in each of the various areas of the park. His crew would no longer be there to help.

"Need you to handle Mammoth on your own going forward," his boss had said, not meeting Nate's eyes. Nate didn't have to ask why. At least Mammoth was the easy assignment—a good place for a man in his mid-forties, who might not be able to keep up with the work in other parts of the park, where the snowfall was often double what it was farther north. Nate had not tried to debate the decision. Instead he had stood, shaken his boss's hand and thanked him.

At least he still had a job—a job he loved. He treasured the solitude of the hours he spent clearing snow—his time and thoughts uninterrupted. He was a man comfortable in his own skin and just as uneasy in the company of others.

Now he stood looking up at the roof of the hotel, where he'd started clearing snow before the latest storm hit. The building was large, and he knew working his way from one end of the roof to the other would take him at least a week—and then he would have to start again as long as the snows kept coming. Back in the Old Faithful area, he might have to deal with a couple hundred inches of snowfall, which—according to his wife, Ginny--amounted to close to seventeen feet of the white stuff.

"Seventeen feet, Nate. That's nearly three times your height," Ginny had pointed out more than once. Ginny liked numbers and she used them freely when making her argument.

Nate had never given much thought to how much snow he'd shoveled over the last twenty-five years. But lately Ginny had. She'd made that and his reassignment part of her case for why it might be time he quit working for the park service so they could live what she had taken to calling "a normal life."

"You're pushing fifty years old, Nate—that's half a century, a quarter of it spent right here," she'd said just the night before, as they sat across from each other at dinner. "On top of that, now they expect you to do it all on your own. And why? Because they knew you wouldn't balk at doing the work by yourself."

"At least I still have a job," he'd reminded her.

"For now," Ginny had whispered. "But, Nate, you're not a young man."

They'd both heard rumors the current owners of the hotels and other concessions throughout the park were trying to sell. Although there weren't nearly as many tourists as in earlier years, the need to maintain the buildings had not changed. Besides, Ginny had a point. He wasn't getting any younger.

He'd started working in the park when he was twenty-four years old, after his discharge from the army. His comrades in arms had been gung-ho, hoping to engage in combat and collect medals for their bravery, but all Nate had wanted was to serve his country. He'd seen his share of combat and he'd done his duty, even when duty meant shooting another human being. It was his commanding officer who had suggested he think about a job in one of the national parks. The park system was fairly new then, and the hotels and shops meant to serve the hordes of tourists anxious to experience adventure in the wilderness were just being built.

"You're a devoted American, Nate," his commander had said. "But you're also a peace-loving man. You need to find some way to serve without the fighting. You just don't have the heart for it."

Nate had bristled inwardly at that. On balance, he had his fair share of stripes to show he was a good soldier. But he held his tongue. "I don't get your meaning, sir."

Captain Garner had smiled. "Now that's just what I'm talking about. I just questioned your dedication to the fighting. You might have taken offense at that, but there you stand—polite and calm as ever. You're a good soldier—one of the best—but there's ways to serve without fighting, Baker—ways you could make a real contribution—and have the solitude better suited to your temperament."

Nate hadn't been able to argue that. When the rest of his unit headed off to some bar to blow off a little steam, Nate found relief in reading and hiking. His father had been a drinker and the drink made him meaner than when he was sober, which was saying something. Nate's childhood had been chaotic—-constant yelling between his parents, never enough food or money, his father sometimes there and sometimes not, and always one more screaming sibling to tend—-and protect from his father's rage. Early on Nate had found refuge in being outdoors.

"You're a loner, Baker," the captain had added. "Find a career that lets you feed off that and you'll be a happy man."

Captain Garner had been right. The first day Nate worked in the park, he felt as if he'd come home. As the months and years went by, he settled into a life that fit him well—a life he couldn't imagine leaving. Even once he met Ginny and they'd married, he'd known this was the life for him.

Now, all these years later, he collected the tools of his trade and prepared to get to work. The ladders he used to scale the roof and work his way from one section to the next had been in place since the first snow had fallen. He removed his skis and clamped on the crampons that would give him traction before climbing the ladder. Once on the roof, he stood in a space he'd cleared a few days earlier and began sawing a chunk the size of an icebox out of the mountain of snow that rose above him. And because the rhythm of the work was ingrained, he gave himself over to his thoughts.

The threat to their livelihood wasn't the only thing worrying Nate these days. It occurred to Nate that ever since Ginny had come back from spending the Christmas holidays with her sister, she'd been going on more than usual about this business of them leaving the park. Always after she spent time back in Chicago, she returned full of talk about "what if" and "maybe we should think about..." Usually that all petered out after a couple of weeks. But this time, things were different. This time it had been months. He suspected his sister-in-law of stirring that pot. Gertie had never warmed to him—always thinking Ginny could have done better.

Truth of it was she probably could have, if "better" was measured by a paycheck and dressing for work in a suit and tie instead of coveralls and a wool-lined jacket with frayed cuffs. His wife had grown up in Chicago's high society—country clubs, debutante balls, the works. They'd met when she came to the park as part of a summer program her college sponsored. He'd been working with the ranger assigned to lead the seminar, responsible for building campfires and setting up picnics out on the trails. Two days after they met, Ginny had told him that she planned to marry him. He'd thought she was joking, teasing him about being able to build a proper fire with wet wood.

But when he'd grinned and told her he might just take her up on that, she'd frowned and laid her smooth hand on his forearm. "I mean it, Nate Baker."

He'd studied her for a long moment. "Why me?"

"Not sure of the reason, but I'm very sure we'd be good together."

He hadn't been quite as certain, especially once he'd met her family. But after a series of letters and a few long-distance phone calls and two more visits back to the park by Ginny, they'd married as she'd predicted. And, although he'd offered to look for something closer to civilization, admittedly he'd breathed a sigh of relief when she'd chosen to follow him to his job in the park.

"I love it here, Nate. I love you and this is where you belong so it's where I want to be and find a way to belong as well."

Ginny—sweet, fiery Ginny.

Just thinking about her made him smile. For the first few years of their marriage, he'd kept expecting her to announce that this wasn't the life she'd bargained for—even though he'd made it plain to her what living year-round in the park entailed. They'd be living in a small cabin, not the hotel. There would be no room service or fancy shops.

"Got it," had been her reply.

And then on their fifth wedding anniversary, she had presented him with a box of eggshells.

"What's this?"

"It's those eggshells you've been walking around on since the day we married, and frankly I am sick to death of it." She went to the phonograph she'd brought with her to the marriage and carefully set the needle on the record. Then she dumped the eggshells out on the floor, held her arms out to him and said, "Dance with me, Nate."

The tune playing was ragtime, not a waltz. He hesitated. She did a couple of fancy steps, stomping on the shells. "Now you," she coached, holding his hands in hers. Soon those eggshells were crushed to sand and they were laughing and breathless from the exertion of their dance.

They made love after that and as they lay together, listening as the wind picked up and the lodgepole pines outside the bedroom window clacked together, announcing a summer thunderstorm, she took hold of his hand, weaving her fingers in his. "Nate, I am so very happy here. This is my life—our life—and sorry to disappoint you, but I'm not going anywhere, okay?"

He'd pulled her closer and kissed her soft hair. "Got it," he'd whispered, and the relief he felt had been as fresh and cleansing as the rain that pelted the roof and rattled the windows as she snuggled against him and fell asleep.

For nearly twenty years now they'd lived in that same little three-room cabin, exploring the park in every season and under every condition. Over time, Nate had added a loft and a greenhouse, so Ginny could grow fresh vegetables year-round. Their closest friends were other staff members and their families, most of them part-time for the season, who returned year after year, and one or two year-round as they were. They'd never been blessed with children, though Lord knows they had tried.

To have children or not had been one of the stumbling blocks of their marriage. They hadn't been married long before Ginny started campaigning for a family, in spite of the fact they'd had this discussion before the wedding.

"You'd be the best father, Nate."

"Ginny, we talked about this."

"I know but..."

"And you agreed," Nate had reminded her.

She'd given him that quirky smile accompanied by a shrug and said, "I lied."

And so, they had compromised. He had agreed to one.

"Okay. I'll pray for twins then," she'd told him.

Nate had groaned but smiled. Ginny would be such a wonderful mother to any child, more than making up for whatever shortcomings he might have when it came to parenting. His own childhood had been brutal and lonely— his father's anger and drinking scaring away the friends he might have had, and siblings always after him to buy them things or settle a score with some bully. "What do I have to teach a kid, Ginny?"

"Oh, for heaven sakes, Nate, how many times do I have to tell you that you are not your father?"

And so, they had tried, and endured the heartache of two miscarriages, and finally Ginny had admitted that perhaps a child wasn't in the cards for them. She'd turned her attention to the children around her——her sister's three and those kids lucky enough to spend their summers in the park.

But they'd been happy, hadn't they?

Still puzzling over his wife's unsettled mood, Nate worked his way to the highest peak of the roof. That way, if there was an avalanche where the heavy wall of snow lost its grip on the roof's shingles and slid, he wouldn't be caught in it. Along with the other winterkeepers, he'd come up with ways of moving large amounts of snow safely and effectively. Sometimes it was as simple as pushing the snow to the edge of the roof and letting it fall. But seasons like this one with unusually large amounts of snow called for more complex solutions. Using the edge of a two-man crosscut saw he'd outfitted so he could use it without a partner, he cut into a wall of snow hardened to rock- solid ice. Each block he cut was six to seven feet tall and almost as thick, and each block weighed probably five hundred pounds or more—the more solid the ice and packing of the snow, the heavier. Each block was capable of crushing a man if it fell on him. Using the square tip of his shovel, he tipped the block and let it slide down the slope of the roof, watching it explode as it hit the ground below.

One of the good things about working alone was that there were no distractions—no conversation, no horsing around. Every so often he took a rest, leaning on his shovel and scanning the eastern sky. The sun was not yet all the way up. As he watched it make its slow climb, he found himself thinking about something Ginny had been going on about a few days earlier.

"Over the holiday when I was in Chicago, I went to the Art Institute, Nate. I realized how long it's been since I visited and the collection there is so incredible. If you could only see these paintings," she'd gushed. "You walk into a gallery, and there before you is a masterpiece from a hundred years ago. I had forgotten how beautiful and different they could be, depending on the artist doing the work."

But the sky he was looking at was real. The lighter blues of daylight shadowed by the deeper gray-blue of the passing night, the clouds streaked with pale violet and orange and even a bit of yellow here and there as the sun peeked out from behind the mountains. The steam rising from the hot springs in the distance created a prism effect that could not be duplicated by any artist, though many had tried. And there was the smell of the clean, cold air undercut at times by the persistent scent of sulfur, the air penetrated by the shriek of a red-tailed hawk or the bugle call of a moose. How could any painting compete with that?

He wondered if maybe Ginny was working in her greenhouse while he worked his way across the flat roof of the hotel. Maybe as she worked, she, too, had paused to study that same scene. Maybe by the time he finished clearing this section of the hotel roof and made the trek home, she would finally remember what it was she'd always loved about living in the park—especially this time of year, with hints that winter would pass and there would be the wonders of spring. She would remember that eggshell dance and know—as she had told him then—that this was home.

-5-

Around noon, Nate stopped to eat the lunch Ginny had packed for him. He climbed down and collected his tin bucket and thermos from the knapsack he carried to and from his job, sat on the top step of the hotel entrance and watched an impressive black car make its way slowly down the partially cleared road to the park headquarters. Chains wrapped around the car's tires bit into the snow and made a crunching sound that was louder than the powerful engine. Nate saw Dan Atwood come out of the building, blowing on his hands as the car came to a stop. He hadn't seen his friend come to work, but lately he'd noticed the ranger was there from early morning to sundown, when usually in winter there was no need for him to keep regular hours.

"In hard times," Dan had told Nate, "there's a tendency for the government to think things like the parks are expendable. I want to do everything I can to be sure this new President Roosevelt knows what a treasure we have here, should he start looking this way for making cuts to the budget."

Nate kept eating his sandwich and watched as the driver got out and opened the back door. The man who emerged was hefty, pushing the limits of his black overcoat with its fur collar and lapels and puffing on a fat cigar. He and Dan spoke for a minute, then the driver pulled a small picture frame from his coat pocket and set it on the roof of the car. Dan stepped closer to get a better look and shook his head. The man with the cigar glanced around, then pointed at Nate.

"Nate!" Dan shouted and motioned him to join them.

Nate packed away what was left of his lunch, twisted the cap back onto his thermos of tea and slowly made his way toward the trio of men. By the time he reached Dan and the two strangers, he could see the bigwig was losing patience, clearly a man used to people jumping to do his bidding. Nate waited for Dan to take the lead.

"Nate Baker, this is Mr. Fitzgerald from Gardiner."

Nate recognized the name. An outfit called Fitzgerald Enterprises was negotiating to buy all the concessions in the park—hotels, shops, restaurants. Technically, if this man was part of that business, Nate might soon work for him.

"Mr. Fitzgerald's daughter is missing." Dan handed Nate the picture of a skinny girl who looked to be maybe ten years old.

"She's awful young," Nate said, as he studied the black and white photo that had been taken at some kind of party.

"She's older now—fourteen" the driver said. "That picture was taken when her mother and the boss here married a few years back." A look from his employer had him shutting up fast.

"So, she's not your daughter, but your step-daughter," Dan said. He frowned. Dan liked things to be factual.

"Toe-may-toes, toe-mah-toes," Fitzgerald said, and took a draw on his cigar. "Have you seen any sign of her?" He stared straight at Nate.

"No sir. How long has she been missing?"

The man shrugged and looked at his driver. "Gus?"

"We think she left Friday," he mumbled.

"Two, three days out in this weather?" Dan glanced at Nate, then back at Fitzgerald. "Did you call the police?"

The man glared at Dan. "You think I'm stupid or what? Of course, I called the police. Who do you think suggested I contact you? Gus here just this morning reminded me her mother brought her to the park once and they talked about coming back."

Gus seemed eager to fill in the blanks. "Her mother died, and we thought maybe in her grief..." The driver broke off when his boss stalked back around the car to the rear door he'd left open. The car's engine was still running.

"Keep the picture and call the police in Gardiner if you see any signs of her," Fitzgerald barked before ducking back inside the car and slamming the door.

"She's a good kid," Gus added, as he hurried to slide behind the wheel. "Been through a lot." His eyes pleaded with Dan and Nate to find her.

"We'll do our best," Dan said, as Gus put the car in gear and drove away. Nate couldn't help but wonder how come the driver seemed more concerned about the girl than her stepfather did.

Dan turned to Nate. "You think a kid could make it here on her own? How would she get here unless she walked? Five miles in this snow?"

Nate shrugged and pointed to the divot he'd seen earlier. "Somebody slipped off the packed trail near here over the weekend, but that could be anybody."

"Well, keep an eye out," Dan said. "Hate to think about her being out there somewhere." They both stared out beyond the village at the endless wilderness surrounding them. "I'll alert the other keepers to check for break-ins over at the lake and canyon."

If she's been out there even overnight, she's not got much of a chance, Nate thought.

"Colder than a…" Dan muttered as he hurried back up the steps.

"Try doing some real work instead of pushing papers around a desk," Nate joked. "That'll warm you up."

Dan laughed.

At the end of the day, Nate stored his equipment, strapped on his skis and headed for home. He was anxious to see Ginny. He was going to just straight out ask her why this time she was so set on them leaving. He chose a path that had him passing close to the same group of bison he'd seen that morning, their mangy beards dripping with frost and icicles as they burrowed their faces in the snow looking for food. Those snowy faces always made Ginny laugh.

Bone-tired, he trudged along until he finally reached the top of a rise overlooking the hollow where the cabin sat. When he could see no signs of life, barely a thin stream of smoke rising from the chimney and no light in the window, his heart hammered with both the exertion of the journey and his concern for Ginny. Maybe she'd gone to visit Bertha Conroy, another winterkeeper's wife, and lost track of time. Of course, she also might have gone off on her own, forgotten the time and would come home after dark. It wouldn't be the first time. She always told him not to worry—that by this time she knew the trails—and how to avoid the natural dangers--as well as he did. Maybe her not being there was a good sign—a sign she was coming back to him and their life in the park.

When he reached the cabin, he removed his skis and leaned them against the porch railing, noting hers were still there. He piled logs into his arms and, once inside, rekindled the fire that, along with the water piped in from the geothermal features nearby, was their main source of heat. As he worked, he decided he would surprise Ginny by making supper—maybe open that bottle of red wine she'd carried back with her from Chicago—a Christmas present to him from Gert and her husband.

"What's the occasion?" he imagined Ginny asking when she walked in, saw the table set with candles and smelled his signature elk stew simmering. He'd grin and say what she always said when she made a special meal for no reason: "Do we need an occasion?"

Yes, he decided. It was the old familiar ways that would help her settle back into the life they loved. The private little traditions they'd established over the years. Eventually, they would have to talk about *after*--after he got too old or too decrepit to handle the work, but not yet.

Revived, he set to work. The stew would take some time, so he tackled that first, and once he'd sautéed the shallots they grew in their greenhouse and added wild mushrooms he and Ginny had collected and dried last fall, he stirred in the meat, potatoes, a cup of Ginny's homemade broth and a splash of the red wine. He pushed the cork back into the bottle and set it aside. When the stew started to bubble, he turned down the heat, covered the pot and took down dishes from the open shelves above the sink.

Expecting any minute to hear the soft whisper of her snowshoes and anxious to tell her about the missing girl, he rushed around, making sure everything would be ready. On his way to the table, he grabbed two cloth napkins and the wine glasses she'd brought to the marriage from that big house in Chicago. He glanced toward the window where two chairs faced each other—where he and Ginny sat most evenings reading or listening to the radio. That's when he saw the envelope propped against the needlepoint pillow Ginny had made for him.

"A proper cushion to support your back," she'd insisted, pushing the small pillow firmly between his lower back and the cracked leather of the chair.

Even from across the room, he could see his name centered on the front of the envelope in Ginny's distinctive half-printed, half-cursive script. And because fear gripped him like a vise, he dropped the wine glasses and heard them shatter on the plank floor as if from a distance. He hesitated, not wanting to know what the note said—but unable to put off finding out anyway.

Whenever Ginny decided he wasn't listening to what she was trying to tell him, she put it in writing. Over the years of their marriage, there had been no more than half a dozen of these notes. But each one had marked a turning point. The first had been after they had tried so hard to have a child. That time she wrote to tell him she wanted to stop trying—if they had a baby, fine, but she didn't need children to know she loved him.

When he'd asked her why she didn't just say that instead of writing to him, she had laughed.

"I've been saying it over and over, but your mind is somewhere else," she told him. "You don't hear me because you don't believe me—or maybe it's that you don't *want* to believe me."

The truth was, it was a relief. With each unsuccessful pregnancy, he'd felt more a failure. And Ginny had seen that relief and admitted she was the one who felt she was disappointing him. They had talked after that—really hearing what the other said.

Another note had come a few years later when they'd fought about her wanting to take a job at the hotel during the busy tourist season. The truth was he'd seen the way the hotel's manager looked at her and flirted with her, and how she laughed and teased in return. Ginny had argued that the man was harmless, but Nate's jealousy had been insatiable until Ginny wrote him a love letter. A letter that described in graphic detail why she could never possibly be with another man. She said he had ruined her for happiness anywhere but with him so he might as well accept that.

He had saved every letter—along with a small vial of those crushed eggshells, and he knew he would save this letter as well—no matter what it said.

He was gripping the unopened envelope and staring down at Ginny's chair, as if expecting her to be there, when the crackle of the two-way radio brought his attention back to the present. "Nate? You there? Over?" Dan Atwood's voice was reedy but clear.

Nate moved to the desk in the corner and switched on the receiver. "Yeah. What's up? Over."

"That Fitzgerald guy earlier this afternoon…what did you think?"

Nate glanced at the envelope, but this was work and work came first. "Bit of a blowhard."

Dan laughed. "That's what I like about you, Nate. Always say what you mean and mean what you say."

"Any sign of the kid?"

"No. I checked all the possible entrances around here. No sign of a break-in. I called around. Of course, with this latest storm everybody's been sticking close to home these last several days, so unlikely anybody would see anything."

"I didn't come across anything on the way home."

"Seems unusual he waited until now to start the search," Dan continued. "Of course, who's to say he hasn't been looking for days now and the idea of the park just came up."

"I suppose," Nate replied, but there was something about the whole encounter that told him different. "Did you talk to Benny?"

Benny Helton was a teenager from Gardiner who had made himself useful doing odd jobs in the park and who had outfitted his tractor to make it possible to travel through the deeper snow once winter set in. Nate wondered if Ginny had maybe had Benny take her somewhere. He didn't want to ask outright if Benny might have mentioned Ginny—didn't want Dan knowing he was worried. Besides, Ginny's skis were where they usually were this time of day—next to his on the porch. And, he realized now, so were her snowshoes.

"Nate, you still there?"

Nate turned his thoughts back to the missing girl. "I didn't trust that guy," he said.

"Me neither. If we find the kid, what do you think we should do?"

Nate took a long breath, closing his eyes as he imagined finding her frozen or dead of an attack by wolves. "Depends on what we find," he said.

"Yeah."

Both men were silent for a long moment. The thing most folks didn't get about the park was that it belonged to the wildlife and the elements. Humans were just visiting, guests of the real residents. And still, those same humans tended to act like the place was a zoo with animals on display but safely separated from them or tame enough they wouldn't do any harm. Through the years more than one tourist had learned that lesson the hard way.

"Well, just keep an eye out," Dan said. "Over and out."

"Got it. Over and out." Nate put down the receiver and glanced out the window. When had it gotten so late? He smelled the stew, realized he'd lost his appetite and turned off the flame. Then he released the death grip he had on the note he'd continued to clutch in one hand while talking to Dan. He smoothed it and slid his thumb under the closing.

Nate,

Got a letter from Milt today saying Gert needs me. I can't explain more now. I just have to get there and get some answers, and I know you will understand that.

Nate could hear her. He could see her. It was as if she were sitting in her chair, perched on the edge of it, her hands on her knees, her whole upper body leaning toward him. Ginny was a passionate person, especially when she felt strongly about something. Her green eyes would sparkle with an intensity that rivaled a clear January sky. Impatiently, she would push her curly red hair away from her face, as if to make sure he could see her features clearly. Her voice—always a sexy, deep, throaty purr— would rise and fall with the heat of her argument. He continued.

I didn't tell you everything about my visit with my family over Christmas. When I was there, Gert and Milt were spending money as if they could always print more.

Now it looks like they've finally realized what's what. I can't just sit here and let everything fall apart. She's my sister, Nate—my baby sister, and you know how flighty she is.

Nate felt a wave of relief as he turned the page over. This wasn't about him—about them—as he had feared. It was about Gert and her family, and as usual Ginny needed to be the rescuer. That was why she was thinking about them moving from the park closer to her sister in Chicago. He read on.

I know this makes no sense to you—it makes no sense to me. All I know is I need to be where I can see what is really going on. I am scared, Nate--for Gert and for us. Milt says we've lost everything. So, Benny's taking me to catch the train to Chicago.

Love you bigger than the great outdoors! G

Sometime while reading Ginny's note, Nate had sat down. He leaned back and felt the small pillow cradle his back. He closed his eyes to trap the tears he felt percolating dangerously close to the surface. He knew Ginny was where she needed to be, but that world terrified him. It was the world she used to know, but he never had. It was a world that was pressing in on all sides of the park. It hadn't intruded yet, unless he counted the cuts in staffing and the reduced number of tourists, but it lurked in the shadows like a wolf pack stalking prey. And because sooner or later the attack on their happiness would come, he wanted Ginny here safe with him. But that was an argument he knew he would never win.

Ginny

-6-

Never would Ginny Baker have imagined that at the age of thirty-eight, after years where everything had gone so well, out of the blue her world would go all topsy-turvy. Even with the country in financial turmoil, her life had seemed about as close to perfect as a woman's could get. For over twenty years, she and her husband, Nate, had lived the promised happily-ever-after in a little cabin deep in the wilderness that was Yellowstone National Park. Talk about paradise!

And every Christmas, although Nate's work prevented him from coming with her, she returned to the palatial house in Chicago where she and her sister, Gert, had grown up. There, she reconnected with old friends and basked in the established holiday traditions and memories of an idyllic childhood. And every year, on the train ride back to Yellowstone, she thanked God for the decision she'd made to leave that life and marry Nate.

But this latest holiday visit had been different—unsettling in ways she couldn't put her finger on. There was an undercurrent of things not being what they seemed. It was as if everyone was going through the motions, simply playing at the joy and delight of the season. Everything felt forced. And on the train ride home, what she'd felt was apprehension rather than gratitude. In the weeks that followed her return to the park, she'd been tense and generally irritable—feelings she was unable to identify—or quell. Everything annoyed her—Nate's stoic silence in the face of her agitation, her friend Bertha's chatter about park gossip that the company running all the concessions was about to sell out and other unsettling trivia, and most of all, her own inability to stop thinking about her sister and whatever was going on with her.

Now, three months later, as once again the train carried her away from her life in the park, she closed her eyes and tried to figure out just what she had missed during that December visit. Something had felt off from the minute she saw Gert waving to her from the station platform three days before Christmas. At first, Ginny blamed the long train ride that had left her feeling exhausted and disheveled. She had been unable to eat more than a few crackers and wondered if she might be coming down with something. But it was more than a physical unease. For one thing, once they were in the taxi, Gert talked non-stop as she kept twisting the gold chain of her pocketbook around her fingers during the entire ride from Union Station to the large gray stone house on Michigan Avenue.

Ginny had so looked forward to this holiday. She especially wanted to talk to her sister about Nate and how, now that they were getting older, she thought the work in the park was too demanding. He'd had some trouble with his back recently. On top of that, there was always the possibility he might fall from the roof of a building where he was clearing snow and be buried beneath the weight of it. Wasn't it past time they started making plans for a future outside the park?

And then there was her worry of how they would pay for that future. Although Gert's husband, Milt—an attorney and the family's investment advisor—had promised that the inheritance left for Gert and Ginny by their parents was secure, Ginny couldn't help worrying if that security might not be breached as the economic crisis dragged on. She had hoped for some private time with Milt to review her finances and reassure herself that everything was indeed still fine.

But that day at the train station, she'd seen at once that Gert was firmly in holiday mode, and Ginny decided not to play the spoiler. She had leaned back in the taxi and looked over at her sister.

"This is new." She fingered the collar of the fox fur coat that covered Gert from her chin to her ankles and suppressed the urge to berate her sister for wearing something that had cost several innocent animals their lives.

"Milt insisted," Gert gushed, stroking the fur. "An early Christmas present. Speaking of which, we must go shopping first thing tomorrow. Milt is taking the children to Marshall Field's to visit Santa while we shop. I haven't even begun gathering the items they listed in their letters to Santa." She pulled three similar envelopes from her purse and handed them to Ginny. Each contained a single sheet written in a child's script.

The lists were longer than usual, and the items were pricier. "I assume 'Santa' is going to pick and choose?" she asked as she read through each letter.

"Heavens, no. Milt says, buy them everything—the bikes, Angela's bride doll and dollhouse, the fire engine for Sammy and train set for Adam…the works."

Gert and Milt had been blessed with three children—twins Angela and Adam, who were nine, and little Sammy—five. The children adored their Aunt Ginny, and the feeling was mutual. Not having children of her own, Ginny doted on her niece and nephews.

Now, on this second trip to see her sister so soon on the heels of her last visit, Ginny looked out the window and watched farms and telephone poles flash by. Milt had always been the frugal one, quietly trying to rein in his wife's overspending and bent toward extravagant entertaining. In December, as the taxi headed east toward Lake Michigan, Ginny had noticed boarded-up shops and men digging through trash cans on the avenues that were usually mobbed at that time of year with well-dressed holiday shoppers. The stark contrast with previous visits had been alarming.

"Gert," Ginny had begun, as she handed her sister the children's Santa letters, "you know Milt would give you and the children anything you asked for—certainly anything you needed, but…"

"How's Nate?" Gert interrupted. "I have never understood why he doesn't join us for the holidays. I mean, doesn't he like us?"

"He works."

"Well, Milt works, but he has time off. Surely in the winter, that wilderness where you live doesn't need as much attention. With the hotel and shops closed, he could take the time, if he wanted to." She folded her arms and pouted as she looked out the window.

Ginny reached over and covered her sister's hand with hers. Gert was wearing soft leather gloves in a fawn color that worked well with the fox fur. Ginny was wearing the wool gloves her friend Bertha had knitted for her. "We've been over this a hundred times. Nate and I have our own way of celebrating," she said.

Gert turned to face her, her eyes glistening with tears. "Oh, Ginny, I always say the wrong thing. It must be so hard for you and Nate—not having been blessed with children. The holidays are really all about the children, aren't they?"

Ginny smiled. "That's right, and you are a dear for letting me play special auntie to your three."

They had spent the next day shopping and stayed up late on Christmas Eve to set out the toys for the children and place dozens of wrapped gifts around the tree. There had been no chance to speak privately with Milt. Now, as she thought about it, had her brother-in-law deliberately put off her request that they find time to talk?

On Christmas morning, the children had tiptoed into Ginny's room, waking her with their giggles and attempts to shush each other.

"Is it too early, Aunt Ginny?" Adam whispered.

Ginny cocked an eye at the clock and realized she had been in bed less than three hours. "Yes," she croaked and held the covers back so her niece and nephews could crowd in with her. She'd managed to keep them there another hour, although she had gotten no more sleep. "All right, go," she'd finally told them, and they scampered from the room and down the stairs.

"See, Sammy," she heard Angela say. "Santa was here. He ate the cookies."

This was followed by whoops of delight as the three of them discovered their loot. Ginny put on her robe and slippers and started down the stairs just as Milt and Gert emerged from their room. "I'll make coffee," she told them. They had given the help the day off to enjoy with their families.

The week after Christmas had flown by in a flurry of visits with friends, dinners out, and more shopping. Gert and the children had claimed all of Ginny's time, and with Milt at work during the day and Gert having made plans for every evening, the time passed.

On New Year's Eve, Gert and Milt had hosted a party that rivaled anything Ginny ever attended. There was a three-piece jazz combo and the champagne flowed freely. Their guests all seemed to be operating in a state of false gaiety—laughing too loud, drinking too much, and dancing with a frenzy that made Ginny uncomfortable. Two of her friends from her days of boarding school and college had confided that they were barely holding on, having lost practically everything when the stock market crashed. And still, they raised their glasses, downing the champagne and holding out their crystal flutes for refills.

Finally, unable to stand the turbulent atmosphere, Ginny made the excuse of needing to pack for her trip home and escaped to her room. The following morning she'd been more than happy to board the train, carrying an extra small suitcase she'd borrowed from Gert to hold the gifts for Nate from Gert and Milt and their children.

But once home she could not shake her sense of foreboding that somehow, she had missed something. Despite Milt's assurances to the contrary in those moments when she had approached him to talk, she worried. Money had never been part of her vision of what life might be when the day came for Nate and her to leave the park. They had never touched a penny of her inheritance--substantial by anyone's measure. They could travel or move to wherever they wanted. Still, after seeing her friends in their reduced situations over the holiday, she had begun to be plagued by doubts—doubts that snuck up on her in the night and left her grumpy and out of sorts the following morning.

She thought of the people she'd seen on the streets of Chicago or closer to home once the train arrived in Gardiner, where the bread lines seemed to have doubled in the short time she'd been gone. Not wanting to worry Nate, she had tried to put a good face on the visit, telling him about the art galleries she'd visited and testing the waters by hinting at the possibility they might consider moving to Chicago.

Ginny was a firm believer in preparing for the worst and hoping for the best. She was not a pessimist, but she did consider herself to be a realist. And the reality these days was that no one's financial status was guaranteed. To her way of thinking, in Chicago they would at least have a roof over their heads. The house Milt and Gert occupied was the one Ginny and her sister had grown up in. Their parents had lived there until their deaths, sharing it with

Milt, Gert and the children with room to spare. There would be room for Nate and her.

Besides this new president—a distant cousin of the first Roosevelt—had promised to turn things around. Surely if they watched every penny they could make do until things improved. But after going over it time and again, she had concluded that a move to Chicago was not the answer. Nate would be miserable there—a fish out of water.

Finally, after months of worry, she'd decided it was foolish to anticipate problems. For now, Nate's job was secure. Besides, nothing would happen until closer to the time the park reopened for the season, and by then maybe things would improve. So why not enjoy the peace and beauty of the winter? On Monday, nearly three months after her return from Chicago as she watched Nate head off for work, Ginny told herself it was high time she set aside her worries about the future and enjoyed the present. She would bake Nate's favorite pecan pie and he would grin, knowing at last she was fully back home.

Then, shortly after she'd taken the pie from the oven that Monday morning, the young man who collected the mail and performed a variety of odd jobs for those who stayed on through the winter—at least until they were so snowed in no one could come calling--knocked at the cabin door.

"'Mornin', Miz Baker. Got a telegram for you." He handed her the familiar yellow envelope along with the rest of their mail, then shuffled from one foot to the other, shy and so very young. "You got anything I can do for you?"

"No, thanks." She couldn't recall his name and that annoyed her. He was a hardworking young man, doing whatever he could to support himself and his father, who had lost his job and taken to drowning his sorrows in drink.

"Well, you have a good day now. Regards to the mister." He headed back to where he'd left the tractor-like vehicle he'd jerry-rigged to travel over snow.

She laid the mail aside as she slid her thumbnail under the flap of the telegram. Inside was a single sheet of paper that read:

Bad news. Stop. Everything gone. Stop. Gert needs you. Stop. Milt.

Ginny stared at the words, rereading them again and again as if that might change their message. *What is happening?* She burst into tears, something so out of character for her that she had to sit down and collect her thoughts.

Everything gone? Everything? Surely that was an exaggeration.

She glanced at the kitchen clock. If she left right now, she could make today's train. She ran to the door, saw the boy still tinkering with his snow vehicle to get it started and suddenly recalled his name.

"Benny! Wait!"

He looked up, holding a screwdriver in one hand. She beckoned for him to come back, which he did without hesitation, moving at an uncoordinated lope that showed his eagerness to be of service.

"Benny, I've had news from my family in Chicago, and I need to leave right away. Can you take me to Gardiner to catch a train?"

"Yes, ma'am." He practically saluted, and that made Ginny smile.

"Thank you. Why don't you help yourself to a cup of coffee while I pack? There are cinnamon buns under that cake cover if you fancy one."

She hurried down the hall to the bedroom, snatching up various items and throwing them into a suitcase. Anything she forgot she could get at Gert's. She changed clothes from her baggy corduroy trousers to the woolen ones she wore when she traveled. She grabbed her coat and the suitcase and returned to the front room.

"Ready?" Benny asked, stuffing fully a third of a cinnamon roll in his mouth and wiping his hands on his pants.

"Just want to leave a note for Mr. Baker. Do me a favor and cover that pie with a towel, then put it in the icebox."

"We could stop by to see him," Benny suggested, as he did as she asked. "He's working the hotel up at Mammoth. We could go by there."

"No time. I can't miss the train. I'll call him once I get to Chicago."

She scribbled a letter for Nate that she knew explained nothing but would have to do until she had more information. Placing the note in an envelope, she checked to be sure the stove was off, and the fire was banked and then said, "Let's go."

Just as she crossed the threshold, she felt a wave of nausea that had her running to the bathroom.

"Maybe I should get Mr. Baker," Benny said a few minutes later, after she emerged wiping her face and hands on a towel. He was young enough to be her son, peach fuzz covering his upper lip in a failed attempt to appear older. The worry lines that marred his smooth forehead seemed out of place.

"I'll be fine," she assured him. "Let's go because I really need to be on that train."

Millie

-7-

By Sunday night Millie was feeling pretty proud of herself. Not only had she managed to find kindling and matches for building a fire, but she'd worked out several other problems as well and developed a kind of routine. At night she would drag one of the sofas close to the fire and wrap herself in the blankets she'd scavenged. She made a kind of tent of one of the canvas dust covers, looping it over two floor lamps she dragged to either end of the sofa. Mornings she replaced the cover and cleaned up from the fire just in case somebody came. In order to stay warm, she ran the halls, starting on the top floor and working her way floor by floor down to her hiding place, then back up again. When she was thirsty, she drank snow she'd melted in a metal pitcher from the kitchen.

Sometimes, when the silence threatened to drive her crazy, she went to the room just off the lobby, where there were tables with checkerboards built into the tops. She found a set of checkers somebody had forgotten to pack away and passed the time by pretending to play a game with Momma. She always made sure Momma won. Other times she would just sit and stare out the windows and think how her view of the outside world had changed.

In Chicago the windows in the front of the house looked out on a street lined with trees. There were sidewalks where she'd roller-skated or played hopscotch in summer and had snowball fights with her friends in winter. The windows in the back of the house looked out over the garden—a place Momma spent many long hours tending her flowers or reading or visiting with her friends. At the place Roger bought in Gardiner, she was hardly ever in the downstairs rooms, preferring to spend the time either in her room, Momma's room or the kitchen. She didn't spend a lot of time looking out windows.

Here in the hotel, she had nothing but time. Over the weekend she'd even found a window way up in the highest part of the hotel—a small window that gave her a sort of bird's eye view of the grounds and buildings below. Every once in a while, some elk or buffalo wandered down the street. Other than that, the town was deserted, and by Sunday night she had pretty much decided that Mammoth Hot Springs was a ghost town. It had been dumb to think she would just come to the park and find Ginny Baker's house, knock on the door and say, "Hi. Momma died and I thought maybe I could stay with you."

She didn't have to look at a map to understand that the park was huge, with mountains and lakes and geysers and hot springs, and who knew where Momma's friend might actually live? Of course, over the weekend, it had dawned on Millie that come Monday it might still just be her and the animals—that the ranger headquarters as well as the hotel might indeed be shut down for the winter. In Gardiner, lots of the stores downtown had closed, and lines of people who looked shabby like the beggars Millie had seen pictured in her story books lined up outside the churches no matter the weather.

Clara had told her those were people who'd lost everything—their homes, their jobs, and even the money they'd put in the bank for safekeeping. They stood in line hoping for something to eat and it would likely be their only food that day. Millie wondered if Clara was standing in one of those lines now that Roger had fired her. She'd taken such good care of Momma and Millie from the day they'd moved to Gardiner, and Millie didn't like to think of her having to wait in some long line because she was hungry. At least Millie was inside and had a pantry filled with tin cans she still hadn't opened.

That first night she'd discovered a large shallow pan in the kitchen that she used for building a small fire. She was afraid to risk lighting a real fire in the massive fireplace, fearing the flue might not be open and she might end up setting the hotel on fire. Besides, smoke coming from the chimney would draw attention, and when she made contact with anybody, she wanted to be sure she saw them first. The pan worked fine.

When she woke, her wristwatch—the one Momma had given her on her twelfth birthday--read half past ten. She was really surprised she had slept so long, but it was finally Monday and she heard snow sliding off the roof. At first, she thought it was a spring thaw—Momma used to talk about that. But when she peeked out the window, she saw ladders propped against the side of the building on the side opposite where she'd found the open door. In the bright sunlight, a man's shadow stretched across the snow, and she realized this was it! The first human she'd seen or heard since Friday was right outside.

Still, she wasn't ready to make contact. She needed time to make sure she'd left everything inside the hotel as she'd found it. And she needed to get a good look at whoever was on the roof—see if she thought she could trust him not to just send her right back to Roger. She figured she shouldn't risk lighting a fire even in the pan, so she'd have to live with the cold seeping in through the windows and walls. In spite of staying busy putting the furniture back where she'd first found it and covering everything, running down to the kitchen to be sure everything looked normal there, and retracing her steps on the upper floors to be sure she hadn't left any evidence behind, by noon her breath was visible—like she was smoking or something. Her teeth chattered as she hurried to get ready to speak to the man on the roof.

Having already figured somebody might show up come Monday and wanting to look as presentable as possible, on Sunday night Millie had collected snow in two tin buckets she found in the bathroom behind the front desk. She let the snow melt and warm up a little by setting the buckets close to the fire before washing herself as best she could. She also washed out her turtleneck, which reeked of smoke and dampness. She draped that over the back of a chair to dry while she wrapped herself in a couple of blankets she'd found while exploring the upstairs guest rooms.

She still hadn't overcome the biggest challenge--she could never remember being so cold at night. Her teeth chattered and she couldn't find enough blankets to wrap herself in.

The snow had kept falling all Saturday and Sunday and, having finished all the food she'd brought with her by Saturday at noon, she'd started raiding the hotel kitchen pantry. The pantry was larger than any room in Roger's house and there was a whole shelf filled with canned goods. Most of them still had their labels but there was this one section full of unlabeled cans. Millie figured somebody might miss a labeled can of beans or corn, but maybe the ones without labels were a kind of last resort.

It had taken her a while to find a can opener and even then, it was the kind with a hooked point on one end, like Roger used to open his beer, not the one intended for opening an actual can. But she made it work, figuring that if she poked the holes in close together, she could get the lid open enough to slide a knife inside and scoop out the contents—usually beans of some sort. Before she ate though, she always heated the can over the fire—even if it turned out to hold peaches or applesauce. She just wanted something warm sliding down her throat--something to make her think about those suppers Momma made for her before Roger.

Mostly out of boredom and to stay warm, over the weekend she had checked all the guest rooms, taking what treasures she discovered that seemed they might be of use as she waited for Monday to come—blankets, a forgotten pair of men's heavy socks, a couple of pieces of soap, the stubs of four candles—and the best treasure of all, a box of matches.

As it turned out, washing the bulky wool sweater was a big mistake because even after sitting there overnight it still wasn't fully dry. Millie put it on anyway, figuring it would warm once she covered it with the pea coat and Momma's poncho. In the tiny bathroom behind the desk, there was a toilet and a sink. Nothing worked, so she assumed it was like when they closed the cottage on Lake Geneva for the winter—the water had been turned off. But it served the purpose. If she left the door open there was enough light to see in the mirror that hung above the sink. She brushed her hair, which also smelled of smoke from the fires she'd made and scrubbed some smudges from her cheeks.

Satisfied that she was ready, she put on the almost dry hiking boots, hat and mittens, made sure the fire was out and everything looked exactly as it had when she'd first broken in to the hotel, even taking the metal pan back to the kitchen, where she made sure nothing was out of place there either. Convinced that she could present herself as if she'd just arrived, she hooked her backpack over her shoulders and was crossing the lobby, headed for that back exit at the end of the long hall of rooms, when she heard the rumble of a car's motor. Running to the windows that faced the park headquarters, she lifted the curtain and peeked out.

A large black car that Millie knew all too well slowed to a stop in front of the gray stone building, where she'd hoped to find someone when she'd first arrived on Friday. A ranger came outside as Gus got out of the car and opened the back door. Roger wore his black fur-trimmed overcoat and a hat pulled low over his forehead. His hands were protected by black leather gloves and he carried a lit cigar that he puffed on while speaking to the ranger. Millie tried to tell herself it wasn't that unusual for Roger to come to the park. He was planning to buy all the hotels and stuff, so he might just be coming to check on them.

But then Gus propped a picture frame on the roof of the car and the ranger leaned close to look at it. Millie saw the man shake his head. Then Roger pointed toward the hotel and her heart pounded in her throat.

Please don't let them come here.

A few minutes later she saw a man with a short gray beard, dressed in a thick-looking canvas jacket and a wool cap with earflaps, follow the path to where Roger, Gus and the ranger waited. Gus showed him the picture. The man turned to the ranger and said something. Gus spoke with them and then Roger threw down his cigar and climbed back inside the car while Gus shook the ranger's hand and gave him the picture. Then everybody went away again.

It didn't take Nancy Drew for Millie to figure out the picture was of her and that Roger had finally noticed she was gone. Now he was hunting for her, and it was important enough to him that he had come himself. Millie thought about the conversation she'd overheard between him and his lawyer. This wasn't good.

She scuttled back to the hiding place she'd found just in case anybody decided to come looking. She'd chosen a room near that back exit, figuring it gave her the best chance to check out whoever might come inside the hotel before that person realized she was there. She had made up a makeshift shelter using an upended mattress that blocked the cold seeping through the window and some of the canvas covers from the dining room. She figured anybody official would come through the front door and into the lobby. So, if they started coming her way as they poked around in the rooms at the other end of the hall and got too close, or if she didn't think she could trust them, she'd just slip out that door.

Earlier, she had replaced the mattress and covers because she thought she wouldn't be back there, so she sat huddled against the wall trying to decide what to do. If she went to the ranger, he was bound to let Roger know she'd been found. It was his job. Millie understood that. Even if she told him why she'd left and what she suspected was Roger's reason for wanting her back, he wouldn't have any choice but to turn her over to her stepfather. On the other hand, she knew she couldn't stay in the hotel forever. Already, she was feeling the effects of being in the cold for so long. Her throat hurt and her chest felt like it was full of water.

Late that afternoon Millie woke and realized she'd fallen asleep and no one had come. From outside she heard a man shout something. She ran down the hall and peered out the window. The ranger stood on the porch of the stone building and shouted something toward the hotel. Above her, the man on the roof laughed and told the ranger to have a good evening. A few minutes later Millie saw the old man climb down from the roof and put on his skis.

Should I let him know I'm here?

Millie's thoughts were a jumble of wanting to and at the same time fearing it would be a mistake. By the time she decided she should maybe take a chance, the man was gone.

As the streetlights came on outside, she flicked the switch on the flashlight. The light sputtered and went out. Feeling her way across the large room to the fireplace as the shadows deepened in the cavernous room, she scavenged for the box of matches she had been overjoyed to discover that first evening. Behind the front desk she'd found a display of advertising brochures she could use for kindling. If she was lucky, it would only take two to get the fire going. Last night she'd had to use six, and there weren't that many left. What if she had to stay here several more days?

Just then, she heard footsteps outside the entrance to the hotel. Someone tried the front door before walking the length of the porch and back again. Millie tiptoed to the window and peeked out. The ranger was walking past, and she leapt back, hoping he hadn't noticed the movement of the drapes. She tried to remember if she had closed the door at the end of the hall tight the last time she went out to get snow for washing up and a couple of small dry logs for the fire. She ran down the hall, swallowing a cough, scared the ranger might hear. The outside door was shut but unlocked and just after she turned the deadbolt, the ranger tried the handle. Had he heard her lock the door? She held her breath and waited. Seconds that seemed more like minutes passed, and then she heard footsteps crunching on the icy path she knew led back to the front of the hotel.

She blew out her breath, ran back to the lobby and watched the ranger leave. Still, she waited to be sure he didn't return before going back to finish starting the fire. When she was sure he wouldn't be back at least until morning, she got the metal pan from the kitchen and set it on the hearth. Cupping her trembling hands around the flame of the match as she touched it to the wadded-up paper she'd placed between the small logs scrounged from the pile outside, she prayed it would catch. She waited and finally heard the wood crackle and then pop. She stretched her hands over the flame, feeling warmth for the first time since morning. Her stomach rumbled and she couldn't help but think she'd give anything for a big ol' helping of Momma's spaghetti and meatballs! Momma wasn't much of a cook, but every once in a while, she would make that for their supper, telling Millie it had been her father's favorite.

As tears rolled down her cheeks, Millie swiped at them with the sleeve of her coat, and for good measure ran the fabric under her nose, which was leaking snot. She'd been crying a lot since first getting to the hotel--tears coming when she wasn't expecting them. "Just can't seem to stop the waterworks," she muttered. That's what Momma used to call her crying.

"Now, Millie, just turn off those waterworks. They won't do you a bit of good."

Oh, Momma, we were doing just fine on our own. For my whole life until you met Roger, it was just us. But then he came along, and everything changed. Why did you have to marry him?

On Monday, when she'd heard somebody on the roof, she'd been so excited. Finally!

But then Roger showed up.

What if Roger comes back?

Of course, why would he unless the ranger called him?

But from her experience, Roger didn't wait for someone to call. If he started putting pieces together that told him she'd gone to the park, he would return and not leave until she was found and delivered to him.

After eating, she made up her bed on the sofa, put another small log on the fire and settled in. If the old guy or the ranger came back, her best chance was to talk to one of them—just come walking around the side of the hotel like she'd planned and ask where to find Virginia Baker.

And what if they called Roger?

Millie jammed her fists into her pockets and felt the roll of money she'd saved. Suddenly she knew exactly what she needed to do. Tomorrow she would make the hike back to Gardiner, board the first train out of town and figure things out from there.

-8-

Eventually she fell asleep, and when she woke it was just starting to be daylight. *Tuesday.* Four days—and nights—since she'd left. Her throat burned and she was so thirsty, she needed a drink, but when she sat up and tried to stand, her knees buckled, and she fell backwards onto the sofa. Fumbling for the covers, she pulled them tight around herself. She was so tired.

She must have slept again because next thing she knew the room was dim with shadows and the last light of day. She figured she was in trouble by the way her breath came out in shallow gasps, like she'd run a race or something. Panic and fear clouded her brain. All she knew was that there was no way she could walk all the way back to town in the dark. Besides, the only train out was a morning train. Could she make it through another night? She was out of fuel for the fire and getting wood and snow to melt for drinking water meant going outside. Getting food meant making the trek to the kitchen, and she didn't think she had the strength to wrestle with the can opener.

From outside she heard the old man making his way off the roof. Realizing she had to trust somebody, she staggered to the window, pulled back the shade and knocked on the glass with her knuckles. But she was wearing mittens covered with that pair of heavy socks she'd found so the sound was muffled. The old man was gathering his things, coiling the heavy rope he used and putting away the large metal hooks. In another minute or two, he'd be gone.

Millie tore off one sock and mitten using her teeth and pounded on the glass with the flat of her hand. He hesitated, then picked up a shovel and funny-looking saw, walked around to the back of the hotel and returned a few minutes later without them.

"Help!" Millie shouted, which sent her into a coughing jag that felt as if her innards would come spilling out any minute, but she kept on pounding, using both hands now, and pressing her face against the cold glass.

After what seemed like forever but was probably not that long, he turned and squinted toward the window. He dropped the skis he'd been putting on and started toward her, motioning for her to go to the front door. But Millie had used the little energy she had to gain his attention. She sank to the floor, coughing until she had to fight to catch a breath as she clutched the blankets closer and kept her cheek pressed against the cold glass of the window.

"Mildred Chase?"

Millie realized she'd been so focused on the effort to stop coughing she hadn't heard the man come inside. But he was kneeling next to her, staring down at her. He wasn't really so old—his beard had some gray in it, but his skin was tanned and smooth and his eyes reminded Millie of her father's eyes.

"Yes sir," she managed. "It's Millie."

"You've got some folks pretty worried, young lady," he said, as he pressed some fresh snow against her chapped lips. "Let's get you…"

Millie clutched the sleeve of his coat and hung on. "No," she whispered. "Please. I need to find Mrs. Virginia Baker."

Even in the state she was in Millie could tell that surprised him. He sat back on his heels and stared at her. "Ginny is my wife. How do you know…?" Then he shook his head and stood. "Time for all that later. Let's get you someplace warm. You up for a little ride?"

Millie nodded. For reasons she would never understand, she trusted this man, and if Momma's friend was his wife, then why wouldn't she do whatever he suggested? Besides, she really didn't have much of a choice.

"Wait here," he said and went outside.

Minutes later he was back. He bundled her up and carried her outside to a small sled. He made sure she was secure, then returned to lock the hotel. "Ranger Dan's gone down to the canyon for a couple of days," he muttered as he covered her with one more blanket. "Otherwise we'd get you to his place down the road there. I'm afraid the next best thing is for me to take you home and once he gets back…"

It seemed he was talking more to himself than to Millie, working things out in his head. He put on his skis and tied the sled to his waist with a long rope before heading cross country, dragging the sled behind him. He didn't say anything more, but Millie could tell he was still thinking because he kept glancing back at her. She wanted to plead with him not to turn her in, and when he passed by the headquarters building and then a cluster of other buildings without stopping, she felt a little relieved. But panic returned as they moved farther and farther away from these signs of civilization. Maybe she'd made a big mistake agreeing to go with him—he might have lied about being married to Momma's friend.

The longer they traveled the more Millie tried to come up with a plan of escape. She considered just rolling off the sled into the snow, hoping he didn't notice, then running back to the buildings they'd left behind. But she kept coughing and he kept looking back, so that wasn't going to happen. Besides, she was in no shape to run anywhere. The man's breath came in white puffs as he climbed a hill. At the crest he paused. Millie looked around and saw a cabin below.

"Almost home," he said, and started forward again.

The small house was surrounded on three sides by tall pine trees with skinny trunks that grew so close together they looked like a fence. There was a little front porch with a large pile of wood to one side of a front door painted a deep red color. Lace curtains hung in the windows, and for some reason that made Millie feel safer.

"Okay, Millie, just let me get these skis off and we'll be inside before you know it." He was still talking more to himself than to her, but he had called her by her name.

"Mr. Baker?" Millie formed the words carefully, mostly to see if he would respond. If he was really married to Momma's friend that would be his name, wouldn't it?

"Call me Nate—everybody does. Ginny's not home just now, but what we need to do first is get you into some dry clothes, warmed up and fed so we can talk."

He lifted her from the sled and carried her inside. She made out a couple of easy chairs next to a big radio, a table and chairs, and the usual stuff she expected to see in a kitchen—stove, sink, small icebox. He set her down on one of the two easy chairs and she began peeling off the layers of blankets while he went to stir the fire in a pot-bellied stove and turn on a lamp. The light revealed a short hall at the far end of the room.

"Bedroom and bath," he said when he saw Millie looking that way. "Got another bed up there in the loft." He pointed toward a stairway. "You okay here for a few minutes?"

She nodded, figuring maybe he needed to use the bathroom, but instead he went down the hall and she heard him opening and closing drawers in the bedroom. Then she saw him move to the bathroom and heard water running. She was halfway to the front door, figuring maybe she should go while she could when he came back down the hall carrying a pile of towels and clothes. "These are Ginny's things but she's not much bigger than you. Are you feeling strong enough to go wash up and change out of those damp clothes while I fix us some supper?"

"When's your wife coming home?" Millie asked, ignoring his question as well as the pile of clothes and towels. "Cause it's her I need to talk to," she added, not wanting him to think she didn't appreciate what he was offering. On the rare occasions when Roger offered to do something nice and Momma turned him down, he got really mad.

Mr. Baker—Nate--let out a long breath and looked beyond her and out the front window where it was pitch dark now. "Ginny had to make a trip to Chicago—she's got family there." He looked kind of lost and sad, and for the first time, Millie felt a little sorry for him.

Then he turned his attention back to her and smiled. "You like elk stew?"

"Never had it," she replied. "I really don't have much of an appetite."

He nodded. "You won't mind if I fix some for me?"

"No sir." She started to cough again and had to sit down.

He put the back of his hand to her forehead and frowned. "Maybe a couple of aspirin and some hot tea with honey will soothe that throat. Steam is good for clearing out your lungs--I ran the water in the bathroom to get it hot. If you soak a washrag in the hot water and then spread it over your nose and mouth and take deep breaths, that might help." He handed Millie the towels and clothes and nodded toward the back of the house. "There's a bottle of aspirin in the medicine cabinet. Just take two."

Then he turned away and began collecting the things he needed for fixing his supper. She waited a couple of seconds, but he just kept working on putting the meal together, so she went down the hall.

He'd closed the door to the bathroom and left the water in the tub running without plugging the drain so that the room was warm and the small mirror above the sink was fogged over. Millie set the clothes–a pair of flannel pajamas, some heavy socks and a thick velour robe—on the little stool next to the tub. She peed and then stripped out of her damp clothes, stood in the tub and washed herself. She tried the trick with the steam and washrag he'd suggested, and he was right. It helped.

After drying off and putting on the pajamas and robe and socks, she spread her clothes over the sides of the bathtub to let them dry before opening the door a crack. Across the hall, she could see he'd set her backpack on the bed. Millie rummaged through it until she found her hairbrush. She could smell onions cooking and her stomach rumbled.

"I made you some tea," Nate said when she inched her way back into the front room that was both living room and kitchen. He nodded toward a mug on the table that he'd covered with a saucer to hold in the heat. Next to it stood a jar of honey and a spoon.

Millie sat on one of two wooden chairs and removed the saucer, then scooped honey from the jar and stirred it slowly into the tea. All the while, she kept glancing at Nate, who stood at the stove stirring the concoction he'd cooked in a large iron skillet. "Did you find the aspirin?"

Millie nodded. "When will your wife be back?" she croaked and noticed how the spoon he'd been using to stir his supper paused in mid-air.

"Hopefully, soon," he replied. He put a helping of the stew on a plate and brought it to the table. "You want some of this?"

It smelled really good--like Clara's home cooking. "I guess."

Nate ducked his head as he set the plate in front of her. Millie was pretty sure he was smiling, and that made her mad. He thought she was just a little kid. She pushed the plate away and wrapped her hands around the mug of tea. "This'll do," she muttered, bending her head so her hair covered her face.

"Suit yourself," Nate said as he pulled out the chair opposite her and started shoveling food into his mouth as if it had been days since his last meal. He washed it all down with a tall glass of watery-looking milk, then leaned back in the chair. Millie could feel him watching her. "So, Miss Millie, how do you know my wife?"

"She and my mother used to be friends."

"Used to be?"

She looked at him. *Was he doubting her?* "They were roommates at the boarding school they went to back in Chicago."

His eyebrows lifted and he leaned forward. "What's your mother's name?"

"Lavinia Chase—well it was Houston before she and my Dad were married."

He nodded. "I remember her. She was maid of honor at our wedding. Lovely woman."

"She's dead." She hoped to shock him, but she couldn't help but choke on the words.

He drew in a long breath and let it out slow. "I'm real sorry for your loss," he said as he got up, and took a pecan pie from the icebox. A big slice was missing. "That's a heavy load to bear, especially for somebody as young as you are."

He set the pie on the table before going back for a knife and fork. "Help yourself," he said, laying the utensils next to the saucer he'd used to cover her tea. Meanwhile he carried his plate and milk glass to the sink and washed them, put away the remainder of the stew and then scrubbed the skillet.

Pecan pie was Millie's favorite and this one looked like it would be at least as good as the one Clara made. She cut a slice. "You want some?" she asked.

"Sure."

He continued scrubbing the skillet, so Millie got another saucer from the open shelf above the counter and a fork from the metal basket. She cut him a piece twice the size of hers. He was a big man, and she kept thinking about all that snow he'd shoveled, and how far he had to walk to his job and back.

"Your wife sent Momma a Christmas card," she volunteered.

This time he made no effort to hide his smile. "My wife sends out a lot of cards during the holidays, fusses about it every year, but she loves it all the same. Still..."

"I can prove it," Millie said, not sure why she was getting so defensive. "Wait there." She shoved the last bite of pie into her mouth and hurried back to the bedroom, where she dug around in her backpack until she found the Christmas card.

"See?" she said, presenting it to him as she slid back onto the chair.

He studied the handwriting for a long moment, and the way he looked at it was like seeing it made him sad again.

"It's from her," Millie said. "You can read it yourself."

He put the card on the table and slid it toward her. "No need. That's Ginny's handwriting." He took a bite of his pie.

"That man who came to the park is not my father," she announced, once the silence had gotten to her. "He's sort of my stepfather, I guess. My real father died in the war a month before I was even born."

"I see. Still, your stepfather seemed quite concerned...."

She wanted to beg and cry, but instead she put on her toughest face and said, "If you try to contact him, I'll run away again."

He frowned. "That would be a big mistake. The park is no place for a girl your age alone, even in the best of weather, and certainly not in winter."

"I'll do it." She folded her arms tight across her chest, smothered a coughing jag and glared at him. "I don't care. I'd rather be eaten by bears than go back to that house."

"I don't think you'll need to go to such extremes. Pretty sure all our bears are still in hibernation."

"Wolves then," she muttered, determined to win this.

He shrugged. "Not too many of those around either—pretty much wiped out back in '26."

He took another bite of his pie.

"How about we table this conversation until tomorrow? It's late, and you need a good night's sleep in a proper bed." He covered the remainder of the pie with a towel and set it back in the icebox. "I'm going to get my things from the bedroom so I can sleep in the loft. Would you mind washing up the rest of these dishes while I do that?"

She did as he asked, keeping one ear cocked for his movement in the back of the small house. She'd seen a telephone on a table near the kitchen next to the radio, so at least he wasn't back there calling Roger. As she was wiping out the sink, he came back to the kitchen. He was holding a pile of clothing and a small blue jar.

"Ginny swears by this stuff for breaking up chest congestion and healing a bad cough. Rub it on your chest before you go to sleep and let it work overnight."

Millie accepted the blue jar, recognizing it as the same remedy Momma used whenever she had a bad cold.

"Sleep tight," he said, as he set the pile of clothes on the steps leading to the loft and waited for her to leave. "I'm going to read for a bit."

Millie was pretty sure she wouldn't sleep a wink. Nate Baker seemed nice enough, but she wasn't in a trusting mood. She held up the jar. "Thanks for this," she said. "See you in the morning."

Later, she thought she heard voices coming from the living room. Panicked, she got out of the big bed and padded down the hall, hoping the socks she wore would make it possible for her to sneak up on Nate before he could hang up the phone.

But when she reached the dimly lit room, she saw Nate asleep in one of the two chairs. The voices were just static coming from the radio he'd left on. Millie tiptoed past him and switched off the dial, then took an afghan draped over the empty chair and covered Nate with it.

She noticed a narrow door under the stairs that led to the loft. A soft light glowed through a frosted glass panel. She tiptoed around Nate and opened the door—and stepped straight into summertime.

A greenhouse! How was this possible out here in the middle of nowhere?

She thought about how Momma would have loved this—the snow all around outside the glass windows and moonlight streaming through. Quietly, she closed the door and tiptoed back to where Nate slept. That's when she saw the letter on the floor and recognized his wife's handwriting. As she read it, Millie understood it didn't take a genius to figure out that Ginny Baker wasn't coming back any time soon.

Ginny

-9-

On her second visit in less than three months, Ginny
arrived at the house on Michigan Avenue at dusk after
spending two days and a night sitting up on trains. She
raised the polished brass knocker and let it fall three times,
and when no one came to answer, she tried the handle. The
door opened and she stepped inside.

"Hello?" she called, expecting to see her sister's
live-in housekeeper come rushing from the kitchen,
apologizing for not greeting her properly. After setting her
suitcase down at the foot of the stairs, she removed her coat
and hat and followed the sound of muffled voices to the
kitchen.

"Hello?" she called again.

"Well, isn't this a nice surprise, children?" Gert said
in a voice that was shrill, tense and anything but
welcoming. Ginny would have expected her sister to be
surprised at her arrival, but Gert acted as if nothing could
surprise her. She had aged ten years in the short time since
Ginny had last seen her. She wore no make-up, had not had
her hair done, and there were deep purple semicircles under
her eyes. Most surprising of all, she was cooking. Gert did
not cook, but she scooped a serving spoon filled with a
sticky mess that was possibly macaroni and cheese onto
three plates.

"What brings you back so soon?" she asked in that
same high-pitched voice.

"Milt asked me to come."

The pan Gert was holding wobbled dangerously and
Ginny stepped forward to take it from her. All the while she
was aware that the twins were watching her intently.

"Angela, Adam, why don't you take your plates, help Sammy with his, and you can all go eat in the solarium?" she suggested. "Pretend it's summertime and you're having a picnic with all the green plants around you."

Reluctantly the children did as Ginny asked. Once they were gone, she led Gert to a chair. "Sit," she said, "and tell me what's happened."

To her shock, her sister laughed—laughter that almost instantly turned to anger. "You just had to come, didn't you? As always, it's Ginny to the rescue. Poor dumb Gert couldn't possibly manage without you-- is that what Milt told you? Well, he has a few things to learn about me."

"He wrote that everything was gone, Gert."

"That's all he knows. He may have lost all our money—everything our parents worked so hard to leave us, but I still have my furs and my jewels, and we have this house and everything in it." She clutched Ginny's hands, her eyes wild. "We can sell it all, Ginny. It's just stuff. The house alone will bring more than enough to see us through these horrid times."

"And if you sell the house, where will you live, Gert?"

Her sister's eyes flitted around the room as if seeking a place right there in the kitchen. "You can take the children to live with you and Nate—such a steady man. I always told Milt that I should have been the one to marry Nate. *He* would have made sure everything was protected, but no. I married *Mr. High and Mighty, Mr. I-need-to-dress-the-part, Mr. Get-to-know-the-right-people-whether-or-not-you-can-stand-the-sight-of-them.*"

Gert was describing herself more than she was Milt, but Ginny wasn't going to debate that point with her. She waited for the tears that didn't come and realized her sister had no more tears. All she had was her fear and her anger—and her hysteria.

"Gert, when's the last time you slept?"

"I can't afford to sleep. In case you missed it, we have no help—no nanny for the children, no cook, no housekeeper, no driver. It's just me."

"And now me. So, I want you to go upstairs, take a nice hot bath and lie down until I come for you."

"The children…"

"Will be fine." She wrapped her arm around Gert and led her to the back stairs. "Go," she urged, and was relieved when her sister did as she asked.

Over the next several hours she made sure the children had a decent supper, got them ready for bed, read them a story and tucked them in, deflecting their questions about why their mother was so upset and where their nanny had gone and why Cook wasn't making the meals like always and when Father would be home. That last question was one Ginny also wanted answered.

Once the children were in bed, she looked in on her sister and found her sleeping soundly. Downstairs, she poured herself a glass of club soda and sat down in the grandly furnished front room to wait for Milt. The room was cold, and after an hour of waiting she lit a fire.

He arrived just after ten o'clock, showing no sign of surprise at finding her there. He dropped his briefcase near the front door, hung his overcoat and hat on the ornate hall tree, and loosened his tie as he walked straight to the bar, where he poured himself a large tumbler of whiskey. He held the bottle up to her, but she refused his offer.

"What happened, Milt?"

To her fury, he shrugged as he took the chair opposite hers. "It's all gone," he said.

"I got that part. What happened exactly?"

He smirked. "There is no exactly in the world we live in, Ginny. You're broke…we're broke…everybody's broke."

Of course, that wasn't entirely true. She and Nate had the small savings they had managed to accumulate over the years. But the cushion from her inheritance after her parents died—the funds she had relied upon to carry them through these hard times should anything happen to Nate or his job—apparently were gone.

"How?" she asked again, clenching her fingers together to keep from screaming the question. After all, it hadn't been so long since she'd been in this very room—a giant Fraser fir Christmas tree in the corner twinkling with lights and the vast collection of German glass ornaments her sister had inherited from their parents, while the floor was covered in the cast-off wrappings of a holiday bonanza.

Milt covered his face with his hands and shook his head. He reached for the crystal glass half-filled with Scotch and drained it. "I don't know, Ginny. Times are..."

"Do not tell me about hard times, Milt. That money was protected. You told me that yourself. After our parents died, I trusted you to secure those funds. You assured me that..."

Her brother-in-law stood and threw the whiskey glass toward the fire that blazed behind her. If he was aiming to break it, he failed, as the glass fell unscathed on the thick Persian carpet.

"I don't know, Ginny," he bellowed. "Do you think I did this? We were fine and then the bank closed. I've been juggling whatever I could salvage ever since, but now.... The investments we made were supposed to be...." The man was near tears.

"How long have you known we couldn't hang on?"

He shrugged. "It became pretty clear just after Thanksgiving." He snorted. "*Thanks*-giving. There's a joke." He collapsed back onto the sofa, crossed one leg over the other and leaned his head on a cushion as he stared up at the ceiling.

"Then what about Christmas? You knew and yet, you let Gert…"

"I didn't *let* your sister do anything. She's the one who always must have the best—the most. She's the one who wore me down time after time when I tried to tell her we needed to watch things."

"She told me you wanted her to buy everything on the children's lists and that you insisted on that fur coat and…"

"Do you know your sister, Ginny? She's impossible. She nags and whines and…"

Ginny did not want to listen to him blaming Gert for what he had failed to protect. She cast about for a ray of hope. "At least we have the house and the artwork and…"

"And exactly who do you think is going to buy any of it? Everyone is in the same boat, Ginny, and even if you could find a buyer, you'd get pennies on the dollar. We're finished—get that through your head. Jesus, I always thought you were the smart one."

He retrieved the tumbler and went back to the bar, where he emptied the last of the whiskey into his glass. He drank it down, set the glass on the bar and headed for the door, where he paused, his back to her. "I'm more ashamed than I can ever say. I really thought this would be over before now. I did my best, Ginny."

She heard him climb the stairs.

She wished he hadn't drunk all the scotch—she could use something a lot stronger than club soda.

Nate

-10-

He'd spent the night in his chair, too worn out to make the climb to the loft or even to change out of his clothes. He woke before dawn and gathered that sometime during the night Millie must have covered him with the afghan his co-workers had given Ginny and him as a wedding present. He stretched as he made his way to the bathroom. The door to the bedroom was closed and he wondered if maybe Millie had taken off again. He was a little surprised to realize he cared. He didn't like mixing in other people's business, especially when that business could get complicated.

When Roger Fitzgerald had shown up, Nate hadn't put it together that this might be the man who had married Ginny's friend, as well as the man looking to buy out the current contract to run all the concessions in the park. The name was common enough, and he'd always assumed the Fitzgerald that Lavinia had married was a Chicago man. But now he knew for certain the two men were one and the same—Millie's stepfather and his potential boss. If that didn't complicate things, he didn't know the meaning of the word.

Easing the bedroom door open, he glimpsed a lump in the bed, though that could be covers stacked to look as if she were there. But as he moved closer, he could make out her hair covering her face and could smell the remnants of the Vick's ointment he'd suggested she rub on her chest. Satisfied, he returned to the steps to the loft, collected the clothes he'd left there and headed for the bathroom. He washed up, changed into the clean clothes and was trimming his beard when he heard a light knock on the door.

"Mr. Baker?" Another knock, more urgent than the first. "Nate?"

"Almost done," he called.

There was something that sounded a little like a whimper, so he opened the door. She brushed past him. "I really have to pee," she said, her eyes pleading with him to give her some privacy.

He dropped his dirty clothes in the hamper and left her to it. In the kitchen, he pulled eggs, bacon, and a pitcher of powdered milk from the icebox. Then he dropped a dollop of the solidified bacon grease from the covered dish Ginny kept next to the stove into the iron skillet and waited for it to sizzle before adding three strips of bacon. While that cooked, he beat the eggs with a little of the milk before adding grated cheese and some chopped chives from Ginny's greenhouse. He was pouring a glass of milk for Millie when she came to the table, still wearing Ginny's pajamas and robe and a pair of thick wool socks. He was relieved to see that she seemed somewhat better, not coughing as much and looking less feverish.

"Sleep well?" he asked, setting the milk on the table before putting the bacon aside to drain while he cooked the eggs.

"You lied," she said, her voice rusty with the effects of her sore throat.

"And good morning to you. How exactly have I lied to you?"

"You let me think your wife would be back soon when you don't know when she might be back."

Nate glanced at Ginny's letter, still lying on the floor next to his chair. He cleared his throat, dished up the food and brought both plates to the table. "Let's get a few things straight, Millie."

She nibbled a slice of bacon and did not look at him.

"First, that letter was private, and you had no right to read it." He poured himself a cup of coffee and sat across from her. "Second, I did not lie—I told you I hoped Ginny would return soon. And finally, when I get to work this morning, there's a chance Ranger Atwood might be back from checking on things near the canyon. He's the park supervisor and the man you saw the other day when your stepfather stopped by. He has a duty to call the authorities in Gardiner once he knows you have been found."

Now he had her full attention. She had dark brown eyes that stared at him in horror. "You can't...please." Tears welled and threatened to spill over.

"The key to what I said just now are the words 'once he knows.'"

She blinked. "You're not going to tell him?"

Nate had spent a good part of the night staring at the phone and trying to figure out why he was hesitating at all to call Dan or the authorities in Gardiner to let them know the girl was safe. Why not let things take their natural course from there? Didn't he have enough to worry about with Ginny's note and the possibility she might have to stay in Chicago for some time? He could feel their idyllic life slipping away, like the ice and snow he pushed off the roofs. Only he wasn't pushing now; he was trying to hold on.

He peppered his eggs and scooped up a forkful. "Do you have any idea what you're asking me to do, Millie? I could lose my job for just what I've done already--taking you in and not making that call."

She poked at her food without eating. "I'm sorry. I don't mean to cause trouble. I just thought if I could talk to your wife, maybe she would be able to...maybe I wouldn't have to..."

"Let's talk about your mother, Millie."

"I told you," she said with an exasperated sigh. "Her name was Lavinia Chase—I mean until she married

Roger. Then it was Lavinia Fitzgerald. But I'm still Millie Chase—Roger never adopted me or anything. That makes a difference, right?"

A memory fired in Nate's brain—a day a few years earlier when Ginny had returned to the cabin madder than a bull moose whose authority had been challenged. She'd been waving a letter around.

"She's gone and married that man," she had ranted. "Known him no more than six weeks and she's married him."

"Who?" Nate had asked.

"Lavinia."

Lavinia and Ginny had been roommates at a fancy boarding school and then college. After graduation, they had gone their separate ways but stayed in touch by letter and the occasional visit. They had served as maids of honor in each other's weddings. Ginny had gone to stay with Lavinia after her husband was killed in the war. When Lavinia met Roger Fitzgerald at some society ball in Chicago, she'd been excited to introduce him to Ginny during the holidays. Ginny hadn't liked the man from day one. She'd tried to warn her friend and they had fought. Then she'd gotten word that Lavinia had married him.

"She is making a huge mistake. At the very least, he'll make her miserable. At the worst, he'll rob her blind."

"You can't know that, Ginny. Do you even know this man?"

"We've met, but I don't have to really know him. Men like him were always sniffing around once we were of age. Mark my words, Nate, this guy is after one thing and that's Lavinia's money."

"Still…"

"Lavinia may never speak to me, but what kind of friend would I be if I failed to make my concerns known?"

That very night she had written a long letter, posted it the following day and, to Nate's knowledge, had never heard from Lavinia again. Not that Ginny hadn't kept trying. The Christmas card Millie had shown him proved that. He suspected there had been other attempts to reconnect as well.

He turned his attention back to Lavinia's daughter. "I only met your mother a couple of times—once at my wedding, and then when she came here for a visit right after you were born. As far as I know things between Ginny and her ended badly a few years ago."

"But your wife still sent that card last Christmas. She sent it to our old address in Chicago and the people living there sent it on to her at the house in Gardiner. Momma cried when she got it. If you'd just read it, you would understand why I have to talk to her."

So, while Lavinia had known Ginny lived in the park, she had never let on that she and her new husband were living just a few miles away in Gardiner. Why? If Nate knew his wife at all, he knew Ginny would have gone to that house and insisted on seeing her friend. He was frankly surprised the two had never run into each other accidentally. Gardiner was a small town.

"All right, Millie. Get the card."

"Wait right there," she said, wiping her mouth on her napkin. She ran down the hall and returned a moment later. She removed the card from the envelope and handed it to him.

This time Nate read it. In her familiar script Ginny had expressed her hope that all was well, and that Millie was thriving. She told her friend that she was headed to Chicago for the holidays as usual, and then had closed with:

Lavinia, I miss you—I miss "us." If there is any chance we might get together while I am in Chicago, you know how to reach me at Gert's. In the meantime, know that I am always here for you and your precious Millie. Nate sends his best wishes. Love, Ginny

He understood now why Millie had thought Ginny would be her salvation. He placed the card back inside the envelope and slid it across the table. Despite his aversion toward getting involved in other people's messes, he knew before he did anything else, he had to make Ginny aware of Lavinia's death and Millie's arrival in the park. The facts were that Millie had come to find Ginny, and it was Ginny who needed to at least be a part of whatever decisions he made going forward.

"I need to speak to my wife, Millie," he said quietly. "I also need to get to work so I'll call her after my shift."

She tucked her hair behind her ears, revealing eyes that were at once hopeful and suspicious. "Does that mean you won't turn me in?"

"Not today," he said. "I assume I can count on you to stay put here, not answer the door should anyone come—which would be unusual, and definitely not get any ideas about going off on your own."

She nodded her head so vigorously that once again her hair covered half her face. She brushed it back impatiently. "I promise."

"Don't get your hopes up, Millie. There's a long way to go before we work things out for you. Ginny has her own family problems she's dealing with right now. You need to get in line, okay?"

"I will. I... thank you." She rushed around the table and gave him a hug.

Embarrassed, Nate patted her back and stood. "Think you can handle cleaning up these dishes? I need to get going."

"Yes. I can make us some supper too. Clara…she was Roger's cook and housekeeper until he fired her…taught me how to cook."

Nate smiled. "Just get some more rest and take another dose of aspirin." He filled his thermos with hot water, took some jerky, an apple and a hunk of the bread Ginny had made before leaving and put them in his knapsack. When he looked up, Millie had gotten his coat, hat and gloves and was holding them out to him. "Plenty of wood out here on the porch," he said as he stepped outside and strapped on his skis. "Just be careful you don't have company when you open the door."

"I don't think Roger could find this place," she assured him.

"Not talking about Roger," he said. "Talking about the real residents of the wilderness here." He waved and started up the trail.

-11-

He was on the hotel roof, sawing through another block of the snow and ice when Dan stopped by.

"Any sign of the kid?" the ranger shouted.

"Not since I got here," Nate replied. It wasn't a lie exactly; just what Ginny might call "stretching the truth to its limits."

Just after noon, the wind kicked up and the sky turned a threatening dark gray. As a shower of sleet fell, Nate took shelter in the park headquarters. He and Dan ate their lunch in Dan's office, and Nate told his friend about the telegram Ginny had received from her brother-in-law.

"She's gone there to pick up the pieces," he said.

Dan shook his head. "You don't think he means everything?"

"Hard to say. Milt's always been pretty steady. Ginny trusts him, but these days, who knows?"

"If you want to go there, Nate, I'm sure your boss would understand."

Nate wasn't as sure. He'd had to make the case for staying on the payroll full-time. The company that owned and ran the hotels and shops in the park was no different than any other business—they looked for ways to cut corners, and lately they'd been working hard to make sure the business was attractive enough to bring a good price when they sold out. To that end his supervisor had hinted Nate's hours might be cut.

"Not much I could do in Chicago, I expect. I'm gonna try calling Ginny when I get home tonight."

"Try her now." Dan pushed the black telephone closer to Nate's side of the desk before heading for the outer office. "I've got some filing to do."

Outside, the wind howled as the icy snow pecked at the window behind Dan's desk. Nate pulled his billfold from his back pocket and took out the paper where he kept numbers he might need but wasn't about to memorize—

Ginny's sister's number topped the list. He dialed the long-distance operator, gave her the information and waited.

"I'm afraid there's no answer," the operator said after several rings. "Would you like me to keep trying?"

"No, thanks. I'll try later." He placed the receiver in its cradle and opened the office door.

"No luck?" Dan asked.

Nate shook his head. "I'm going over to the hotel. With this storm coming, I want to check inside to be sure there's no water leakage from ice dams on the roof."

"Sure thing." Dan pulled out a file drawer and began thumbing through the folders until he found the one he wanted.

The real reason Nate wanted to check the hotel was to be sure there was no evidence that Millie had been there. With the concessions up for sale, who could say when Fitzgerald or some other prospective buyer might decide they wanted to examine the property?

Once inside he saw immediately that she'd done a pretty good job of making sure things were put back the way they'd been. Other than the sofa she'd slept on and the remains of a small fire, everything was in its place. What she'd forgotten was to observe the trails she'd left in the dust accumulated on the floor when she dragged the sofa closer to the fire or made her trips back and forth to the kitchen, bathroom or guest rooms.

He found a dust mop and scattered the dust. No one would question his footprints. In the kitchen he checked the pantry and chuckled when he realized how she had replaced the tin cans she'd opened behind those not yet used. Trouble was she hadn't thought to rinse them out and the remains were sure to attract critters, so he gathered them and placed them in a covered metal trash bin. He would make sure they were properly disposed of before the hotel staff came to reopen for the season.

Truth was he couldn't help being impressed with Millie's resourcefulness. She'd found her way to the park—on foot—and been clever enough to find shelter and food. That alone told him she was awfully determined not to end up living with her stepfather. In spite of his resolution not to, Nate found himself thinking of ways to keep her away from the man, at least until he'd had a chance to discuss things with Ginny.

He was just coming out of the hotel when he saw Dan headed his way. "Look at this," he said holding up a single sheet of paper.

Nate took the paper Dan handed him and unfolded it.

If the kid turns up, call this number—not the police.

Taped to the paper was a business card for a lawyer from Livingston.

"There's no signature," Nate noted, turning the paper over.

"Benny brought it with the mail," Dan said. "I studied the envelope, but it just had my name and the park address. I think it might be from that driver—the one who brought Fitzgerald here the other day."

"Could be." Nate was trying hard to figure out what to say.

Dan folded the paper with the business card inside and stuffed it in his pocket. "I'll hang on to this just in case she turns up. You want to try calling Ginny again?"

"Yeah." Calling from the office where Millie wouldn't be there to hear made sense. "Thanks."

"I'm going to head home. Lock up when you leave." Dan was a confirmed bachelor and he'd taken up residence in one of the former military houses at the far end of the village, so he had a short trip. "Say, after you talk to Ginny, come on over for supper."

"Another time. I left something unattended back home."

Dan grinned. "Did you forget Ginny wasn't there to handle things?"

"Something like that." He waved to his friend and hurried inside to try calling Ginny again. It was five o'clock in the park, meaning it was an hour later in Chicago, and how many times had Ginny fussed about the fact that the world might explode if Gert and Milt didn't sit down for supper right at six? It was his best chance to reach his wife.

But once again the phone rang several times with no answer, and the operator suggested he try later. Nate felt a flicker of worry, then thought maybe Milt had taken them out to eat one last time before they settled in to deal with their financial disaster. Ginny often said how much her brother-in-law liked eating in restaurants, especially places where he might be recognized. Milt had a flashy side despite his tendency toward conservative decisions when it came to investments. He and Gert both liked what Nate had once heard Milt call "the finer things," and if he could afford such things, he planned to enjoy them. Still, it was odd none of the servants had picked up the phone.

Nothing he could do now and besides, he had Millie to worry about. He wanted to ask her what she knew about the lawyer listed on the business card Dan had showed him. *Alvin Stoner.*

When he reached the cabin, the windows were steamed over from the inside and he could hear music coming from the Victrola. After removing his skis, he opened the door and had to duck to keep from getting slapped in the face with the sleeve of a dripping wet shirt.

"Millie?" He worked his way through a makeshift clothesline she'd stretched from one end of the cabin to the other—a line filled with her clothes and some of his.

"Oh hi. Sorry about this. I thought everything would be dry by now." She frowned.

He grasped the tail of an undershirt and squeezed it so that water dripped steadily onto the planked floor. "Helps if you really wring stuff out first," he said.

She blinked and then giggled nervously. "I slept most of the day and just got started on this a little bit ago. Guess I didn't squeeze things hard enough." She started snatching clothes down and running back to the bathroom. She sure was a nervous kid.

He took off his coat, gloves and hat and went to help her. "My hands are stronger, so you bring me a piece. I'll wring it out and then you rehang it."

"I'm sorry, Nate. I'll clean up the mess, I promise." Her voice shook and he realized she was afraid of him.

"How about you turn down that music a little before you scare the neighbors?"

She hesitated. "I thought you didn't have neighbors—I didn't see any other cabins or houses or…"

"Millie, you need to understand that it's the animals who own this land—not us. We're just visiting."

"Oh."

"And while you probably won't see many people, there's a young man who does come by a couple of times a week to bring the mail and supplies. Although, since he knows Ginny's gone, he's more likely to deliver anything to me at headquarters."

"What if he comes here anyway?" Her voice shook.

"Like I said, don't answer the door. He won't come inside, but you need to wait 'til I'm home to play music or the radio, okay?"

"Okay." She stared at him, as if waiting for another shoe to fall.

"Turn down the volume," he reminded her as he headed for the bathroom.

They made short work of the laundry. She didn't have that much and Ginny—as usual—had already taken care of any dirty clothes Nate had left in the hamper the day before she left.

"Seems to me you promised me supper, so what are we having?" Nate thought it best to keep the tone between them light and unthreatening. He would ask her about the lawyer later.

She had put together a meal from canned goods— lima beans and corn, Spanish rice, and Spam, with tea for him and milk for her. "Is it enough?" she asked, studying the plates she set on the table. "I didn't want to take anything from the greenhouse unless you said it was okay."

"It's a feast," he assured her. "Maybe some of that bread there and some oleo. How are you feeling?"

She paused, seeming to consider this. "Better. Maybe sleeping all day and the Vick's helped. Oh, and I took another dose of the aspirin so that probably did some good." She hurried to add to the meal and then sat across from him, pushing aside the legs of her corduroy pants drying on the line behind her. He noticed she was still wearing Ginny's pajamas, although she had abandoned the robe for a red and black checked wool shirt that Ginny wore sometimes. He also saw that her face was not as flushed as when he'd found her, and she seemed to be coughing less. Still, he'd have to watch to be sure she didn't have a relapse.

Once they started to eat, she turned shy, glancing at him from under lowered lashes, as if waiting for him to say something. When he complimented her on the meal, she sighed. "Are you gonna call your wife or not?"

"Tried two times from work but didn't get an answer. I'll try again tomorrow." He'd decided as long as Dan was okay with him calling from the phone at headquarters, that was the best idea.

"You could try now."

Nate glanced at the clock. "It's already after nine there. My sister-in-law has three young children. Ginny probably just got them settled for the night. I'll try again tomorrow."

Millie pushed her food around her plate. "Are they all right? Those kids? I mean, are they sick or something? Is that why she had to go to Chicago?"

"I expect they'll be fine."

Nate was touched by her concern. At a time when he wouldn't blame her for focusing solely on her own troubles, she was thinking of others. He didn't know much about kids, but he figured that was rare.

"Millie, did you ever hear your mother speak of a lawyer by the name of Stoner?"

She froze, and Nate saw how her hand trembled as she guided a fork filled with food to her mouth. "He's Roger's lawyer," she mumbled.

"I see. Did Mr. Stoner and your mother ever have any meetings or conversations that you know of?"

She leaned back in her chair and hooked her hair behind her ears. "He came to see Momma when she was sick. Roger wasn't there, and Momma told me not to tell." She frowned. "Why? Did you talk to him?"

"No. Ranger Atwood mentioned him."

She twisted her hair around one finger and refused to look at him. He could practically hear the wheels turning in her mind and feared she was planning to run.

"Nothing has changed, Millie."

She looked up and he knew she didn't believe him, so he decided to take a different tack. "Seems to me like you and Roger aren't exactly close, so what do you think is going on here? I mean, why should he care if you run away?"

"I told you. He wants to get at Momma's money."

"And what makes you think he needs you to do that?"

"Because the day I ran away, Roger and Mr. Stoner had a meeting at the house, and Mr. Stoner told him

Momma had left everything to me and there was nothing he could do to change that. Mr. Stoner said she'd left her friend back in Chicago in charge and mentioned your wife's name. That's when I remembered about the card. I think she put Mrs. Baker—Ginny—in charge."

Nate felt an actual shiver of apprehension move up his spine. A man like Roger Fitzgerald might be capable of bending the law or doing things Nate didn't care to consider to get his hands on a fortune the size of Lavinia's—assuming her fortune was still intact. Ginny had always laughed when she told him that she and Gert were rich, but Lavinia was *rich* in capital letters. He wondered if Lavinia had named her husband to inherit should anything happen to Millie. He also wondered if the whole business wasn't some wild goose chase. After all, if Ginny and her sister had lost all their money, wasn't it just possible Lavinia's fortune had suffered the same fate, since, as he recalled, Milt handled Lavinia's finances too?

It was a question he was not about to raise with this child.

"I got to thinking today that you're missing school," he said, and was pleased to see that the change in subject had caught her attention. "Since you might be here for a few days with not much to do, there are some books there on wildlife and natural history and such you might take a look at." He nodded toward a bookcase that practically filled one wall near the front door.

"I'm a good student—I can catch up once this is all over."

"Still, it will help give you the time you need to fully recover and regain your strength. I'm not much of a teacher, but I'd be glad to quiz you some in the evenings. You pick out something and let's come up with a plan."

"Yeah, okay." She didn't sound exactly thrilled at the idea.

They cleared the dishes and washed and dried them, mostly in uncomfortable silence. Afterwards, Nate turned on the radio and sat down to listen to the news. Millie knelt next to the bookcase and ran her finger along the spines, occasionally pulling a book out until she had a stack of about half a dozen. She held up one titled *Pride and Prejudice*.

"Have you read this?"

"Not my cup of tea, as Ginny might say. It's her book. I think she's read it more than once so it's probably pretty good."

"Momma had a book just like this." She opened the cover, gasped and read the words scribbled on the fly leaf out loud. "Look at this! *Property of Virginia Dodson, St. Thomas's Boarding School, September 1904*. Gosh."

"That's where your mother and Ginny were in school together. In 1904 they would have been a couple of years younger than you are now."

He saw how Millie closed her eyes as she hugged the book to her chest.

"If you want to go on to bed and read awhile, I'll be fine," he told her.

She nodded and stood. "I can sleep in the loft," she said. "I was up there today—not snooping or anything."

"Did you like it?"

"I did, and I was thinking if somebody did come around, if all my stuff was up there, they wouldn't know I was here and you wouldn't get in trouble and besides, you wouldn't have to climb up and down. I'm not saying you're old or anything, but you already do a lot of climbing when you work so…"

Nate felt an urge to embrace the girl but settled for paying her a compliment. "Millie Chase, did anyone ever tell you that you are a very intelligent and considerate young lady?"

She blushed. "Momma used to say things like that."

"Well, your mother was right. How about a glass of warm milk before you say goodnight?"

"I can fix it," she said, setting the books on the step and hurrying to the kitchen.

He watched as she took down a small saucepan from a hook over the stove, measured out two cups of milk and set the pan to heat. "Clara sometimes added vanilla to the milk," she said.

"Now that sounds nice. Look in the cabinet there next to the sink."

When the milk was warm, she stirred in a splash of vanilla and then filled two mugs. She handed one to him and waited until he took the first sip. "Is it all right?"

"It's just dandy," he assured her.

She grinned. "Okay, then see you tomorrow." She started up the narrow staircase but stopped midway, set down her milk and the books and hurried back to where he sat. She gave him another hug. "Thanks, Nate. I'm really glad you're the one who found me."

He patted her hand. "Sleep tight, Millie."

He waited to hear her settle into the single bed above him before he leaned forward, buried his face in his hands, and wished with all his might that Ginny would come home.

Ginny

-12-

"Really, Ginny! Surely, you realize that everyone in this room has been waiting for you," Gert snapped as Ginny hurried into the richly paneled and lavishly furnished lawyer's office. She and Gert had arrived together for the reading of the will, but Ginny had rushed into a restroom they passed, telling Gert to go on. The lawyer—one of Milt's partners--stood and waited for Ginny to take her seat.

"I'm sorry," Ginny murmured as she pulled out a straight-back chair next to Gert's. What she really wanted to ask was, what did it matter if she was late or not there at all? They had come for the reading of Milt's will. Gert, dressed in widow's black, kept dabbing at her eyes with a lace hankie.

Everything was happening so fast. In the week since Ginny's arrival in Chicago, things had gone from bad to unbelievable. The day after their conversation, Milt had committed suicide. The funeral had been poorly attended and it had fallen to Ginny to try and comfort the children and calm Gert. Thankfully, Milt's mother had moved into the house and taken charge of Adam, Amanda and Sammy.

The lawyer cleared his throat and began reading: "…being of sound mind *blah blah blah…*"

But was Milt truly in his right mind when he took the elevator to the top floor of the building that housed his offices? Was he thinking straight when he climbed the flight of industrial metal steps leading to the roof, removed his gold Rolex watch and the diamond cufflinks Gert had given him for Christmas, and set them carefully on top of his suit coat—also removed?

Had he hesitated at all, Ginny wondered, before stepping onto that ledge and falling seventeen stories to his death? Had he even for one minute realized he had chosen to do this horrid thing on his wedding anniversary?

The reading of the will took less than fifteen minutes. But it took nearly an hour for the lawyer to try to explain to Gert that, other than the house and furnishings that were in her and Ginny's names, she was broke. Finally, the lawyer stood, signaling the end of the meeting. Gert ignored the proffered handshakes of the attorney and Milt's other partners and stormed out. Ginny hurried to catch up with her.

"Selfish, cowardly bastard," Gert muttered as she tottered on her high heels toward the elevator. "Did not even have the decency to…"

She paused for a breath and Ginny opened her mouth to speak—to try and repair this broken world her sister was living in, but Gert was moving at close to a trot now, hurrying to catch the elevator before the doors closed.

"How am I supposed to pay for the next semester at St. John's for the twins?" she fumed, then turned on Ginny, wagging a gloved finger in her face. "And do not for one minute think any child of mine is going to a public school, Ginny. I'll contest every word that lawyer uttered today— you can bet he collected his fee before declaring us broke."

They stepped inside the elevator and the automated doors closed. Another man's job gone, Ginny thought, and then shook her head that such an idea would occur to her at a time like this. She pressed the button for the lobby and turned to find Gert pounding the polished wood of the wall with her fists. "Damn you, Milton Dodge," she repeated with every beat. She was still at it when the doors opened and Ginny dragged her out the door, which was already starting to slide closed.

"Stop this right now," she whispered. She led Gert past a half-dozen people waiting for the elevator and witnessing her sister's hysteria.

"What am I going to do?" Gert moaned as they left the building. It did not escape Ginny's notice that not a single passerby seemed to think Gert's tirade was anything unusual. Over the years, as the Depression deepened, public displays of grief and hysteria had become commonplace.

Ginny hailed a cab and waited for her sister to get in. "Go home and lie down. The children will not be home from school for several hours. Use that time to pull yourself together."

"You're not coming?"

Ginny sighed. "Somebody has to go through things at Milt's office. His secretary is waiting for me there." She gave the driver Gert's home address and handed him more than enough cash to cover the fare. They could not afford such luxuries, but at that moment she would have paid anything to be free of her sister's refusal to even begin to come to terms with reality.

As she walked the three blocks to Milt's office building, she mentally chastised herself for her impatience with Gert. The woman's husband had committed suicide and left her and their children deeply in debt. At least Ginny still had a roof over her head—and she had Nate.

She pushed the revolving door that opened onto the lobby of Milt's building. There was a reception desk but no one behind it, so she went directly to the bank of elevators and pressed the call button. It took some time but finally doors at the far end of the row opened and an elderly, uniformed man slid back an old-fashioned cage door and waited for her to come in.

"Sixteenth floor, please." *At least one operator still has work,* she thought.

The man nodded and they ascended in silence. When they reached Milt's floor, he held back the doors and waited for her to exit. "Sorry for your loss, ma'am," he mumbled.

"Thank you. That's kind of you." She supposed he thought she was Milt's widow—the way she was dressed in a black coat and hat that belonged to her sister and the fact that she and Gert looked a lot alike. She would be sure to tell her sister how kind the old man had been.

She introduced herself to Edith Wilson, Milt's longtime and devoted secretary, and followed the gray-haired woman down a carpeted hall to a corner office with a spectacular view of the city and Lake Michigan.

"I took the liberty of canceling all of Mr. Dodge's appointments," she told Ginny. "There has been a flood of condolence calls—some genuine, others looking for gossip." She shook her head in disgust. "Some people have no sense of decency."

Ginny saw that Milt's massive, hand-carved mahogany desk was covered with several neat stacks of file folders—each stack clearly labeled with a card that indicated what it was: current client projects in progress, closed client files, files pertaining to the running of his business, and the smallest stack, marked *Personal.*

"I'll start with this stack," Ginny said as she pulled a leather chair close to that end of the large desk and opened the first folder in the personal pile.

Edith placed a pad of paper and several freshly sharpened pencils within reach. "I made tea," she said, "or would you prefer coffee?"

What a jewel this woman is!

"Tea would be lovely," Ginny replied. "Thank you. I hope Milt knew how blessed he was to have you."

The older woman's eyes teared up and her lower lip quivered, but she said nothing as she left the room, closing the door behind her. Had Milt given any thought to what his suicide might mean for someone like Edith? She was clearly in her fifties and jobs were scarce.

An hour later, Ginny leaned back in her chair and let out a long breath. She sipped the tea Edith had brought for her—cold now. Most of the folders in the stack contained routine information—receipts, the children's birth certificates, Milt and Gert's marriage license and passports. But as she worked her way through each folder, she was surprised to find one labeled simply *Ginny.* Where all the other files were perfectly organized with handwritten notes and clips to separate information by date or situation, her folder was a jumble of miscellaneous items, everything mixed together as if he'd simply stuffed things inside, perhaps intending to sort through them later.

There were copies of documents she had signed after her parents died, giving Milt permission to invest her part of the inheritance. There were copies of checks he'd deposited on her behalf in the bank the family had trusted for generations—the bank that had closed without warning. And buried in the mess was a pale blue envelope she recognized as Lavinia's signature stationery.

It was addressed to Milt. Curious, Ginny lifted the flap of the envelope and removed the single sheet of monogrammed paper.

Milt,

I hope you and Gert are well and the children are thriving. I know you must be busy, so I'll come straight to the point. I have met with my husband's attorney, Alvin Stoner, here in Montana to finalize my will. Mr. Stoner is a man of integrity, but he works for my husband and to that end his loyalties are divided. Therefore, I am letting you know that despite our estrangement over the last few years, it is and has always been my wish that should anything happen to me, I still hope Ginny will agree to the will's terms that she serve as my daughter Mildred's guardian and protector.

For reasons I choose not to discuss, I prefer to leave this in your hands rather than to contact Ginny directly. I am enclosing a copy of the will for your files, knowing that when the time comes, I can count on you to help Ginny and Millie sort everything out. Thank you in advance.

> *Best to Gert and the children,*
> *Lavinia*

Ginny stared at the letter.

Montana?

Lavinia was in Montana? When? How long?

Ginny searched through the file, dumping the contents out on a side table. There was no sign of Lavinia's will. She had to believe that Milt might have stored the document with more official paperwork. After all, Lavinia was his client. She searched through the files in the other stacks of folders. When she found nothing, she opened the connecting door to the outer office.

"Edith, if Mr. Dodge had custody of an important family document—a will-where might he store that?"

"Family?"

"Yes. Something that would mention me?"

Edith followed Ginny back into Milt's office. "You checked all the personal files?"

Ginny nodded.

"This is the will of a family member?"

"A close family friend but it involves me."

"And this friend was a client of Mr. Dodge's?"

"At one time she was. Her name is Lavinia Chase, although she remarried so now it is Lavinia Fitzgerald."

Edith went to a locked cabinet in the outer office that held more files, leafing through them quickly before closing the drawer. "I'm afraid there's nothing under either name. Perhaps you might want to contact your friend— hopefully she kept a copy for her files, especially if she's moved away."

Ginny didn't have the strength to explain the complications of her relationship with Lavinia, so she simply nodded. "That's a good suggestion. Thank you."

Edith left, closing the door behind her. Ginny sank into a chair and reread Lavinia's letter, then gazed out the window. She wondered if Lavinia still wanted her to act as Millie's "protector," or had she written a new will—one that gave that responsibility to Roger Fitzgerald? She shuddered at the thought. She searched the note and envelope for a date. Nothing on the note and the stamped date on the envelope was smudged, but she saw that it had been mailed earlier that year—and that gave her hope.

There was a light tap on the door and Edith stepped into the office. "You have a call," she announced as she approached the desk and moved the telephone within Ginny's reach. "It's your husband," Edith added with a smile. "He sounds like a keeper."

"Thank you, Edith." She waited for the secretary to leave before putting the receiver to her ear. "Nate?"

"How's my girl holding up?"

Tears of exhaustion and frustration rolled down her cheeks. "How did you know where to find me?"

"I've been calling the house a couple of times a day since you left, but no answer. Finally, today Milt's mother answered and said you were at his office and gave me the number."

Gert had often complained about her mother-in-law, but as far as Ginny was concerned, her sister was lucky to have this woman's support.

"Ginny? You still there? Did you get my letter?"

"Still here, but no letter. Oh, Nate, Milt committed suicide earlier this week and with the funeral and all, the truth is we've barely glanced at the mail. Right now, I'm at Milt's office going through some files that Milt's gem of a secretary organized for me."

Nate let out a breath. "I got your wire. I can't believe it. Milt always seemed so—sure of himself. How are Gert and the kids holding up?"

"You know Gert—she's sure he was punishing her. She's angry and scared and hasn't even begun to face her loss. The children are spending most of their time with Milt's mother—bless her. They seem to be subdued but okay. I found a file in Milt's office with my name on it."

"And what's that all about?"

She told him about the documents and about Lavinia's note. "But there's no will attached. Milt must have taken it home, and for all I know she's probably changed it by now. I haven't had a word from her since she married Roger. I have to contact her and see if she wants this destroyed or…"

Nate cleared his throat. "Ginny, there's something I need to tell you. Lavinia died."

Ginny felt as if someone had punched her hard in the stomach. "How? When? No!" A rush of emotions that blended regret, denial and gut-wrenching grief assailed her.

"What details I know are in the letter I sent. Apparently, she had been ill for several months. Anyway, that's not everything." He lowered his voice. He was almost whispering. "They were living right here in Gardiner. He's the Fitzgerald looking to buy out the concessions here in the park. Anyway, after the funeral, her daughter ran away. She came here to find you and, well now she's with me and nobody knows. I don't know what to do, honey."

Ginny's head was spinning with all these loose ends of information that she had no hope of weaving into some rational plan for moving forward—there were too many people on different paths and all of them seeking help. When Nate had come home one day that fall with the news that his bosses were thinking of selling out to an outfit called Fitzgerald Enterprises, neither of them had put it together that there could be a connection to Lavinia's husband. Fitzgerald was a common name and besides,

Roger lived in Chicago and had certainly never struck Ginny as the outdoorsy sort.

"Ginny? Look, I know Gert needs you, but I need you here. Lavinia's daughter needs you."

Could the web that held her life get any more entangled?

"Is she all right? It's Millie, right?"

To her surprise, Nate chuckled. "She's quite a kid, but…"

Static filled the line, breaking Nate's next words into disjointed syllables.

"Nate, I'm losing you," she shouted, as if that would do any good. And then the line went dead.

She replaced the receiver in its cradle and sat down. *Lavinia gone?* And how long had she been only a few miles from where Ginny lived—where she *knew* Ginny lived? Oh, how she wished she had insisted on them finding some way to work out their differences. And now Millie had run away and was with Nate? He could lose his job—something that a couple of weeks ago did not hold the threat it did now that they did not have her inheritance to sustain them.

She stood, put on her coat, hat and gloves and opened the connecting door to the outer office. "Edith, I'm taking this folder with me, since it contains documents related only to me."

Edith produced a large manila envelope and placed the folder with Ginny's name on it inside. "Anything else?"

"No. Thank you for your support and loyalty. I wish we could have met under different circumstances." She hugged the diminutive woman as together they walked to the elevator.

At the funeral Milt's partners had assured Gert she should not worry—they would see to everything. But Ginny had noticed they looked as haggard and shell-shocked as Milt had that night they'd talked. She'd also seen the way their wives clung to them, as if afraid they might contemplate the same escape Milt had taken.

Outside, she decided to walk back to the house. The weather was mild, with hints of spring popping through the slushy gray snow, and she had a lot of thinking to do. There was Gert and the children and now Lavinia's daughter, and there was the one additional fact she had avoided facing because it seemed impossible.

Ginny was fairly certain she was pregnant.

Nate

-13-

Although Nate had had a telegram from Ginny telling him about Milt's death and her need to extend her stay, he was breathing a little easier now that he'd finally reached her by phone. He had just replaced the receiver in its cradle in Dan Atwood's office when he noticed the head ranger coming up the steps, kicking the snow off his boots as he prepared to enter the building. Nate hurried to open the door. Millie had been with him for nearly a week now. It was past time he shared that secret with Dan.

"Afternoon, Dan. Hope you don't mind, but I tried calling Ginny again."

"Did you reach her this time?"

Nate nodded.

"Good." Dan hung up his coat and filled a percolator with water. He seemed distracted and out of sorts.

Nate hesitated. "Something going on?"

"Poachers," Dan grumbled. "Want some coffee?"

"Sure."

Dan measured out the grounds and plugged in the pot. "There have been signs for the last week now, but nothing definite," the ranger continued. "Then Benny found a decapitated bison this morning over near Steamboat."

"Sounds like trophy hunters," Nate said.

"Yep. They left the body—just took the head. Damn their selfish hides. Benny said vultures had already been at the carcass."

"You think the culprits are still in the park?" Nate thought immediately of Millie alone in the cabin. She enjoyed spending time in the greenhouse while Nate was at work, studying Ginny's gardening books to know how best to care for the plants. She'd taken a shine to it and that was a relief. It meant she was occupied during the day while he was gone, and not tempted to explore beyond the confines of the cabin. But he sure didn't like the idea of men on the hunt maybe coming upon Millie, watching her through the glass of the greenhouse.

Dan was still talking. "From what Benny could tell, there are at least two of them, so yeah. I'd bet they plan to collect a few more 'trophies' before they leave. Trouble is, we're stretched thin and they know it. Tracking them won't be easy."

"They might head for that abandoned ranger station up near my place."

Dan nodded and stared out the window. "Another storm moving in and it'll bring enough snow to cover their tracks, but it'll also force them to hole up somewhere 'til it passes." He turned to face Nate. "Look, I know it's not your job, but…"

"It's right on my way back to the cabin. I can check it out. Just want to get rid of that cornice that's hanging off the north side of the hotel before I leave today." Nate stood and reached for the jacket he'd hung on the coatrack.

"There's time for you to have your coffee first," Dan said as he filled two mugs and handed one to Nate. "How's Ginny?"

"Not entirely sure—line went dead before we could finish talking. Did I tell you her sister's husband committed suicide?"

Dan shook his head as he blew on his coffee. "Can't imagine anything getting so bad, but then that world out there isn't one I know much about—or care to."

Nate raised his mug—a gesture of agreement. "Her sister's taking it hard, as you would expect. And there are three kids. Ginny said Milt's mother has been a big help, so that's one good thing."

"When's Ginny coming home?"

"Not sure. But I'd rather it be sooner than later."

"I know how you must miss her, Nate, but I expect Ginny's where she needs to be right now."

"Yeah."

They drank their coffee. Dan continued to stare out the window while Nate tried to decide if telling Dan about Millie was really the best thing. Surely another couple of days would make no difference.

"Never heard anything about that girl, did we?" Dan said. "What's it been—a week?"

And just like that Dan opened the door to an opportunity. "Just over." Nate drank the last of his coffee and set his mug down. He buttoned his jacket. This wasn't the time, he decided. He couldn't tell Dan until he could offer a plan that would keep them both from being fired. "Best get to that cornice."

"Don't take any chances, Nate—not dealing with that cornice and not looking for the poachers. Just see if anything looks out of place or you find any signs of human trespassing, and radio me once you get home."

"Sure." Outside, he climbed onto the hotel roof and then onto the smaller roof that covered the top floor of the hotel. He worked his way carefully over to the north side and considered how best to attack the problem.

Snow cornices were one of nature's more beautiful and fragile creations. They began with windblown snow that accumulated on roof's edge. Over time, as the wind packed on layer after layer, the cornice hung off the edge, forming a valence or drape with no more to support its weight than the frigid temperatures and that original fall of snow frozen solid and clinging to the upper roof. This particular cornice was thick enough that finding the true edge of the roof took some doing. From there it unfurled in a curtain of snow and ice that covered the windows of the floor below. All told it probably weighed several hundred pounds, and if Nate tripped or missed his step, he could go tumbling off the roof, unsettling the cornice as he fell and landing just in time to have the mountain of snow bury him. Usually there were at least two men to handle this dangerous task, but he was alone.

For all those reasons, Nate tried to put Millie and Ginny and their problems out of his mind and focus only on his work. It started to snow again just as he found the edge. Carefully, he backed away, knowing if the cornice fell it could take him with it. He'd already cleared much of this section of the roof, sawing through block after block of hard-packed snow and moving each block off the roof. But the snow overnight had laid another six to eight inches of fresh deposit on the roof and it made the surface slippery— and dangerous.

Using the edge of his shovel, he worked at loosening the cornice that stretched several feet in each direction. As he worked, his worries crowded to the front of his mind. He probably should have told Dan about finding Millie. Every day he'd thought of telling. He didn't like keeping something this important from his friend, but he'd wanted to talk to Ginny first. And the fact was that he'd enjoyed the evenings with Millie. She was a quick learner and always full of chatter about some book she'd read that day or consulted to know how best to tend to the greenhouse plants. A couple of nights earlier she'd even asked him to show her how the pipes he'd rigged to bring heat to the greenhouse worked. On his way to and from the cabin, he often found himself smiling as he thought about the way she rambled on, carefully avoiding asking when he might tell others she'd been found.

Tomorrow, he thought. First, he'd talk to Millie— let her know the time had come. He owed her that much. Then he'd sit down with Dan. Having made his decision, he dug his shovel under the edge of what he thought was the top of the cornice.

That's when he heard a crack followed by a rumble. In his haste to back away before the breakaway snow could carry him over the edge, his crampon caught, and he stumbled backwards just as the massive cornice detached and fell with an explosion of snow and ice chunks that shot up and showered over him as he slid down the roof and landed on top of the avalanche. He lay there, fighting to catch his breath. Maybe Ginny was right. Maybe he was getting too old for this work.

"Nate?"

"Yeah, Dan! Over here!"

In minutes Dan had scaled a ladder and was standing on the lower roof near where Nate had landed. "You okay?" He knelt next to Nate, brushing snow away— easier now that it had broken apart into chunks.

"I'll live. Kind of twisted my back. Sure glad you were still here."

Slowly, with Dan urging caution, Nate got to his feet while holding on to Dan and using the shovel as a cane. Both men were breathing hard, their faces red with exertion and cold.

"Let's get you to my house where you can change and warm up," Dan said as he helped Nate down the ladder.

"I'll be fine," Nate insisted. "Ginny might try to call back tonight, and I don't want her worrying." He could see Dan thought this was a bad idea.

"You can try her from my place."

Nate clapped the man on his shoulder as the two of them walked back to where Nate had left his skis. "That storm's coming, Dan, and no offense, but if we're going to be snowed in, I'd like to be in my own bed."

"All right. Go home," Dan said. "I'll take care of the poachers--not your job."

"Neither was getting me off this roof yours," Nate replied. "Thanks." He strapped on his skis, trying not to show Dan how every move sent pain shooting across his back and down his legs.

"At least come inside, take a couple aspirin and warm up before you head out," Dan said.

Nate hesitated. He really should stay, but if there were poachers out there and Millie was on her own... "Thanks, but it's coming on dark." The snow was coming down harder now and visibility was limited.

Dan squinted into the glare of the falling snow. "All right, but no need to try and come back here until this storm passes. Get some rest. Take a couple of days."

"My bosses might not agree," Nate said, reminding them both that he did not work for Dan or the government. "I'll be all right," he assured Dan as he headed east toward a horizon where the sky was already dark as twilight.

Covering terrain that was as familiar to him as another man's back yard might be, he pushed through the pain in his back and legs. He would pay a price come morning. To get his mind off his aching body, he thought about his call to Ginny. She sounded so exhausted and stressed. Her sister was challenging under the best of circumstances and now facing financial ruin and dealing with her husband's suicide, she had to be impossible. Nate wanted Ginny home, where he could care for her instead of her taking on all this. That life back in Chicago was no longer her life. Her life was right here in the park—with him. Here they were safe from all the chaos that had enveloped the outside world. But he knew his wife—knew that she was worried not only about Gert but about those three children, knew that even now her mind was racing with possible solutions, and knew that he should not have added to her stress by telling her about her friend's death—and about Millie.

I'll call her tonight after Millie's in bed, he thought.

He was approaching a trail that, if followed, would bring him within sight of the abandoned cabin he'd mentioned to Dan. *Might as well have a look.*

He thought about what Dan had said about taking a couple of days off. Truth was he'd been wishing he could maybe take Millie out into the park now that it was pretty clear she was fully recovered—let her see what he saw on his way to and from work. Just last night, she'd come back downstairs after saying goodnight, holding a book about the park. She'd asked him to explain how come there were geysers and hot springs and such in this part of the country, but nowhere else.

"It's like we're on another planet or something," she said.

"The truth is that probably as much as a third of the park sits inside the caldera of a volcano. That's what gives us such a unique landscape."

Her eyes went round with surprise. "A volcano?"

"Yep."

"Holy moly," she whispered.

That had set her to quizzing him about his personal life. "Were you born here in the park?"

He laughed. "Sometimes it feels that way, but no. My parents had a sheep ranch north of here in Montana. I grew up there. Came to work here right after I got out of the army."

"And you never left? I mean you never wanted to leave?"

"Never saw any reason to go someplace else. Had everything I needed or wanted right here."

She'd let that sink in for a moment, then asked, "What about Ginny? I mean, she was like Momma-- growing up in a big city with parties and lots of people and things to do. Didn't she miss that at all?"

"Sometimes. That's one reason she goes to Chicago a couple of times a year. But she always comes back here— and seems pretty happy to do so."

Millie had let out a long breath and said softly, "Momma and I used to live in Chicago—until she met Roger."

And it was his turn to ask her the questions he'd been holding in reserve, waiting for her to give some sign she might be ready to talk. "Do you have other family back there, Millie?"

"No. It was just me and Momma after my grandparents died. She had a lot of friends, but friends and family aren't the same, are they?"

He thought about that now as he climbed up the trail. He remembered how sad Millie had looked, as if she had just realized all over again how truly alone she was in the world. Strange, how for him being alone—as long as he had Ginny—posed no threat, but for a kid like Millie, it had to be pretty terrifying.

He pressed on. So far, the landscape where he'd veered off his usual route was pristine and undisturbed by even a hint of human presence. Maybe the poachers had realized the storm was coming and left or maybe they'd moved deeper into the park. Certainly, the territory was vast enough that they could be anywhere and one man trying to find them was futile. Still, he was headed in the right direction to reach home, so he walked on. In some ways he and Ginny were both on a mission—hers to comfort and maybe even save her sister, and his to do what he thought best for the land he loved—and for Millie.

When he saw the abandoned ranger cabin, he stayed close to a cluster of juniper bushes, positioning himself for the best view of the cabin several yards away. The snow had let up and the sky was less leaden and gray, although in another hour it would be pitch black. He took out the binoculars he always carried with him and studied the small wooden structure.

A thin stream of smoke rose from the chimney—a sure sign of occupancy. There was other evidence as well—

rabbit pelts hanging from a rafter on the sagging porch, and a dim light showing through a ripped shade in the lone window. No way to tell how many poachers were in there, but he'd have good news for Dan.

He skied a little way back down the trail where he saw a red fox pause and glance his way. Even with the fading light, the red fur against the fresh snow made Nate think of Ginny and the way her red hair fanned over the pillow when she slept.

God, he missed her.

He hadn't gone three steps when he sensed something—or someone--behind him. He slowed and tightened his grip on his ski poles, prepared to turn and lash out at his stalker. But even as he was deciding his defense moves, he felt something heavy strike his neck and shoulders. He went down in a heap and rolled to his back, his head landing next to the large tree branch used to hit him. Through blurred vision, he tried to focus on the form of a man. Then he saw another man pulling a sled. Nate was tangled up in his skis and in no shape to take on two of them, so he pretended to be unconscious as his attackers stepped closer and debated what to do with him.

"Leave him," one growled. "We got work to do and this storm's getting worse."

The men moved away. Nate opened his eyes and watched them disappear over the rise. Just before they were out of sight, he made out the silhouette of the head of an elk on the sled one man pulled.

Another trophy, he thought as he unfastened his skis, rolled to his stomach and got to his feet. A wave of dizziness from the pain of the blow in combination with his back injury threatened to bring him to his knees, but he leaned against a tree and put on the skis, then struggled on. He had to radio Dan—and he had to get home to Millie.

Millie

-14-

The cabin didn't exactly make for good pacing, but Millie paced it anyway. Nate had never been this late. Even that one day when he'd come home over an hour after what was usual and she'd started to worry, he'd told her she needed to understand that his routine could be irregular. But now he was more than two hours late. Their supper was ruined but Millie didn't care about that. What she cared about was Nate.

That thought was not as noble as it might sound. It was true that she had started to like Nate, but that morning he'd told her that even though he'd had a telegram from Ginny telling him about the death of her sister's husband, he planned to keep trying to call his wife until he reached her. What Millie really wanted to know was what Ginny Baker had to say about her and her situation.

She peered out the window, trying to see through the darkness, hoping for some sign of Nate. She'd been cooped up in the cabin for a whole week now and had to keep telling herself that being there was ever so much better than being in that big house in Gardiner. She filled the days with routine chores—cleaning, working in the greenhouse, reading and listening to the radio. Even though Nate had said she shouldn't play the Victrola or radio unless he was home, Millie kept the sound way down and didn't see how it could hurt. Sometimes she would put a record on the Victrola and dance around the small space like she and Momma used to do back in Chicago.

At night she and Nate would sit in the two matching chairs, listening to the news or music or one of Nate's favorite shows—*The Shadow*. They didn't talk much except over supper—a meal Millie spent at least an hour every day planning and another hour or two putting together. Nate would talk about his day—things he'd seen on the trip to and from work. He'd ask her about a book she was reading, but when she asked if he'd gotten through to his wife or maybe gotten a reply to the letter she knew he'd sent, the answer was always the same. "Not yet."

Outside the window Millie thought she saw something moving. She shielded her eyes from the lamplight inside the cabin and leaned closer to the glass. A giant moose approached the cabin, stood for a moment as if trying to decide which way to go and then wandered off. Nate had told her it was the stillness and solitude of life in the park during winter that he loved most. To Millie, it was just dark and lonely.

Suddenly the two-way radio squawked to life— scaring the bejesus out of her.

"Nate, you there? Over."

Millie edged away from the machine Nate had told her never to touch and definitely never to try and answer. She slunk back into the shadows, as if the voice coming through might be able to see or hear her breathing or something.

"Nate? Over."

She heard static and another voice in the background. Broken words that sounded like the people on the other end of the wire were upset had Millie reaching for her boots. There was no reason to believe they were upset about Nate, but what if they were?

The radio went dead and all she could hear was the wind whistling around the cabin. She dressed quickly in her outer garments, grabbed a flashlight, and stepped outside. She put on Ginny's snowshoes that Nate had pointed out to her should she need to leave the cabin for some reason— although he added that he couldn't come up with a reason in the world she might need to do that. As she hobbled into the black of night trying to adjust to the snowshoes that Nate had assured her would be easier to manage than skis,

Millie was pretty sure Nate would be mad at her. But what was she supposed to do? That call on the two-way surely meant the ranger thought he was home. What if he'd fallen or been attacked by some animal? Of course, maybe whoever had tried to reach him on the two-way was thinking along those same lines and a ranger was a darn sight more qualified to track Nate than Millie was. Maybe she should go back to the cabin and just wait. Wouldn't they bring him home?

Not if he's really hurt.

She hadn't gotten far when she heard voices— men's voices. They were some distance away, but the sound carried, especially when the world was mostly silent. She could tell they were on the move. She stood still and listened, and while she couldn't make out the words, Millie knew for sure neither of the men was Nate. Not knowing what to do, she stayed where she was, trying to figure out which direction those men were moving, praying it was away from her, but scared it might not be. She listened hard to catch their conversation, thinking it might just give her the clue she needed to find Nate. Maybe it was Ranger Atwood. She stood very still and strained to hear what the men were saying.

"...shoulda just finished him off," one man shouted to the one following him, his words slurring like Roger's did when he'd had too much to drink.

"Just shut up, will ya?" the other man yelled, and then he swore, and Millie knew this was not the ranger.

She pressed herself closer to a boulder and held her breath. She watched the two men drag a sled past. They were hunched against the cold, their heads and faces covered. On the sled she saw the head of an elk—just the head. She felt vomit rise in her throat and swallowed it. She waited for them to move farther down the unmarked trail they were following, then started following her own tracks back to the cabin. Because she was afraid those men might turn around and see her made the trek back slow going. Besides, the falling snow had already pretty much covered her tracks. The wind picked up, tearing at her scarf and hat, and the icy snow blinded her, making it nearly impossible to find her way. A couple of times she figured she must have taken a wrong turn because she knew there was no way she had gotten so far from the cabin.

Finally, she saw a glimmer of light and headed straight for it. When she was almost there, she heard a pop and more shouts from somewhere in the distance. She'd never heard a gunshot, but what else could it have been? She staggered on, seeking the safety of that light. The falling snow coated her clothes and froze on the scarf she'd used to cover her face.

When Millie finally stumbled into a clearing and saw the cabin, Nate was leaning against a post that held up the porch roof, a bundle of something pressed to the back of his head.

"Nate," she whispered, all her relief at seeing him alive coming out in that single word. Once she got close enough, she noticed he was holding a towel wrapped around something and grimacing as he pressed it firmly to the back of his neck. "What happened?" she shouted, plunging forward until she reached the step up to the porch.

His head jerked up at the sight of her. "Millie, get inside. Now." He'd never spoken to her that way.

Scared, she hurried to unfasten the snowshoes and put them away, then went inside as he'd instructed.

"Loft," he added as she shook the snow from her coat.

It was clear this wasn't the time to ask questions, so Millie scampered up the steep, narrow stairs and lay on her stomach across the bed so she could see out the small window.

She watched Nate push away from the post and enter the cabin. Then seconds later, he stepped back outside into the yard, and this time he was carrying a gun—a rifle or shotgun. She'd never been sure of the difference. With the light spilling out of the open door of the cabin, she watched as he balanced the gun on his arm, opened it and shoved a shell into each chamber before snapping it closed. Then he walked toward the place where Millie had heard the shouts and that crack sound that she was more and more certain had been a gunshot.

No!

He was going to get himself killed. There were at least two of them and only one of him. She ran back down the stairs and just as she reached the door, the two-way squawked to life.

"Nate, good work. Thanks to you, we got 'em. Over."

Static and then, "Nate? Benny's..."

Voices crackled in the background and then the disembodied voice swore and the two-way went silent.

She saw no reason why she shouldn't shout to let Nate know it was over, so she ran through the greenhouse and out the back door to the cluster of lodge pole pines, where she cupped her hands around her mouth. "Nate! They got 'em," she yelled, deliberately using the words the voice on the two-way had used. "Nate! Come back!"

Millie heard a branch coated with ice crack behind her and turned, prepared to see Nate. Instead she looked up and into the face of a startled young man. He was carrying a gun and it was pointed right at her.

"Who are you?" the two of them said in unison, and behind her Millie heard Nate say, "Oh, damn."

Nate herded her and the young man he called Benny back to the cabin, ordered Benny to sit, scowled at Millie and went immediately to the two-way.

"Dan? Over."

"Yeah. You all right? Thanks to your call, we got them. Benny's still out there so..."

"I'm fine. Benny's here with me. Can you come over?"

"We'll talk in the morning. Me and the other rangers need to get these guys processed."

Millie held her breath. Nate looked at her, closed his eyes a minute and then said, "Yeah. It can wait. Over and out."

"I'll make coffee," she said.

"You go to bed, young lady. I'll make the coffee. And close the door up there."

She saw the towel he'd held to his neck lying on the drain board next to the sink, the snow he'd stuffed it with slowly melting and trickling down the drain. She sniffed back snot—and maybe the beginnings of tears--and headed for the stairs.

"Millie?" His voice was kind and gentle as usual. "Just get some sleep, okay?"

And that's the moment she understood. Nate might be her best hope, but Nate wasn't the one in charge. She nodded without looking back at him, and climbed the stairs, closing the door at the top, knowing he meant for her not to hear whatever it was he would tell Benny tonight and Ranger Dan the next morning. As the door clicked shut, she was already wondering if she could fit herself through the window that was not even as big as a breadbox, and how hard of a fall it might be. She figured if she could fit through the window, she could tie the sheets together and use them as a rope to shimmy down the side of the cabin. She'd seen that in a movie once. She decided maybe the best plan was to wait for just before dawn while Nate was still sleeping. She could borrow Ginny's snowshoes and make her way back to Gardiner. There she would leave the snowshoes at the station with a note saying they belonged to Ginny, then she'd catch a train to anywhere that took her away from Roger. She still had all the money she'd saved.

With her plan made, she packed her stuff, lay down with all her clothes on and listened to the voices below, unable to make out what Nate was saying. After a while she heard water running in the bathroom, then the light that leaked beneath the loft door went out and everything was quiet. She got to work tying the sheets and securing one end of them to the iron headboard of the bed, ready to toss the rest out the window.

Then she realized that the way the wind had kicked up and the snow was falling, making it all the way back to Gardiner wasn't going to be easy. For one thing, since Nate had brought her to the cabin, she had no idea of direction. Two fat tears plopped onto the backs of her hands as she tied the last knot.

He hasn't told Ranger Dan yet, she thought. Of course, there was Benny to be reckoned with. No matter how Millie looked at things, she was doomed. The only thing that might buy her some time was the weather. If this was what Nate had described as a major spring storm, they could be trapped here in the cabin for days—time enough to change Nate's mind and get Benny on her side.

For the first time since arriving in the park, she found the sound of the howling wind comforting. She untied the sheets and made up her bed, put on Ginny's pajamas and tiptoed to the door.

Opening the door a crack revealed only darkness downstairs. She could see just the edge of the afghan and knew that meant Nate or Benny was sleeping in one of the chairs. So, she crept down the stairs, trying hard not to make any noise.

"Bathroom?" Nate said when she reached the bottom step.

"Yeah." She walked down the hall past the closed bedroom door to the bathroom.

When she came out again, Nate had turned on the reading lamp next to his chair. "Let's talk, Millie," he said, indicating the other chair.

She sat, and Nate handed her the afghan.

"Here's the thing, Millie. We both knew sooner or later this would have to be faced head-on—so here we are."

He waited, but Millie didn't know what to say, so she just huddled under the afghan, letting her hair fall over her face in an attempt to cover how scared she must look.

"I have to let Ranger Dan know I found you."

"But with the storm and all, we've got some time, right?" She was clutching at the edge of a cliff, hanging on by her fingernails.

"I had hoped to tell him in person, but if the storm socks us in, then I'll need to call him tomorrow morning so we can decide how best to move forward."

"What about Benny?"

"Benny has no part in this other than he knows you're here. I explained the situation to him tonight. You two have something in common. His mother left him and his dad a year or so ago when his dad lost his job. Benny dropped out of school and works odd jobs wherever he can find them to support the two of them."

"Did you talk to Ginny?" Millie was desperate to keep him from saying what she knew he was going to say—that she needed to face the fact that with no other family, Roger was her most likely choice.

"She knows, but Millie, we're beyond that now."

"What about Momma's will that put Ginny in charge?"

"That's for the courts to sort out, but in the meantime…"

Sobs broke through the dam she'd built trying to keep them from coming. "I don't want to live with Roger. He was mean to Momma and he never liked me. He fired

Clara and Momma said I could depend on Clara to watch out for me."

Nate moved forward in his chair and placed his hand on her knee. "Who's Clara again?"

"She was Roger's housekeeper, but he fired her the night after Momma's funeral—fired her for lighting a candle in Momma's bedroom."

"Do you know her last name or where she lives?"

Millie shook her head, unable to speak around the hiccups that accompanied her crying.

"Gardiner's a small town so it shouldn't be hard to find her." Nate was talking more to himself, but Millie felt a spark of hope.

"Maybe you could make Roger hire her back and then at least I'd have her—and Gus."

"The driver?"

She nodded.

"Ranger Dan got a note from somebody telling us to call that lawyer if we found you. He thought the driver might have sent that."

"Gus likes me, so yeah, maybe."

"What about Mr. Stoner—the lawyer?"

"He works for Roger." Millie folded her arms over her chest and scowled.

"So, does Gus. So did Clara," Nate reminded her. "You've got to trust somebody, Millie."

"I trust you—or I did," she grumbled. But then she had an idea. "If you call Mr. Stoner, then he has to take this to the courts, right?"

"Not sure how these things work, Millie, but I would expect he'd have to file some papers."

"Whether or not Roger liked it?"

"If he's a man of honor, he would do what the law requires no matter what your stepfather says."

She remembered how Mr. Stoner had tried—and failed—to stand up to Roger that morning at breakfast.

"But, Millie, you're going to be back at your stepfather's house—at least in the beginning."

She shivered in spite of the afghan. "Yeah, I know that, but...."

"Here's the plan, Millie. I'll call Ranger Dan and talk it over with him, but I think he should call Mr. Stoner and let him know you are safe. Then we'll let him tell your stepfather. In the meantime, I'll call Ginny again and fill her in on what's going on. If I can't reach her by phone, we'll send a telegram—either way if I know my wife, she'll find a way to be in touch with you—and your stepfather's lawyer--right away."

"She knows about Momma?"

Nate nodded. "And she knows you're here and we're both in a heap of trouble, but Millie, it's like I said before, Ginny's sister needs her there."

"But she can talk to the lawyer long distance?"

"Yeah, I suppose."

Millie began to relax. How hard could it be staying back in that house for a few days? She could make sure Momma's things were not thrown out or given away. She could try to figure out what had been taped to the bottom of the nightstand drawer. She could start getting ready to come live with Nate and Ginny.

"It'll be all right, Nate." She handed him the afghan and headed for the stairs, then turned and hugged him hard—and held on.

"How about we both get some sleep?" Nate returned her hug, then moved a little away. "It'll be morning before you know it."

She nodded. "Nate, will you be in trouble for hiding me?"

"Maybe."

Millie liked the way he was honest and didn't treat her like a little kid by saying something like, "Now, don't you worry about that."

"If you lose your job, don't worry, okay? Once the court gives me the money, we'll be fine."

Ginny
-15-

"Gert, we have to start making some decisions," Ginny said.

The two sisters sat across from each other at the oversized dining room table their parents had bought to accommodate family gatherings. Milt's mother had taken the children upstairs to do their homework.

"What decisions?" Gert poured the last of a bottle of wine into a crystal glass and leaned back in her chair. She sounded bored—more to the point, she sounded unconcerned. Her lack of any sense of urgency was slowly driving Ginny mad.

"Paying the back taxes on this place, finding a school for the children…"

Gert's fingers tightened on her wine glass. "The children are *not* changing schools. How many times must I say that, Ginny?"

Ginny forced herself to take a deep breath. "They can finish out this term, but come fall…you cannot afford the tuition, Gert. That aside, right now the tax issue is the most pressing."

"The house is paid for, Ginny. Papa saw to that."

"That doesn't stop the city from requiring taxes. I think I may have a solution, but it requires sacrifice."

Gert squinted at her and downed the rest of her wine before standing, bracing her palms flat on the table and leaning close to Ginny's face. "I have sacrificed more than my share, Ginny. No more." These last two words were delivered on a rush of air that fanned Ginny's face. Gert lingered there a moment, her expression shifting from determination to confusion. She collapsed back into her chair and fingered the lace tablecloth.

"Remember when Mother brought this back from Brussels?" Gert had always insisted on calling their parents the more formal *Mother* and *Father*.

Ginny reached across the table and stroked her sister's hand. "Gert, I am so very sorry for all the suffering you've had to endure these last several days. I wish there were something I could do, but the fact is...."

"The fact is that we have both lost money, Ginny. The difference is that you have a place to live and a husband with a job and no dependents." It was the most rational point Gert had made since Milt's death. Ginny wasn't sure what to say.

"Gert, I want to go home—I *need* to go home, so please work with me."

Her sister rolled her eyes and sighed loudly. "Very well. Call my friend, Peter Walton—the number is in my book. He has an auction house. Make an appointment to have him come assess what we have—the art, the furnishings, my personal items, such as jewelry and furs. Surely there is enough in all that to pay the taxes—and keep the children in school next year."

Ginny was astonished. Her sister had moved from refusing to even consider making any changes to offering a plan that just might work. "I'll call him first thing tomorrow," she said.

"Call him now. He stays late at his office and we may as well get his thoughts. Tell him I'll pay him in vintage wine—that will bring him on the run. Peter has a wine cellar to rival any other and he was always after Milt to sell him those bottles of vintage port we brought back from Paris in '25."

Ginny did not hesitate. She made the call, introduced herself, mentioned Gert and wine, and the man was at the front door an hour later. For the first time since arriving in Chicago, she felt that maybe—just maybe—there might be a way out of this mess.

Peter strolled through the main rooms of the house, making notes in a small notebook, then Gert brought him to her bedroom and opened her closet—practically the size of Ginny's entire cabin in Yellowstone. Peter sighed and kept writing. Afterwards she led him to the attic, where she and Milt had stored furnishings and paintings from the time Gert and Ginny's parents had been alive. Then they went down to the cellar. Rather than follow them, Ginny returned to the kitchen and put together a light refreshment of cheese, fruit and wine.

"Well?" she asked, when Peter and Gert emerged from the cellar several minutes later. Peter was carrying three dusty bottles of wine that he set on the table before retrieving his notebook and pen from the pocket of his double-breasted navy jacket. He wore a pale blue shirt and a bright yellow ascot, and his gray flannel trousers had a sharp crease running down each leg. When he'd first arrived, he'd removed heavy black galoshes and a camel-colored overcoat before stepping into the front hall.

"The verdict is," Gert said, as she pulled out a kitchen chair and reached for the plate of cheese, "that we have valuable stuff. Of course, we knew that already."

Peter focused his attention on Ginny. "The problem, Mrs. Baker, is one of finding buyers who can afford such fine things."

While Ginny had greeted him informally as Peter, he had insisted on referring to her as Mrs. Baker, and she noticed he called her sister Gertrude.

"I understand. Well, it was worth considering," Ginny said. Seeing that Gert was not inclined to move beyond the kitchen, she indicated a chair. "Please have something," she offered.

"Well, let's not throw in the towel just yet," Peter said with a smile. He pulled out a chair, sat and reached for the wine Ginny had opened for them. "There are a few collectors who are still in the black. Give me a few days."

"Are you thinking of doing an auction?" Ginny asked.

"Nothing so crass," he replied. "Private transactions are far more genteel—especially in these times."

Ginny was not sure if she should be insulted by his patronizing tone, but decided if the man could help them, she would forgive him a good deal.

"You'll have to pardon my sister, Peter," Gert confided, leaning in close and taking Peter's hand. "I'm afraid she has spent so much of her adult life living off the land in the wilderness that she has forgotten how things are done here in civilization."

"I haven't forgotten everything about this life, Gert," she snapped, and regretted her tone immediately. "Sorry." She directed this to both her sister and Peter. "I seem to be on edge."

"Understandably," Peter replied, and for the first time since he'd arrived, he looked at her with something approaching sympathy and understanding. "Allow me to assure you both that I believe I can be of service. Your treasures will not bring their true value, but if you will trust me, I am convinced I can raise a substantial amount of money for you."

"In the near future?" Ginny asked.

"In the very near future," he replied and smiled. "Let me make some calls and I'll contact you in a day or so. Will that suffice?" He was speaking directly to Ginny.

She nodded.

"Excellent. And now, could I prevail on you lovely ladies to join me for a proper dinner at the Drake?"

Gert clapped her hands. "Yes! I'll just get my coat." She hurried from the room.

"And you, Mrs. Baker?" He spoke softly, with an intimacy that was in sharp contrast to his earlier demeanor.

Ginny knew that look. It was the gaze of a man who found her interesting—a man who wanted to explore the possibility of a personal relationship. She was flattered. Peter Walton was tall and broad-shouldered, with Scandinavian good looks—piercing blue eyes, and blond hair that he had a habit of sweeping back from his forehead.

"I have some files from Milt's office that need my attention," she said. "Thank you for including me, but the truth is that Gert will enjoy the evening a good deal more if I am not there. I'm afraid she views me as something like her jailer these days. I do tend to keep reminding her she has no money." Ginny smiled and offered Peter a handshake. "Thank you for whatever you can do to help."

He took her hand between both of his, his manicured nails catching the light. "A rain check then."

It was not a question.

She withdrew her hand as Gert burst into the room. Her sister had not only retrieved her coat. She had rouged her cheeks and applied lipstick and changed into a silk dress with a deep V-neckline that revealed a good deal of skin. She wore diamond earrings and a cluster of gold bracelets. When she saw Ginny's raised eyebrows, she tossed her hair from her face and said, "May as well wear them while I still own them."

"I couldn't agree more," Peter said, offering her his arm. "Shall we?"

Ginny followed them to the front door and stood there watching as Peter donned his galoshes and coat, then helped Gert into the passenger seat of his car. As he got behind the wheel, he looked back at Ginny, raised his hand in farewell and smiled.

She closed door, shivered a little and stood in the dim foyer—a place that held so many memories for her. She lingered on an image of the day she had come home from the seminar in Yellowstone. She had run up the front steps and into her mother's waiting arms.

"Oh, Momma, I met the most incredible man," she had gushed.

"That's nice, dear," her mother had replied with a laugh. "I take it you also learned things pertinent to your studies?"

"I'm serious, Momma. This is the man I'll marry. I know it."

Gert had come running down the stairs. "You're back," she'd squealed as she hugged Ginny and kept talking. "The cotillion is next Saturday, and you don't even have a dress yet, so we'll need to go shopping right away. What have you done to your hair? It looks a fright. Never mind. Come with me. Let's get you a bath and then I can repair the damage." Her hand had hovered near Ginny's hair, not quite touching it, as if there might be critters nesting in its tangled curls.

Ginny had gone to the cotillion. She had danced with half a dozen boys, but her mind had been on Nate. Did he dance? What might it be like to be in his arms? The cotillion boys were awkward and cocky. Nate was so self-assured and yet humble. With him, she had felt anything was possible. She'd never fit the properly ambitious mold that society dictated for a woman of her station. But with Nate, Ginny had seen ways she might succeed outside that mold, and the prospect had been so thrilling.

Shaking off the memories, she closed the inner door that separated the foyer from the reception hall of the massive house. Upstairs, she heard Milt's mother urging the children to get ready for bed so she could read them a story. To her left was the darkened parlor where she'd had that last conversation with Milt. To her right, the large formal dining room and the library that her father—and Milt—had used as an office. Now it was her turn to sit in the high-backed swivel chair, the worn leather seat cool to her touch. It was her turn to pull a file from the stack and spread out the contents, sorting them into categories—file, discard, address.

She reached for Lavinia's note and opened it. Tears welled. She had been so caught up in handling things for Gert that she had not allowed herself even a moment to mourn her friend. But someone else was attending Gert's needs at least for an evening and it was time Ginny gave some thought to what *she* needed, how everything that had happened was going to affect her life—and Nate's.

Although she and Nate had agreed that she could not add to Gert's expenses by making long distance phone calls, just this once she needed to hear his voice. She needed to take herself away from Chicago and back to Yellowstone.

She had not yet told Nate about the baby. With all the stress she was under, she had simply assumed another miscarriage was in the offing and decided not to place that burden and heartbreak on Nate when he had his own problems.

But was that fair?

He answered on the second ring and she burst into tears.

Nate

-16-

The one thing Nate could never deal with was Ginny's tears. She rarely cried, but when she did, the floodgates broke. He would hold her and urge her to let it out, knowing the only solution was for her to cleanse herself of whatever pain had become too much for her. But this time she was hundreds of miles away and holding her was not an option.

"Hey," he said, his own voice breaking with the emotion of all the days they had been apart and all each of them had been forced to face alone. "I'm here, Ginny. Just let it out."

"I'm sor-r-ry," she stuttered.

"Shhh." He closed his eyes and tightened his grip on the phone, his only link to Ginny. He could hear Millie moving around in the greenhouse. The storm had been a big one and they were snowed in for at least another day—meaning Millie had a reprieve and was happy. The weather had also given Nate's pain from the injuries sustained in the fall and poacher attack time to ease.

"Ginny? Are you okay? I mean, you're not hurt or anything?"

"I'm pregnant," she managed between hiccups.

Nate was pretty sure he had misunderstood. "Honey, say again—must be some static."

"You heard me," she said.

The emotions that leapt to his throat ran the gamut from elation to panic and back again. "You're sure?"

She let out a hoot of mirthless laughter accompanied by another hiccup. "Bad timing, huh?"

Nate did the math. By the time the kid was Millie's age, he would be almost sixty and Ginny would be in her early fifties—the ages of grandparents, not parents. And yet...

He felt something unfamiliar—a kind of joy he had never associated with the idea of parenthood. He thought about Millie and imagined his son or daughter at fourteen—all arms and legs and curiosity.

"Well, that's just swell, Ginny."

"Of course," Ginny continued, "I don't exactly have a good track record for this so there's every possibility..."

"Don't think that way. We'll take this one day at a time."

"You do know that your habit of taking life minute to minute drives me nuts?"

He chuckled. It was just one more difference between them—he was a firm believer in living in the moment while Ginny tended toward long-range planning—and dreaming.

"When you coming home?"

She sighed and didn't answer. "How's Millie?"

"Benny knows," he told her. He hadn't intended on saying anything, not wanting to add to her worries, but it just came out. "We had some poachers last night and Benny was helping Dan. He kind of stumbled onto Millie."

"Does Dan know?"

"Not yet. He's tied up with processing the poachers, plus we got hit with a spring storm and we're snowed in until day after tomorrow probably. I asked Benny to let me handle it. He stayed the night and left this morning."

"Nate, you have to tell Dan."

"I know—tomorrow."

"I was reading the letter Lavinia sent Milt. Not sure if it's still in effect, but if it is, she appointed me as Millie's guardian, should something happen to her. Trouble is, I can't find the will."

Nate frowned. "If Lavinia's lawyer has a copy, it may be a way of keeping Millie from having to go back to living with her stepfather."

"Where would she live then?"

"With us."

Ginny was quiet for a long moment.

"Ginny?"

She cleared her throat. "Nate think about this. We have a baby on the way. Not only that but if Roger Fitzgerald acquires the contract to run the park's concessions, he can make life miserable for us."

Nate chuckled. "Babe, he'll fire me, so what else can he do to us?"

"Men like that are not satisfied with simple solutions, Nate. He'll want to make an example of you. And where will we live once you're no longer working there?" Her voice was shaking, and he was afraid she might start crying again.

"Ginny, we'll work it out. You and the baby come first, before anything else." He heard her sniff back tears. "Tell me what's happening there," he said, hoping a shift in focus would help.

She told him about Gert's friend, Peter, who seemed to think he could find buyers for art and furnishings from the house. He barely heard a word she said, his mind still back on her startling announcement and the repercussions that came with the news.

She had always hoped to have children, but for that wish to come true now? It wasn't just their ages; it was the uncertainty. Early in their marriage Nate's reasons for not wanting children had to do with his own upbringing. These days, his fears ran deeper—how would he provide for a child, especially in these desperate times?

Millie came in from the greenhouse, saw that he was on the phone and gave him a little wave, dirt clinging to her palms and fingers as she hurried down the hall to the bathroom and shut the door. He could hear the water running and guessed she was washing up.

"Ginny? Millie just came in from the greenhouse so I should probably get off the phone."

"Let me speak to her."

"Not sure that's a good idea until you and I come up with a plan for what we're going to do about—well, everything."

"She's going to know you were talking to me. I should at least express my sympathy about Lavinia."

The water shut off and Millie opened the bathroom door. She was still drying her hands, but something made her look at Nate, her eyebrows raised. "This is a mistake," he muttered into the receiver, but beckoned Millie forward.

He handed her the phone. "It's Ginny. She wants to speak to you."

Millie was still holding the towel, but instead of using that to dry her hands she ran her palm down the leg of her pants before accepting the phone. "Hello," she murmured, her voice faint and shaky.

Nate could hear Ginny's voice but not her words, although it wasn't hard to figure out her side of the conversation as he listened to Millie.

"Yes, ma'am," she said, hooking her hair behind her ear. "Do I?" She smiled and visibly relaxed. "She had such a pretty voice. Most people tell me I favor my father—in looks anyway."

Nate couldn't help noticing how Millie always said *father* as if the man were a stranger—which, of course, he was.

Ginny went on for several seconds, probably sharing some memory of Lavinia. Millie perched on the arm of the chair nearest the telephone table. "She never told me that," she said. "She did say we were going to come see you once she got well." Tears brimmed and wet her lashes as Ginny said something more. "Yes, ma'am," Millie whispered, and handed the phone back to Nate as she slid fully into the chair and wiped her eyes with the towel.

"Ginny?"

"Now Nate, listen to me. We need to get things straightened out for Millie as soon as possible. When I think what that child has been through and how terrified she must be of what's to come… I want you to call that lawyer. Tell him we know all about Lavinia's will and unless his client can produce something more recent, we will be proceeding under those terms."

"Ginny, I…"

"That girl has no one but us, Nate."

There was no point arguing with Ginny once she'd made up her mind, and clearly this was such a case, but this time Nate was going to stand his ground. "Ginny, we need to think about you right now—getting you home."

She let out a long breath. "I know. I'm working on it, honey."

Any time she called him honey he knew she was trying to get around him. "I'm sending you money for a train ticket, Ginny. I want you on that train."

"I need time to make sure Gert…" she began.

"Gert is a grown woman—one who needs to take some responsibility. Besides, it'll be a couple of days before I can get up to Gardiner and have the money wired to you."

She chuckled. "Okay, you win this one—I'll come home as soon as I receive the funds."

"Get some rest, okay?"

"Nate, we're going to be all right," she said, although there was no conviction in her words.

"We will be," he assured her. "Whatever happens, babe." He heard the kiss she blew him across the miles before hanging up.

"Millie, day after tomorrow you'll be coming with me when I leave for work."

Millie pushed herself more firmly into the chair and folded her arms across her chest. "But I heard you tell Ginny to come home. You're sending her the money and everything."

"True enough, but that doesn't change your situation. You knew the day would come when we would have to face things head on—that day is here."

"But…"

Nate smoothed her hair back from her forehead. "It may turn out better than you think, Millie. Ginny and I are in your life now. We're not going to abandon you, but you have to understand that we can't very well help you if I end up in jail."

Her eyes went wide with surprise. "You think that might happen?"

Nate shrugged. "Maybe. Hopefully not, but we have to consider all possibilities."

She grabbed his hand. "I won't allow that," she announced. "I'll tell the judge you were just doing what anybody would have done. I'll tell him you…"

Nate eased his hand free. "Let's not get ahead of things, Millie. I'm hungry. How about we finish off the rest of that cake you made the other day?"

Millie
-17-

Millie divided the last hunk of the lopsided chocolate cake she'd made a couple of days earlier and filled two glasses with milk. Suddenly everything she did took on special meaning. Was this nearly the last time she and Nate would sit across from each other at this table—the table with one leg Nate had told her he'd never been able to get level? Would she make just one more supper for the two of them? And day after tomorrow when Nate set breakfast in front of her, would she be able to force down more than a bite without gagging?

Maybe that was the answer. If she got sick, started throwing up and stuff, Nate would have to postpone taking her to see the ranger. But what was the point? Even if she stayed in the cabin, Nate would go to work. He would tell Dan about her—if Benny hadn't already.

Benny.

They hadn't really gotten acquainted. Nate had sent him off to bed right away that night, and the next morning breakfast had been eaten in silence—a quiet only Nate seemed to find normal. All through the meal Benny had watched her from under probably the longest eyelashes she'd ever seen. One more piece of evidence that life was not fair. Why should a boy get long, thick lashes when every girl she knew would practically kill for them?

Benny ate his food like every bite mattered— chewing slowly and taking his time. He took his coffee with a lot of milk and sugar. When he finished, he wiped his mouth on his napkin and stood. "I'm gonna try to make it out," he said, addressing Nate.

"You're sure?"

Benny nodded. "Yes, sir. Need to check on my dad." He put on his coat and hat, wrapped a long wool scarf twice around his neck, and shook Nate's hand. "Hope everything turns out the way you want," he said, lowering his voice as if he didn't want Millie to hear.

Nate nodded and patted his shoulder. "Call me so I know not to send out the rescue dogs."

Benny smiled. "Yes, sir." He glanced at Millie. "Good luck, Millie."

She'd waited for Benny to leave, then turned to Nate. "You've got rescue dogs? Like St. Bernards or something?"

"It's a joke, Millie." Nate started putting on his coat. "I'm going to shovel the path."

"I can help."

"No, thanks. I need to do some thinking," Nate said, and she remembered how he'd told her he liked using the time he spent alone to work out whatever problem he might be facing. He'd hinted it might be something for Millie to try.

The rest of the morning had been pretty normal. Over lunch Nate quizzed her on some math and wiped the dishes as she washed them. Then, just after lunch, the sky started to clear. He tossed her Ginny's shearling coat and said, "Let's take a walk."

Outside he helped her strap on Ginny's snowshoes before putting his on, and they headed out. As he led the way, she started to ask him when he thought Ginny might get back. He raised his hand, stopped walking and pointed to something in the distance. "No talking out here, Millie," he whispered. "Just watch and take it all in. There are lessons to be learned—lessons that you might find useful."

Millie snorted. "I'm not exactly going to be…"

Nate held up his hand and she stopped talking.

Over the next hour he pointed to things she never would have noticed on her own. There was a slender weasel-type animal the color of the snow that burrowed deep into a drift and emerged with something small and squirmy. Millie shuddered and Nate grinned before pushing on. After climbing a steep rise, they stood for a minute catching their breath. Nate picked up a handful of snow and stuffed it in his mouth.

"Helps with the altitude," he said. "You're looking a little peaked."

"I know that about sucking on snow. Clara taught me."

Millie followed his lead and ate some snow, letting it melt in her mouth and then stooping down to grab more.

Nate chuckled. "Ready to press on?"

She nodded, grabbed another handful of snow and followed him along the ridge. She was getting the hang of the snowshoes and feeling pretty proud of herself when Nate stopped and pulled out a pair of binoculars. He focused them on something in the distance before handing them to Millie.

"Watch," he whispered.

In the distance she saw a herd of elk moving slowly across a hillside. Nate had told her about the huge elk refuge that had been established farther south near the Teton Mountains. "Are they going to the refuge?" she asked.

"More likely leaving there," he replied. "Do you see the wolf pack? First, I've seen in some time. Maybe they're starting to come back."

Millie raised the glasses again and adjusted the lenses. "They're gonna kill the elk," she protested. The wolves were moving closer when suddenly the elk took off. But the wolves were gaining on them. "No," she muttered, her eyes glued to the action. Nate rested his hand on her shoulder.

"Keep watching," he said.

The wolves focused on the slowest in the herd—a smaller animal having trouble keeping up with the rest. Suddenly one of the wolves lunged and missed. Millie let go of the breath she hadn't realized she was holding as the elk scampered away and the wolves seemed to give up. She grinned as Nate took the binoculars without comment, put them away and then started down the trail that would lead them back home.

Home.

Later, as Millie fixed their supper, Nate sat at the kitchen table watching her. "Tell me what you saw today, Millie," he said, and though she knew he was deliberately trying to distract her from what was coming, she decided to play along. The truth was he'd be facing some tough stuff, just like she was.

She laughed as she set their plates on the table and scooted her chair closer. "Well, I guess even though I felt sorry for the mouse, I understood the weasel wasn't being mean."

Nate put oleo on the potato she'd harvested from the greenhouse. "The thing is, when spring is fully here, he'll turn colors—to brown so he blends into the spring foliage same as he does the snow. One of the ways we know spring is on the way is when we see that little fella starting to turn."

"That's amazing," Millie said, shaking pepper onto her baked potato. "Nate, wouldn't it be swell if people could turn different skin colors?"

"Might solve a whole bunch of problems," Nate agreed. "What did you think about the elk herd and wolf pack?"

She heaved a sigh of relief. "That was a close one. I thought that little elk was a goner. Even though they ran fast, seemed like the wolves were faster."

Nate nodded. "They've got big padded feet that give them a lot of traction in the snow. Come spring, after the snow melts, the elk will easily outrun them. Even in the snow the wolves are only successful maybe ten percent of the time."

"Good." Millie drank the last of her powdered milk.

"So, you're willing to forgive the weasel, but not the wolf?"

"Uh…" He had her. Just because the weasel was small and sort of cute…

"There's a lesson there for you, Millie, especially given what you're about to face."

She didn't want to hear this, so she stood and begun gathering the dishes.

"Sit, Millie."

She did as he instructed, but she'd fiddled with her napkin rather than looking at him.

"Look, Millie, that world we walked in this afternoon is all about survival—finding food and shelter, making it through the storms, finding another way when the first one doesn't pan out."

He reached across the table and placed his hand over hers. "Those wolves failed today but they'll keep working at it because that's the way the world works—it's all about survival," he repeated, emphasizing each word. He didn't say more, just left her to think about that. She'd gotten used to Nate making these statements and then just leaving them hanging there as he went off to do something else.

After supper he turned on the radio and settled into his chair to listen to the news. Usually once Millie had done the dishes, she sat in Ginny's chair to read until bedtime. But tonight, she was restless, so she told him she was going to do some work in the greenhouse before bed. He nodded. And when she came back inside an hour later, he was on the phone. Her hands were covered with dirt so she hurried down the hall, but she had the oddest feeling he might be talking to Ginny. Inside the bathroom her heart hammered against her chest and she closed her eyes tight while she let the water run over her hands. Millie prayed Ginny would persuade him to keep her there until she got home.

But once she and Ginny had talked, Millie sat across from Nate eating that chocolate cake—the same way they'd shared Ginny's pecan pie that first night. That night she'd been so sick she hadn't much cared what happened to her. All she wanted was to be warm and safe from Roger. Nothing much had changed, but she knew really, everything had. Nate would have no choice now.

"I know you have to do this," Millie mumbled around a bite of cake. "But couldn't we maybe wait 'til Ginny gets back? What can a few more days matter?"

"It matters, Millie. It matters that I've kept this from others for so long. It matters that what I've done could impact those people—their careers."

"You're talking about Ranger Dan."

"Yes, and Benny as well. But there's something neither of us has considered, Millie. If you disappear without a trace, what's to keep your stepfather from claiming your mother's estate?"

"He can have it. I'll give him everything if he'll just let me stay right here with you and Ginny."

"That's not the way these things work, Millie."

"Well, it's the way they ought to work," she muttered, pushing the rest of her cake away.

Nate pulled the plate to him and finished the cake, using the back of his fork to press into the crumbs and eating those as well. He drank his milk and wiped his mouth on the sleeve of his flannel shirt. "Go pack up your stuff, Millie and then let's get some sleep," he said.

With a sigh she hoped might make him reconsider, Millie trudged up the stairs to the loft. She made a big show of slamming around although she had packed most everything the night she'd intended to run away—again. She gathered her few remaining belongings and stuffed them into Momma's knapsack. Downstairs, she heard Nate wash up the cake dishes, then go into the bathroom. While he was in there, she carried the knapsack down the steps and set it by the front door.

"All set?" Nate came down the hall as she started back to the loft.

Millie made a face—one meant to show her disgust at the way things were going. But as it turned out she burst into sobs and grabbed Nate around his waist. "I'm so scared, Nate."

He wrapped his arms around her and held on. "I know," he said, and it sounded as if he might cry too.

They stood like that for a long moment—Millie bawling and Nate gently patting her back. Finally, when her crying shifted to shudders, he said, "Hey, Millie, you any good at babysitting?"

She was so surprised she leaned back and looked up at him. "Why?"

He shrugged. "Ginny's expecting and I was just thinking we might be in the market one of these days. Can't think of anybody I'd rather take care of our kid than you—I mean once we get everything with your situation all straightened out."

Millie knew what he was doing, but it worked. It was going to take some time getting used to the idea that Nate, who was definitely older than Momma had been, and Ginny, who was Momma's age—so almost forty, could have a baby.

"Ginny's having a baby? I mean—wow. That's big news. I've never done any babysitting, but how hard can it be? I played with dolls right up to a year ago."

Okay, that was about the dumbest thing she could have said, but Nate just nodded.

"Well, when the baby comes, we'll talk about what your duties might be. Better yet, once Ginny gets back maybe you two could get together."

Her breath caught. Nate was telling her something a lot more important than that he and Ginny were expecting.

He was telling her that even after tomorrow—even after he handed her over to Roger or whoever—he was planning to be in touch. "What if Roger won't allow you or Ginny to see me?"

He shrugged. "Seems like your mom made sure at least Ginny would have something to say about that." He patted Millie's shoulder and steered her toward the steps to the loft. "Now, tomorrow's going to be a long, hard day—for both of us. So, head on up and no reading, okay?"

"Okay." She wrapped her arm around his waist. "It's probably going to take some time, Nate, but we'll get this all worked out, right?" She knew she kept saying that, but it was the one thing she most needed to hear.

"That's a promise," Nate said, as he bent down and kissed her forehead.

Nate

-18-

Breakfast was a silent and somber business. Nate dished up the food and Millie picked at it. Nate wolfed his down without really tasting it. He just wanted to get this over with. While Millie finished dressing, Nate scraped the dishes and stuck them in the dishpan to soak. After he loaded her knapsack on the sled, he put on his skis and waited for her to come out.

"Millie?"

"Be right there," she called.

He heard her scrambling around inside. "Come on, Millie. We need to get going."

She rushed out of the house, her coat unbuttoned and her scarf trailing down her back. She was carrying his lunch bucket. "You forgot your lunch," she said as she climbed aboard the sled. "Mush," she added with a nervous giggle.

Nate had to give her credit for trying to put the best face on this. "Yes, ma'am," he replied and tied the rope of the sled around his waist before setting off.

The sky was a clear blue and the sun rising in the east promised an end to the early spring blizzard that had kept them housebound. Nate glanced back at Millie and pointed to an elk in the distance, hoping to remind her of their conversation about survival. She pulled the lap robe more firmly around her shoulders and nodded. But he saw how her lips were set in a thin, hard line and she barely glanced at the elk.

As they approached headquarters, Dan stood on the porch watching them come. "You found her?" he shouted as he came down the steps, his arms raised in a gesture of disbelief. "How?"

"Can we talk inside, Dan?"

Something in his tone must have told Dan this was a lot more than just finding the kid. He waited for Nate to ski to a stop, then offered his hand to Millie to help her out of the sled. "Mildred Chase?"

"Yes, sir."

"I'm Head Ranger Dan Atwood, and I am very glad to see you."

Millie glanced at Nate, then squinted up at Dan. "Thanks."

"Let's get you inside, young lady," Dan said and led the way.

Once in the outer office, Dan looked around as if not quite sure what to do, so Nate figured it was up to him to take charge.

"Millie, could you give me a few minutes to bring Ranger Dan up to speed on things?"

She sat in a wooden chair that faced the window and folded her arms over her chest—a gesture Nate didn't need words to understand. He indicated to Dan that the two of them should talk in Dan's office. The ranger nodded but kept watching Millie. "Want some water?" he asked.

Millie seemed to know the question was for her. She shook her head and scooted further into the chair, folding her legs so that she could rest her elbows on her knees.

As soon as Dan reached his desk and Nate took the chair opposite, he leaned in close and whispered, "Nate, what the hell were you thinking? When did you find this kid? Where was she? Is she hurt?"

"She was hiding out in the hotel there." Nate gestured toward the structure visible through the window behind Dan. "I found her one night a little over a week ago. She was half-frozen, so I took her home and...she's fine."

"Before or after her stepfather came here?"

"After."

"What about the business card I showed you from the lawyer—did you have her then?"

"I did."

Dan ran his fingers through his thinning hair. "Nate, do you have any idea what trouble you're in? What trouble you've created for me?" He kept his voice low, but there was no mistaking his agitation as he clenched his fist and stamped the desk with it to make each point. "Does Ginny know?"

Nate nodded. "But she's not been involved. She's still in Chicago."

"She's involved because you're about to lose your job, Nate, and that means losing your home and then what?"

Nate let out a long breath. He hated this. It was non-productive going over the territory he knew all too well. "There's something you don't know, Dan. Millie's mom made Ginny her guardian—that's why she came here in the first place. That's probably why somebody sent that lawyer's business card. Ginny found a note Millie's mother wrote to Milt about wanting Ginny to become Millie's guardian."

Dan sank back into his chair and drummed his fingers on the arm as he looked past Nate at Millie in the outer office. Then he flipped through a list of contacts, pulled the phone toward him and started to dial.

Nate reached across the desk to stop Dan from calling. "Can we talk about what comes next before…?"

"You lied to me, Nate. I don't appreciate that." But he put the receiver back in place and sat back in his chair.

Nate got up and closed the office door, giving Millie a signal to stay put. "You're right and I'm sorry for that. Truth is, the kid got to me." He stood behind the chair, bracing his hands on its wooden frame. "If she's telling the truth…"

"That's a big if, Nate. She ran away. Don't you think she'd say whatever she thought might help her?"

"I suppose, but the thing is a lot of what she's told me has been backed up by Ginny. The kid's mother and Ginny grew up together, went to college together, stood up in each other's weddings. Ginny was even there for Millie's father's funeral."

"Still…"

"All I'm saying is couldn't we start with the lawyer? If the will is invalid…"

"I need to call the authorities, Nate. You know that. Besides…"

Nate held up his hand for silence and moved quickly to the closed door. When he opened it, the outer office was empty. "She's gone," he said, grabbing his jacket as he headed out. He didn't wait to see if Dan would follow but had barely hit the bottom step before the ranger was there next to him.

"Which way?" Dan asked scanning the landscape for some sign of Millie. "There," he said pointing.

She was headed back toward Gardiner. She hadn't gotten far before she slipped and fell, and Nate caught up with her.

"You hurt?" he asked as he knelt next to her.

She wiped away snot and tears with her sleeve. "Ranger Dan is going to turn me in to the police and they'll call Roger and he'll be furious and…" She was choking on her sobs and unable to finish.

Dan had caught up to them and he too knelt next to Millie. "Now listen, young lady, there are laws we can't ignore, but…"

"He hit Momma and he'll hit me," Millie shouted at him. "And there's nobody there to stop him."

Dan looked at Nate, seeking confirmation, but Nate only knew what Millie had told him and like Dan said, the kid wanted to get away from Roger Fitzgerald.

"Millie, listen to me," Nate said. "Let's go back to the office and have a cup of tea to warm us up while you tell Ranger Dan the story…"

"It's not a story—it's the truth." Millie gritted out each word.

Nate again looked at Dan, seeking his approval of the plan.

"Okay, Millie, I'm ready to listen to your side of things before I call anybody, but it's cold out here so how about that cup of tea?"

"You got any honey?" Millie looked up at the ranger.

"I think I might. I've also got milk." He offered Millie his hand to help her stand. "Ever have your tea with milk, Millie?"

"That's coffee."

"Not in England. The Brits like their tea with milk. I served in the army during the war over there. Never got used to it, myself."

The three of them were walking back to headquarters. "You were in that war?" Millie asked.

"Yes, ma'am. Nate tells me your father also fought overseas."

"He died."

Dan placed his hand on Millie's shoulder as he led the way to his office and the chair across from his desk. "I'm real sorry about that. Sometimes we forget the price those left behind must pay—like you and your mother."

"I'll make the tea while you two talk," Nate said.

"I want to try it with milk," Millie said. Then she looked back at Dan. "Momma always promised we'd go to England and other countries in Europe one day and see the places my father might have seen when he was over there. Maybe he even drank his tea with milk. Momma said he liked trying new things."

The need for her to cling to something of her dead parents nearly broke Nate's heart. He looked at Dan over Millie's head, his eyes pleading with his friend to keep an open mind.

"He sounds like a swell fella," Dan said, as he took his place behind the desk. And just before Nate closed the door between Dan's office and the outer room, the ranger nodded to him. Nate let out a breath of relief. Dan was upset with the way Nate had handled this whole thing, but he would be fair about it. He would hear Millie out.

Ginny

-19-

Within a few days of Peter Walton's visit, the walls of the mansion showed only the outlines of framed paintings that had hung for decades and the floors were stripped of the hand-dyed Oriental rugs their parents had collected on their travels. Small treasures were carefully wrapped and boxed and carted away as well. Gert's furs and jewelry gradually found new owners. Meanwhile, the two sisters met with Milt's partners and the family accountant to establish a plan for paying off the taxes and other debts.

Ginny began to feel as if she could breathe again and started to believe she could finally go home without leaving her sister in the lurch. Thankfully, her morning sickness had passed, making it easier to face the many challenges each day brought. But she was certainly not prepared for Peter's news delivered just days after their initial meeting that he might have a buyer for the house—furnishings and all.

"But, where will we go?" Gert moaned.

Peter was clearly surprised at her reaction. "I thought this was what you wanted, Gert. Selling the house will not only pay off your remaining debts but leave you—and your sister--with a stake for starting fresh." He glanced at Ginny, who shrugged, having by this time grown used to the fact that nothing was going to fully satisfy her sister.

"It is mortifying enough to have our neighbors watch from behind their lace curtains as our treasures get hauled away day by day," Gert argued. "Now you want them to watch me and the children bundled away as well?"

"I hardly think…" Peter began.

"Gert," Ginny said softly, placing her hand on her sister's as the three of them sat around the kitchen table sharing a bottle of wine, "this could be very good news. Think of it—a fresh start. You wouldn't need to stay in Chicago."

"That's true," Peter agreed. "As a matter of fact, your money will go a good deal further in a smaller setting."

"You mean move away from my friends, the children's school, everything?"

Ginny rolled her eyes. "Gert, your so-called friends have not called or come by since Milt's funeral. The children are young, and they will adjust. There are good schools in other places."

"Maybe you could move closer to Ginny," Peter suggested. "Family," he added weakly when he obviously caught Ginny's horrified expression.

"Or a smaller community here on the rail line so you and the children could come into the city from time to time," Ginny hastened to recommend. The last thing she needed right now was getting Gert and the children settled while she dealt with her pregnancy and the consequences she and Nate were bound to face related to Lavinia's child.

But Gert was paying her no mind. "You're suggesting a complete change in lifestyle?" She addressed this to Peter.

He hesitated, glancing nervously at Ginny. "Well, nothing so drastic as all that. Ginny has the right idea—your life as you've known it but pared down a bit."

"That's so boring and sad," Gert announced, refilling their wine glasses until the bottle was empty. "No, something completely new is the answer. It will look more like a choice rather than something I'm being forced into because of circumstances."

"Whatever you do will be a choice, Gert," Ginny said. "And since when do you care what others may think? The truth is they may find your determination to move forward inspiring—even courageous."

Gert twirled her wine glass around, focusing on the burgundy liquid, then suddenly set the glass aside and clapped her hands together. "I've got the perfect solution," she announced. "Ginny needs to get home—she's been gone far too long. Milt's mother has been suggesting for days that the children stay with her for the duration of their school year so that they don't have to witness the dismantling of the house."

Ginny felt her stomach tighten. She did not like where this was headed. "Gert, maybe you need to…"

"So," her sister continued, "Peter, you can handle everything here while Ginny and I take the train back to Montana. I think I might just be ready for life on the range." She raised her glass in a toast. "Yee-ha!"

After Peter had taken his leave, there was no dissuading Gert from her plan. "Don't you see, Ginny? Finally, I can do something for you. You've sacrificed so much for me and the children. Please allow me to repay a small part of that devotion."

Ginny had not told Gert about either her pregnancy or Nate's news that Lavinia's daughter was staying with him. "Things at home are somewhat more complicated than I've told you, Gert. This may not be the best time for you to visit."

"Oh, Ginny, for once in your life, stop playing the heroine and let someone help you. Your health has not exactly been great since you got here—you're constantly running to the bathroom, and even Milt's mother noticed how you barely eat. We are worried about *you*." She accented the word by pointing her finger at Ginny.

Ginny sighed. "Gert, come sit down. I have a couple of things to tell you, beginning with I'm not sick—I'm pregnant."

Gert scowled at her. "If you're going to make a joke of this, Ginny, then…"

"No joke. I'm a nearly forty-year-old expectant mother."

Gert's mouth opened and closed several times, reminding Ginny of a goldfish—and making her smile. "Nothing you can say would be anything I haven't already thought. *I'm too old* heads the list."

"I wasn't going to say that."

Ginny quirked an eyebrow.

Gert grinned. "Okay. It was what popped into mind, but a baby, Ginny. Finally, a baby!"

"Yeah. It's pretty incredible."

"How far along…and did you tell Nate?"

"I figure about four months and yes, he knows." She hesitated. "I think he's scared—we both are. It's a lot to take in."

"What does your doctor say?"

Ginny looked away. "Well, the thing is I didn't really realize I was pregnant until just recently. I mean, I knew something was different, but I thought it was stress and…"

"You haven't seen a doctor?"

"There's time for that. I feel fine."

Gert uncurled herself from the sofa and headed to the hall. She flipped through a black book, stopped at a page and ran her finger down the entries. Then she picked up the receiver and dialed a number.

"Who are you calling, Gert?"

"My doctor." When Ginny started to protest, Gert held up a finger and spoke to the person on the other end. "This is Mrs. Milton Dodge. I need an appointment as soon as possible. This afternoon would be best."

She listened a second and then shook her head vehemently. "This is an emergency. My husband just jumped off a building, in case you haven't heard."

Ginny heard the person on the end stumble for a response.

"Lovely," Gert said. "One o'clock today. Oh, and let Dr. Morgan know it's quite possible this is about a pregnancy. That's right. Well, aren't you sweet! Toodles, my dear."

"Gert, you are deliberately misleading your physician. I'm sure he's quite busy and..."

"We are going to keep that appointment, Ginny. And then we are going to check train schedules and make plans for getting you home."

"If I see the doctor in Yellowstone, we won't be charged. It's part of Nate's contract and..." But suddenly she realized that by the time she got home, Nate might no longer have a contract. Besides, it would relieve his mind to know she'd been checked out and pronounced healthy. Truth was, it would give her some comfort as well.

"All right, Gert, you win. I'll go change."

"Good." She watched Ginny climb the stairs and then said, "How does it feel to have me taking care of you for once?"

"Pretty damned good," Ginny admitted and retraced her steps to give Gert a hug.

But what she had failed to calculate into her sister's uncharacteristic take-charge attitude was that it would not stop with the doctor. By the time Ginny had been examined and Dr. Morgan had pronounced her and baby healthy and had also agreed with her timeline of four months, Gert had come up with a whole new reason for traveling to Montana.

"Who's going to take care of you once the baby comes?"

"Nate and I..."

"Nate will be working and neither one of you knows the first thing about handling a baby. For once I have the edge here—three children?" She raised three fingers to make her point.

Ginny didn't want to remind Gert that she'd had a nursemaid from the minute each child came home and a full-time nanny once the children were older. "My friend, Bertha, has two children and…"

Gert heaved a sigh of exasperation. "Are you going to shut me out of this, as you have everything else in your life, Ginny?"

"I don't…I didn't…is that how you see me?"

"I don't think it was intentional, but we had different interests and our friends were never the same. You've no idea how left out I felt."

Ginny could not have been more surprised. "But Gert, you were the popular one—the pretty one. The house was always so filled with your friends, their laughter and the parties and…"

"Do you remember Lavinia?"

Ginny's heart skipped a beat. "Of course."

"The two of you were so close that sometimes it felt more like she was your sister and I was the friend. There were times when I hated her," Gert admitted, her voice dropping almost to a whisper.

Given her sister's reaction to the news of Ginny's pregnancy, she had decided against telling Gert about Lavinia's death and Millie running away. But the admission of Gert's combination of jealousy and hurt gave her pause. "Lavinia and I lost touch a few years ago."

"I'm sorry. Was it after she married again?"

"Yes. I guess I made my feelings too clear regarding the man she chose. She didn't appreciate that and cut all ties. I didn't even know she'd left Chicago."

Gert's eyes widened. "She did? I just thought we moved in different circles."

"She was living just outside Yellowstone in the town of Gardiner."

"Lavinia? Oh, did that scoundrel leave her? Did she lose everything and have to start again?"

"They moved there together. Her husband is a businessman and he saw an opportunity out west, so they moved."

"And she never let you know? I mean, she knew where you were, right?"

"There's more. Nate told me Lavinia died a week or so ago. He didn't know details. Just that she had taken ill and never recovered."

"How horrid! She had a daughter, right? I remember you came back here to be with her when that child was born."

"Yes, a daughter—Millie." Ginny did a quick mental calculation. "She must be fourteen now...."

"Lavinia's parents died shortly after she remarried—died within months of each other, right?"

"That's right. So, Millie has no one—Lavinia had no other children and no siblings, so the child is alone."

Gert thought a moment. "Well, at least she has the second husband—what was his name? Robert? Ralph?"

"Roger Fitzgerald," Ginny replied. "And Millie does not want to live with him."

"How is that her decision? Seems to me... How can you know that?"

"She ran away, Gert. Just after the funeral. She remembered seeing the Christmas card I sent Lavinia and I guess Lavinia may have told her she had a friend who lived in Yellowstone. It's all pretty jumbled right now, but the end of the story is that she found her way to the park, hid out for several days, and nearly froze to death until thankfully Nate found her."

Gert stared at Ginny for a long moment. "And immediately called the authorities, I hope."

Ginny's silence was her answer.

"Oh, Ginny," Gert said softly. "This is not good."

Gert's grasp of the obvious had always annoyed Ginny. "So, you can understand why it's imperative that I go home as soon as possible."

"Of course."

"And you understand why this would not be the best time for you to embark on this adventure to see if you might like life in Montana?"

Her sister scowled at her. "That's all changed. I would be coming there for you. Or do you think I'm just too dumb or self-centered to appreciate the mess Nate may have made for you?"

True to form, her sister had found a way to turn the tables so that the discussion shifted from Ginny's worries to Gert's hurt feelings. And true to form, Ginny hurried to reassure her.

"That's not it. It's just that…"

"Peter has a buyer for this place, Ginny. Where am I supposed to live?"

She was tempted to remind Gert that a buyer meant money—funds enough to pay rent or even buy something. Instead she said, "It's not forever, Gert. First of all, whoever this buyer is, the actual sale will take weeks if not months to organize, and if worse came to worse, you could stay with Milt's parents in their place. There's plenty of room for you as well as the children and…"

Gert let out a loud sigh and rolled her eyes. "I have no intention of being any further in the debt of that woman than I already am."

"Then I don't know what to say. I need to go home, and I have enough to deal with without worrying about you." Ginny picked up her sweater and prepared to leave the room.

But when she reached the stairs, she stopped, because Gert asked the one question Ginny had refused to even consider. "And once Nate is fired for harboring this child, where exactly will the two of you live?"

Ginny did not turn back to face her sister. Instead, she started climbing the impressive, curved stairway. "Well, the good news is that if Peter can sell this place, hopefully the division of the proceeds will be enough to ensure each of us has a place to live, Gert. Goodnight."

Millie

-20-

It was stupid to try and run again. All she'd gotten for it was wet and cold. Millie wrapped her hands around the mug of tea Nate had brought her before leaving her alone with the ranger and stared out the window behind Ranger Dan's head. While Nate was making the tea, she had told him the whole story—how Roger and Momma met, what things were like when they were first married, how they had started to fight that night Momma accused him of using her money, and how he had hurt Momma— then and all the other times Millie had seen the bruises.

"Did he ever hurt you, Millie?" Ranger Dan asked, as if the idea had just popped into his head.

She snorted. "Most of the time he seemed to forget I was around. At first—after we left Chicago, Momma made sure we did things together—as a family, she liked to say. But I don't think Roger liked that and after a while he would make excuses or just not show up when Momma planned some outing for us. Mostly it was Momma and me during the day—and Momma and Roger at night."

"Were you ever afraid of him?" Ranger Dan leaned forward, and Millie could feel him watching her closely.

She sighed and looked directly at him. "You met him. He can be pretty scary when he's not getting his way."

Ranger Dan's eyes widened in surprise. "So, you were aware he came to the park—you saw him and did not reveal yourself then?"

"I ran away," she answered, deliberately emphasizing each word. "From him," she added just in case.

"I understand that. I just thought maybe after a couple of days on your own out here, you might have reconsidered."

Then it was Millie who leaned forward. "I would rather be anywhere—even dead—than have to live with Roger."

He sighed and swiveled away from her to stare out the window. He did this thing with his fingers like a game Momma used to play when Millie was a little kid. *Here's the church and here's the steeple; open the doors and see all the people.*

For reasons she didn't understand, she started to cry, and when Ranger Dan heard her sniffling, he turned around again. "Millie," he said as he fumbled in his pocket and handed her a clean white handkerchief, "we have to let the authorities know you're here."

"I know," she blubbered.

"So here are my choices. I can call your stepfather's lawyer—Mr. Stoner—or I can call the police in Gardiner or I can call Mr. Fitzgerald."

Suddenly Millie had an idea that would solve everything—at least for Nate and Ranger Dan. Her plan to get on the train could still work. "I've got money. I could take a train back to Chicago and…"

"And then what? Nate tells me you have no contacts there."

She searched her mind for something else. "Or you could take me to the edge of town—maybe the railroad station—and let me just walk from there. Then everybody would think I just came back on my own and you and Nate wouldn't get in trouble and…"

"And where would you go, Millie?"

She hadn't thought of that. "Maybe Clara's—she was our cook and housekeeper and Roger fired her, but she lives in town and…"

"…and she would be in more trouble for taking you in," he reminded her. His voice was gentle, and his eyes were kind. Millie understood he was trying to get her to face the fact that there was no way out of this.

"I need to talk to Nate," she said, her voice breaking and her chest feeling so full of panic she thought it might explode.

Ranger Dan went to the door and opened it. Next thing Millie knew Nate was standing next to her. She looked up at him. "I don't know what to do."

He shook his head. "That's okay because neither do I. But the decision isn't up to us." He looked at Ranger Dan, who cleared his throat and sat on the edge of his desk.

"Millie, why don't I call Mr. Stoner and let him know the situation? Then he can advise us on the best way forward."

She looked up at Nate. "Okay?"

"Best of a bad situation, Millie," he replied and sat in the chair next to hers while they both watched Ranger Dan pull a business card from his desk blotter and start dialing.

Once he'd made the call and told them Mr. Stoner would be coming to the park, Ranger Dan heated some soup and sliced some bread. After they ate, Nate suggested Millie lie down on a bench in the outer office and read. "It'll help pass the time," he said.

"Where are you going?" she asked.

He smiled. "Thought I might get a little work done." He put on his coat and hat. "I'll come back when Mr. Stoner gets here."

Ranger Dan went back to his office and, after reading for a bit, Millie fell asleep—until she heard the familiar growl of Roger's big black automobile.

She ran to the window and saw Mr. Stoner step out of the back seat followed by Roger. Ranger Dan came out of his office. "You lied," she shouted, even as she glanced around, frantically searching for an escape. He caught her and held on as she flailed away at his chest with her fists.

"Millie, I didn't know your stepfather would be here. Mr. Stoner must have…"

"I want Nate." She broke away and ran for the door, but when she wrenched it open, Roger was standing there blocking her way. At the same time, she saw Nate coming up the steps behind Mr. Stoner. Roger led the way into Ranger Dan's outer office the same way he entered any room—like he owned it. He glanced around, then turned his full attention to Millie.

"Well, at least you're in one piece. Did you enjoy your little adventure, Millie?" he asked in that voice she knew meant trouble.

Before she could say anything, Roger struck her across her face with his leather gloves.

Nate

-21-

When Roger hit Millie, Nate felt his insides roil with rage. Without a thought as to the consequences, he charged like a bighorn sheep protecting his family and shoved the man to the ground.

"You feel like hitting somebody, hit me, not her," he growled, his spit landing on Roger's cheek. After that all hell broke loose. The driver dragged him away while the lawyer and Dan went to Millie's aid. Nate observed it all from his position on the ground where the driver had dropped him before going to Fitzgerald and offering him a hand up.

Roger brushed off the offer of assistance and got to his feet, swiping at his cheek with the back of one hand as he stood over Nate. "Who are you again?" he asked.

"Nate Baker." From the corner of his eye he saw Millie trying to push past Dan and the lawyer. "I'm okay, Millie," he said, without taking his eyes off her stepfather.

"How exactly do you know my stepdaughter?" Roger was standing so close that the toes of his shoes were touching Nate's fingers. It would be impossible to stand so Nate flattened his palm to the floor and stayed where he was as he glared up at the man.

"Her mother and my wife went to school together and were close friends. Maybe you've heard of my wife— Virginia Baker?"

Fitzgerald frowned. "Virginia Baker," he muttered and glanced over his shoulder at the lawyer. Alvin Stoner nodded. "And where is your wife now?"

Dan stepped forward. "Perhaps we should all just calm down. We're upsetting the child."

Fitzgerald continued to stare at Nate. "I am perfectly calm, Ranger Atwood, and the child ran away from home, so I don't think she has much to say about what happens next here. Gus, take Millie to the car."

"No!" Millie made a break for the door.

Gus grabbed her.

Nate tried to get up, but Roger stomped down hard on his hand and pressed his knee to Nate's throat. "Alvin," he said with deadly calm, "I want this man arrested for abducting my stepdaughter and for assaulting me." He stepped away then and slowly pulled on his gloves. He scowled at the driver, who was holding Millie firmly but gently.

"Let's go, Millie," Gus said, as he half-carried her from the room.

Roger turned his attention to Dan. "Ranger Atwood, I hope this is not an example of the way you manage things in this park. As a citizen and someone with friends in Washington, I would hate to see you transferred or demoted."

He did not wait for Dan's response as he strode out the door. The lawyer gave Dan an apologetic glance before following.

As soon as they heard the car doors slam and the engine roar to life, Dan knelt next to Nate, who was still struggling to catch his breath. "Nate, what possessed you? I mean, do you have any idea how much trouble you're in? I can't…"

"I know. It was just… He hit her, Dan. He didn't even hesitate." Nate stood and walked to the window in time to see the tail lights of the large black car disappear. He was thinking about Millie, but he was also remembering a scene from when he'd been about her age—a day when his father had nearly beaten his mother to death before driving away.

"What are you going to do?" Dan put his hand on Nate's shoulder.

He shrugged. "Wait, I guess."

"For what?"

"You heard the man. Likely the police will be here before sundown. Maybe you could ask Benny to check on our place at least until Ginny gets back. He knows where we keep the spare key."

"Can you post bail?" Dan asked.

"Depends on what they set. Any way you look at it, I'm likely to be in jail overnight, and even if I get out tomorrow, I want to check on Millie—be sure she's all right."

Dan stepped in front of him, forcing Nate to look at him instead of the scene outside the window. "You need to stay as far away from that house—that man—as possible. So far, you've still got a job and a place to live. You need to be thinking about Ginny."

And the baby.

"You heard any more about the sale of the park concessions, Dan?"

"Only that it's not a deal yet and that's all to your favor. Fitzgerald can't fire you if he doesn't own the business."

Nate crossed the room, pulled a paper cup from a stack on the side table and filled it with water. He drank it down and refilled it, flexing his fingers, hoping nothing was broken. He noticed his hand was bruised where Roger had stepped on it. He also noticed how badly he was shaking.

Millie

"Sit up front with me," Gus said as he guided Millie toward the car.

"No. I won't go, and he can't make me and…"

Gus wrapped his arm around her shoulders. "Oh, but he can, Millie. At least right now he can, so be smart about this, okay?"

Survival.

She nodded. "Okay." As Gus opened the passenger door for her, she saw Roger and the lawyer leave Ranger Dan's office. She slumped low in the seat and pulled her hat over her forehead before wrapping her arms tight around her chest. Mr. Stoner took the seat behind her while Roger climbed in behind Gus. Millie could feel him glaring at her as he struck a match and lit his cigar. "Drive," he ordered.

When they reached the outskirts of Gardiner, Millie noticed green leaves of snowbells peeping out from the soot-colored banks of ice and snow in some of the yards they passed. Once the weather warmed up, she could leave and this time, she would board a train to anywhere but here. Thanks to her, Nate would probably end up in jail, and Ginny had the baby and some place for her and Nate to live to worry about. They didn't need to add Millie to their list of troubles.

In the meantime, she would find a way to endure the days and weeks she'd have to spend in Roger's house. The stench from the cigar wafted forward and surrounded her.

Survival.

She cleared her throat and made a show of sniffing back the remains of her crying jag. Gus glanced at her with a worried frown. She half-turned in the seat so she could see Roger, who was now staring out the window.

"I'm sorry, Roger," she said softly. "I don't know why I ran away. After the funeral I didn't know what to do...."

Slowly he turned his gaze on her, assessing her the way he so often had looked at Momma when he was upset with her. "I am a busy man, Millie. I do not have time for your shenanigans. It's high time you grew up and faced facts. Your mother is dead. You have no other family. I should think you might be grateful that you have me and a roof over your head and food in your stomach. A lot of people in this country aren't nearly so lucky."

"I know. I was wrong." She ducked her head and sniffed again. "I'm really sorry."

"There will be consequences, Millie. New rules. Gus will take you to school and pick you up at the end of the day. If you need something, you'll let Nan or Gus know and they will see that you have it. You will not leave the house unaccompanied—ever. Is that clear?"

She nodded, thinking these rules weren't new at all. They were the same rules he had applied to Momma.

"I didn't hear you," he said.

"I understand," she replied. "Thank you," she added, not because she meant it but because she hoped it might help her cause.

Roger went back to staring out the window as they approached the house. Gus pulled onto the drive and left the car idling while he got out and opened the door for Roger. Mr. Stoner also got out. Millie hesitated.

"Well, come on," Roger grumbled, and when she emerged from the car, he was waiting for her. They climbed the front steps together, his hand gripping the back of her neck. She figured to anybody watching it might look like a fatherly touch, but it was more like a clamp and a definite signal that he was in charge.

Nan opened the door, but where Clara would have hugged her, Nan just stood there like a soldier waiting for orders.

"Take her to her room and see that she has a bath and changes and then burn those clothes she's wearing." Roger handed Nan his overcoat and gloves and fedora before heading for his study. Mr. Stoner gave Nan his outer garments and then followed Roger without so much as a glance at Millie.

She waited for Nan to hang the coats and hats on the hall tree and then followed her up the stairs. She started down the hall to the stairway leading to the third floor, but Nan stopped her.

"He wants you in here," she said as she opened the door to her mother's room.

"Really?" It was a gesture so out of character for Roger—a kindness Millie would never have expected. "You're sure?"

"He wants you close so he can keep an eye on you," Nan added, as she went directly to the bathroom and turned on the taps.

Millie dropped her knapsack on the closet floor and kicked it to the back, hoping Nan wouldn't notice. There were things in there she didn't want her seeing.

"Get out of those clothes," Nan said, going to the dresser and pulling out what looked like new undergarments. "I don't have all day," she added, and Millie realized with Clara gone, Nan had taken on two jobs. She sounded tired and she looked older than she had when Millie left, even though it had only been a couple of weeks.

As soon as Millie was undressed, Nan bundled up the clothes and hurried away, closing the door behind her. Millie heard a click and realized Nan had locked her in.

So that's how it's to be, she thought. She checked the windows and saw they had been sealed shut as well. She was a prisoner—for now. But thanks to Nate and the books he'd given her to study and that day in the park, she'd learned enough about how animals survive to know things could change.

After she'd had her bath, she discovered that Momma's clothes had been pushed aside and her meager wardrobe hung in the space left. She picked out a plaid pleated skirt and a white blouse to wear for dinner. Of course, she was assuming she would be having dinner with Roger in the dining room. Maybe not.

Once dressed, she brushed her hair and sat on the end of the chaise lounge to wait for the door to be unlocked. While she waited, she slowly looked around the room, seeking things that still spoke of Momma, but also checking for other changes Roger might have made. That's when she realized Momma's jewelry box was missing.

The really valuable stuff was kept locked up in the wall safe in Roger's study, but her favorite pieces—a bracelet Millie's father had given her and the wedding ring she'd worn right up to the day she married Roger had been in that blue satin-covered box.

Millie checked the small side drawers of the dressing table, but neither the jewelry box nor the pieces she sought were there. The lock clicked and the door swung open behind her. She looked into the mirror and saw Roger filling the doorway.

"You can join us for dinner, assuming you can mind your manners."

All Millie heard was "us." Maybe Mr. Stoner was staying. But while she was dressing, she'd heard Roger speaking to the lawyer outside the front door and then she'd heard the door close and footsteps moving away from the house.

"Who else is coming?" she asked.

"Not that it's any of your concern, but Mrs. Glover will dine with us." He stepped to one side, waiting for

Millie to head downstairs. "Well, come on," he said impatiently.

She wanted to ask him what had happened to Momma's jewel box, but the news that the woman who had stood so close to Roger at the funeral was now there for dinner gave her other concerns. Mrs. Glover was divorced. She'd once heard Clara tell Momma, "that woman is on the prowl, so you'd best keep an eye on her and your mister."

As she entered the dining room Millie hesitated, because Mrs. Glover was sitting in Momma's chair. Then she felt Roger give her a push forward. "Sheila, you remember Lavinia's daughter, I'm sure," he said, as he guided Millie to her usual place on one side of the long table.

Mrs. Glover held out her arms to Millie, although she remained seated. "Darling girl, what an ordeal this must have been for you."

Millie gave her an awkward hug, trying hard not to actually touch her. She smelled of perfume and wore too much powder. "I'm fine," she said, and hurried to take her seat.

"Well, you're home now and that's all that matters. Isn't that right, Roger?"

He grunted and started slurping his soup. Millie saw Mrs. Glover frown as she picked up her spoon.

The soup was watery, with shreds of carrots floating in it. Also, it was too salty, but Millie hadn't eaten much since breakfast, so she scooped up a spoonful. But before she could swallow, Mrs. Glover said, "Mildred, napkin." She pantomimed dabbing the corner of her mouth.

Millie felt her cheeks go hot with anger and ducked her head, so her hair covered her face to hide it. She had to be careful here—figure out the lay of the land, as Nate had once said when explaining about the animals in the park.

"And at mealtime, it may be best to pin back your hair, dear."

Not that Millie expected any help, but she shot a look at Roger, who sighed and leaned back in his chair while Nan removed the soup bowls. The only one who had finished was Roger, but that's all that mattered.

"Is Mrs. Glover…" Millie fumbled for words that would not make him mad.

"Mrs. Glover is staying with us while her home is being redecorated. In return, she has kindly offered to take you under her wing and make sure you receive the lessons in etiquette and decorum a girl your age needs."

"She lives here?" Millie almost shouted the words and immediately saw her mistake when Nan, balancing a tray filled with serving dishes, froze halfway through the swinging door that led to the kitchen. Millie turned to Mrs. Glover. "I mean, I hope you'll be comfortable. Momma used to say one of the hardest things in life was being away from home." She forced what she hoped was a concerned smile.

"Well, aren't you sweet! Roger, this child is a gem and we are going to get along famously, aren't we, Mildred?"

Roger glared at Millie as he attacked the slab of meat Nan set before him, carving the beef into slices and flopping them onto the plates Nan held and then delivered to Mrs. Glover and Millie. Once the meat was served, Nan made her way around the table offering portions of mashed potatoes and limp-looking green beans from a can. Millie couldn't help thinking about Ginny's greenhouse and what Nate had called "root" vegetables that the two of them had enjoyed almost every night.

That, of course, made her think about Nate and wonder if Roger had had him arrested. But she knew better than to raise the question, so she pushed her food around her plate, taking a bit and forcing it down whenever Mrs. Glover or Roger glanced her way.

"I've spoken to the school, Mildred," Mrs. Glover said after they'd eaten the main course in silence and Nan had returned to remove their plates. "Do you feel up to attending classes tomorrow?"

"It's not her choice," Roger said. "She will be in class tomorrow. She has a lot of work to do in order to catch up and I fully expect her to be back on track within the week. Is that clear?"

He was talking to Mrs. Glover, but somehow Millie figured this last was for her, so she muttered, "Yes, sir." And then she saw a chance to put in a good word for Nate. "Mr. Baker had me reading and doing reports and stuff while I was with him, so maybe…"

Roger was on his feet and looming over her before she finished the sentence. "Let me be perfectly clear about one thing, Millie. I do not wish to hear anything about what happened while you were away. That unfortunate piece of your life is finished. Do you understand?"

She nodded. Her heart was pounding. He wouldn't hit her in front of Mrs. Glover, would he?

"Shall we have our coffee in the front parlor, Roger?" Mrs. Glover's voice shook as she twisted her napkin around her fingers.

And that's when Millie noticed she was wearing Momma's bracelet. Millie stared hard at it—so hard that Mrs. Glover noticed and smiled. She held out her arm for Millie to see. "Isn't it lovely, Mildred? It was a gift from your stepfather."

Millie felt vomit rise in her chest and throat and swallowed it back. "May I please be excused?" she managed as she glanced up at Roger. Something in his expression told her he was aware that she had recognized the bracelet. A slow smile spread over his face as he stepped away from her chair, freeing her to leave. Millie ran up the stairs, threw herself onto Momma's bed and burst into tears.

Ginny

-23-

Finally, they had a plan. The children were settling in with Milt's mother. Peter had set up a meeting for Gert, Ginny and Milt's partner to meet with the prospective buyers. He had also presented the sisters a check for a sizeable amount, covering the sale of art, antiques and other items. On Friday, Ginny and Gert would leave for Gardiner. Ginny would be home by Sunday.

Home to Nate!

She couldn't wait to see him, to feel his arms around her. Of course, there was Millie to deal with, but that could wait. She was determined to have at least twenty-four hours where it was just Nate and her—and the child she carried. After that they could tackle everything else.

Early Friday morning they had barely settled into their compartment in the sleeping car Gert had insisted they book when her sister announced, "I didn't care for that man and his wife."

Ginny searched her mind for some couple they might have encountered in the station, or while boarding the train now rolling slowly into bright morning sunlight from the tunnel that covered the platforms of Union Station.

"They simply are not the right sort for our home," Gert continued as she unpinned her hat, placed it in its box and stored it above the bench seats that would later fold down for beds. Ginny realized she was referring to the prospective buyers.

"They are willing to pay an enormous price for the property—especially in these times. That is money we can both use, Gert. I don't see the problem." Ginny was so tired—tired of trying to solve problems for Gert, tired of

Gert agreeing with something and then questioning it after, and so very tired of trying to make things work so she could get back to Nate.

Gert snorted. "Can you really see them there, Ginny? Of course, they seem nice enough but really, are they…suitable?"

"The right sort? Suitable? When did you become so biased about other people?"

Gert sat on her side of the compartment and straightened the seams on her stockings. "I am not biased, Ginny. In fact, I am thinking of their comfort and happiness. You know how people can be in that neighborhood."

"What I know, Gert, is that ours is not the only home to be put up for sale recently. What I know is that the neighborhood is changing—has already changed. What I know is that I do not wish to rethink what is already in place."

"Well, excuse me, Miss Grumpypants." Gert stood and looked around. "I'm going to the lounge. Perhaps that will give you the opportunity to nap and wake in a better mood in time for lunch."

With that she slid open the door and looked both ways, as if preparing to cross a busy street before heading off to her left.

"The lounge is the other way," Ginny murmured, knowing Gert would soon realize her mistake. She rested her head against the cool glass of the window as the train left the city behind and settled into its top speed. Farm pastures dotted with grazing livestock flashed by.

She closed her eyes, abandoning the scene outside the window and focusing instead on thoughts of Nate and Millie and what she might face once she and Gert arrived in Gardiner. She was frankly worried. She had tried calling Nate, ringing him late, in the hope that Millie would be in bed, but there had been no answer. Earlier, before she and

Gert left to catch their train, she had called Dan Atwood's office—again with no success. Milt's mother had offered to send a telegram, letting Nate know the sisters were on their way and would arrive the following afternoon—an offer Ginny had gratefully accepted as she followed Gert into the back seat of the taxi.

But she could not shake the nagging feeling that something had gone terribly wrong back home. She knew Dan well enough to understand that he would not be happy that Nate had kept the news of Millie from him. Dan was a rules-oriented man. As Nate said, he did things by the book, and in this case the book had no provision for rescuing a child and keeping her discovery from those who were her guardians. Of course, the idea of Roger Fitzgerald being Millie's only guardian was nauseating.

She dosed off and woke to see clouds had covered the sky, turning the light gray. She wished there were some way she could find out what had happened when Nate told Dan about Millie. Ginny was a planner—she could handle just about anything as long as she had information. She was also a realist, and the reality was that until she reached Gardiner sometime tomorrow, there was nothing she could do, even if she had all the information in the world.

She glanced at her watch and realized it was nearly noon. Gert had not returned, meaning in all likelihood she'd met someone who amused her in the lounge car. In some ways Ginny hoped whoever that person was, he or she—or they—might join the sisters for lunch. It would make the meal so much more pleasant if she didn't have to try and ease Gert's second thoughts about selling the house.

The lounge car was almost empty. In fact, Gert and a younger woman dressed in trousers and a bright orange silk blouse styled like a man's shirt were the only occupants other than the young man behind the bar. All three looked her way as Ginny opened the door connecting the lounge to the sleeping car.

"Ah, here she is," Gert announced. "Ginny, this is Helen from Helena." She giggled and the white wine in her half-empty glass sloshed dangerously.

The other woman stepped forward and extended her hand. "Helen Matthews," she said. "I've heard quite a bit about you, Ginny."

Ginny returned the woman's handshake and smiled. "All good, I'm sure."

Helen chuckled. "I have five sisters," she confided. "There's not a one I would trust to tell a stranger the truth, but Gert seems quite fond of you." She led the way to a small round table anchored to the floor and waited for Ginny to take a seat on the banquette behind it. "What can I get you?"

"Oh, please, I really…"

Helen smiled. "Ah, yes, I forgot—Gert told me you have a bit of a queasy stomach. The baby perhaps? Howie, white soda, if you please."

The bartender prepared the drink in a tall slim glass he'd filled with crushed ice. He capped it off with a lemon slice and presented it to Ginny on a small silver tray.

"Thank you."

Helen patted the seat beside her. "Come, join us, Gert. Howie, can you rummage up some crackers? Maybe some cheese?"

Howie grinned and nodded.

"Well, now," Helen said as soon as Gert had taken the seat next to Ginny, "here we are—three women on a train bound for Montana." She laughed. "Sounds like a title for a novel."

She had a deep, husky voice, but her laugh was more of a giggle. Ginny smiled. "You live in Montana?"

"Helen from Helena," Gert mumbled, and polished off the rest of her wine before holding up the glass for Howie to refill.

"Let's all switch to white soda," Helen suggested, relieving Gert of the wine glass as Howie brought the crackers and cheese. "We want to be able to enjoy our lunch. The chef on this train is the very best—should be in some fine restaurant on Michigan Avenue, if truth be told, but he's not, so prepare yourselves for a wonderful meal, ladies."

Howie returned with glasses of white soda for Helen and Gert.

"Do you have family in Chicago, Helen?" Ginny asked.

"Heavens no. My family wouldn't be caught dead east of Bozeman. But as the black sheep of the clan, I fell in love with art, so I make regular treks to Chicago a couple of times a year to feed my passion."

"You're an artist?"

"If taking pictures can be considered art, I guess you could say that. I'm all fired up with a new idea I have of taking pictures in Yellowstone as the season changes from winter to spring."

Gert leaned in closer. "Helen has rented a house in Gardiner. Isn't that wonderfully serendipitous?"

"And not to spoil your sister's surprise, but the place is far too big for my needs and Gert tells me she's looking for a place while she decides if she's Montana material, so…" Helen grinned as she lifted her broad shoulders—made more impressive by the shoulder pads lining her shirt.

In some ways it was the first truly good news Ginny had heard in weeks.

"And that's something you might consider?" she asked her sister.

Gert snorted. "Consider? I've practically moved in already. The house is furnished and there's an apartment above the garage…"

Ginny thought it might be too large a leap for her sister to make from a mansion on Michigan Avenue to a small apartment above a garage in Gardiner. "It's certainly worth considering," she managed.

"The garage is all mine," Helen said. "Apartment above and downstairs will be my darkroom and studio. "Gert gets the house—which I have to say is a relief, because the thought of keeping up more than one or two rooms has been a little daunting."

"And if it all works out, there's plenty of room for the children once school lets out," Gert added. She took a cracker and topped it with a slice of cheese. "Furthermore, if you and Nate ever need a place…"

Ginny frowned at her and Gert pantomimed zipping her lip. "Just a thought," she muttered.

The porter entered the car and rang a small bell. "Ladies, lunch is served," he said, and waited for them to precede him through the connecting door to the dining car.

There were two men seated at separate tables. They wore suits and ties and Ginny assumed they were traveling for business. Otherwise the tables with their starched white cloths and napkins and their china hand- painted with the Northern Pacific logo were deserted. The porter indicated a table set for three and seated each of them in turn, snapping open their napkins and presenting them with a flourish.

"Thank you, James," Helen said.

"Always a pleasure, Miss Matthews," he replied with a wide grin.

"You seem to know everyone working on this train," Ginny noted after James had left them to consider the menu.

"I've photographed most of them," Helen replied. "That's been my subject matter ever since the crash— working people struggling to stay afloat, taking pride in their labor."

"You'll have to photograph Ginny's husband then," Gert said.

Helen quirked an eyebrow with interest.

"Nate is what is known as a winterkeeper for Yellowstone," Ginny explained. "It's his job to make sure the tons of snow and ice we get there during the winter doesn't damage the buildings."

"For the entire park?"

Ginny smiled. "No, there are others working in the same capacity, although since the crash there have been cutbacks."

"He works for the government then?"

Ginny took a sip of the water from a heavy crystal glass that reminded her of crystal her parents had once owned. "No. The concessions in the park—the lodges, hotels, restaurants and gift shops and such—are privately owned by an outside company. Technically, I suppose the company works for the government, since they sign a contract, but Nate and the others work for that company."

"I see. And in summer?"

"In summer he works wherever he's needed anywhere in the park."

James had returned to take their orders, murmuring "very good," before leaving them.

As they ate, Ginny learned that Gert had confided quite a lot to Helen, telling her about their financial losses and Milt's suicide, and how her children were finishing the year in the private school she preferred, but would need to attend what Gert referred to as "a local school" once she had decided where they would settle. Ginny could not help thinking how mature and self-assured Gert sounded—a far cry from the insecure and childish woman Ginny had been dealing with for days now. Was it an act for Helen or had she finally hit her stride as a responsible adult?

"You certainly have had to make some hard choices," Helen said as they enjoyed their entrees. "I think you are both quite courageous. I've been blessed not to have had the Depression touch me or my family. Oh, we've struggled—the weather has been horrific, but I'm not sure I could have met the challenges the two of you have faced."

They talked about how Ginny had come to live in Yellowstone and Helen's photography as they finished their fish with boiled parsley potatoes and green peas. While they waited for James to clear their dinner plates and deliver their desserts, Ginny thought about the challenges still awaiting her once she got to Gardiner. "I wish I had some way to contact Nate," she said, as the three of them devoured a luscious chocolate pudding and lingered over cups of hot tea.

"Oh, but you can call him," Helen said.

"Perhaps when we make a stop, if there's time."

"You can call from the train," Helen said. There's a phone for the use of first-class passengers."

"Ginny hasn't traveled first class in some time," Gert said.

"I usually come and go coach to save money," Ginny explained.

"Translation? She's cheap," Gert muttered and then tried softening the criticism with a sly smile.

"She's thrifty," Helen corrected. "Nothing wrong with that—especially these days." She signaled James.

"Anything else, Miss Matthews?"

"Yes, James. Mrs. Baker here needs to make a phone call. Can you see that the line is available?"

The man's perpetual smile faded. "I'm afraid the lines are down—at least in this area. I'll let you know when service is available," he said.

"And please tell Leonard how much we all enjoyed our meal."

One of the businessmen signaled James, so he smiled and hurried away.

"Who's Leonard?" Gert asked, covering a yawn.

"He's the chef I mentioned earlier. If you thought this food was good, wait until you see what that man can do with powdered eggs—his omelets are divine." She dabbed the corners of her mouth with her napkin and stood.

"No more food for me until morning then," Gert announced. "I am stuffed."

Helen stood. "I have some work I want to do so I plan to retire to my cabin for the rest of the day and night. Shall I see you both at breakfast?"

"It's been a harrowing few weeks for me," Gert said. "I'm going to sleep in if that suits?" She directed this to Ginny.

"You've earned it," Ginny replied and then turned to Helen. "I, on the other hand, tend to be an early riser, so I would love to have breakfast with you."

Helen beamed. "Lovely. Eight o'clock then." She gave a little wave and left the dining car.

"Well, that was a happy accident," Gert said, as she and Ginny returned to their compartment. "Who would have guessed I would already have a friend for my stay in Gardiner?"

Ginny laughed. "Oh, Gert, you have always made friends and connections wherever you were. It's one of your talents."

"It's one of my *few* talents," Gert replied, with no hint of self-pity.

"That is simply not true," Ginny argued as they entered their compartment, kicked off their shoes and stretched out on the seats that faced each other. "You have many gifts, and once this little person comes, I am counting on you to show me some motherly skills."

Gert laughed. "Well, I can certainly teach the kid how to shop," she teased.

Ginny threw a pillow at her and they giggled like the girls they had once been when they shared a room in that house on Michigan Avenue.

Nate

-24-

About an hour after Millie left with Roger, Nate had just finished clearing the hotel roof when he heard the distant bleat of a siren. Leaning on his shovel, he watched the police car come slowly down the road. Dan came outside and glanced his way. Nate nodded and climbed down the ladder, stored his tools and the crampons that allowed him to move over the snow and ice in the shed and walked over to where Dan waited.

"Sorry, Nate," Dan muttered, as the police car came to a stop and the siren petered out.

Nate shrugged. "No regrets," he said softly.

The sheriff stepped out of the car. He was holding a clipboard and he was alone. "Mr. Baker?"

"Yes, sir."

The officer referred to the document on the clipboard. "Mr. Roger Fitzgerald of Gardiner has filed a complaint against you. The charge is kidnapping and falsely imprisoning his stepdaughter—Mildred Chase—for an extended period of time." He glanced at Nate.

Dan stepped forward. "Sheriff Wilson, this is all a misunderstanding. The girl ran away after her mother died. She hid out in the hotel there for several days. When Nate found her, she was half-frozen, and it was night. I was away from headquarters and there was no one else around. He did the only thing he could. He took her home in order to administer care."

"For over a week?" Wilson turned back to Nate. "Why not call it in?"

Nate had had time to consider how he would handle the inevitable fact that Fitzgerald would file charges. After the fracas in Dan's office, he'd needed to think, and the solitude of cutting and moving snow gave him the venue, but he'd come up with nothing. "I had my reasons," he told the sheriff.

Wilson frowned. "Mr. Fitzgerald also claims you assaulted him." He tapped the clipboard against his thigh and stared at Nate. "What do you have to say about that?"

"He struck Millie. I reacted. I should have held my temper but it's not right to hit a child." Nate knew he wasn't helping things. If Ginny were there, she would be explaining things to the sheriff—making a case. Nate understood his reluctance to give fuller explanations was hurting him, but he didn't know what to say.

"The man hit that girl with no warning," Dan said. "He…"

The sheriff held up his hand to stop Dan from saying more. "Nathan Baker, I am arresting you on a charge of assault." He stepped away and opened the door to the police car.

Nate was surprised the sheriff focused on the one charge but not the other. He expected it was because he'd admitted that one—and the officer only needed one reason to take Nate into custody. He held out his hands, expecting handcuffs.

"I don't think that's necessary," Wilson muttered. "Just get in the car and behave yourself."

Nate followed directions, nodded to Dan as the sheriff shut the car door, and then stared straight ahead and said nothing more during the ride back to Gardiner. The jail was a single-story small rock and sandstone block building set a couple of streets over from the town's center. The sheriff pulled up to the front door and got out.

"Come on," he said, as he led the way inside.

A stove sat in one corner of the space. The rest was pretty much taken up with a single metal cage divided into three cells.

"Cell by mail," Wilson said when he saw Nate studying the structure. "It's built at the factory and shipped in."

One cell was set up with four pulldown iron bunks while the other two smaller cells could hold two prisoners each. Nate guessed the whole place couldn't be more than five hundred square feet. At least there was light--four windows, two on the north wall and two more on the south. All of them were covered with iron bars running both horizontally and vertically in a checkerboard pattern. It was clear he wasn't going anywhere—even if he was of a mind to do so.

"I'll need your personal effects," the sheriff said, and Nate pulled out the pocket watch his grandfather had given him, his keys and wallet and handed them over. He noticed the outer door they'd entered was made of heavy steel with a fan-shaped barred opening at the top that Nate figured allowed the sheriff to look in without unlocking the building. Each cell door featured a slot Nate assumed was used for the delivery of meals. *Very efficient.*

Wilson plucked a set of keys from a hook near the door and indicated one of the smaller cells. "You'll have the place to yourself for now. Later I expect you'll be joined by one or two drunks. Pretty much happens every night. They can't feed their kids, but they can drink themselves stupid." He shook his head and waited for Nate to enter the cell.

The paint was peeling off the plaster walls, on which former prisoners had left their marks. Nate chose the cell closest to the potbelly stove and pulled down the lower bunk. It squealed in protest. Wilson handed him a rough wool blanket and a flat pillow.

"Your night bucket's in that tin cabinet there. I'll bring you an extra blanket with your supper." He stepped outside the cell and locked it. Then he locked the second door that gave access to all three cells, lit a kerosene lantern and set it on a square wooden table. "I'll be back directly," he said, as he stepped outside and locked the outer door.

Nate stretched out on the bunk—its metal webbing curved to better fit his body. He was still wearing his coat and hat, giving him some padding in the absence of a mattress, and he figured with night setting in he might need them despite the fire the sheriff had stoked in the stove. Staring up at the corrugated metal ceiling, he thought about Ginny.

He'd considered asking Dan to call her and let her know what had happened, but the way he figured it from their last phone conversation, she wouldn't be leaving Chicago for a few days yet, and maybe by the time she got home he'd have everything worked out. Why add to her worries? On the other hand, if he was locked up, how was he supposed to solve anything?

He wondered how Millie was doing and hoped Roger Fitzgerald had decided to leave her alone. The sooner Ginny could meet with the lawyer, the better. In the meantime, he supposed there was little he could do.

Maybe an hour had passed when he heard the jangle of keys outside the main door. He sat up.

"Suppertime," a female voice trilled.

By the dim light of the lantern Nate watched a small, bent woman balance a tray as she pushed open the door. "Good evening," she said cheerfully.

"Hello," Nate replied.

"Louise Wilson—Sheriff Wilson's better half." She set the tray on the floor before passing him a thin blanket through the bars. "It'll help some," she said.

Suddenly Nate had a thought. "Do you know a woman named Clara?"

"I know three Claras," she replied, as she fed the tray through the slot. "What's the last name?"

"I don't have a last name. She used to work for the Fitzgerald family."

"Oh, Clara Royce—poor soul. That man cut her loose without so much as a final paycheck. She's got no family close by. Who treats another human being that way? Especially one who has given her heart and soul to her work. When the missus was still living, I can tell you we all thought Clara had found her place. Mrs. Fitzgerald was an angel, and Clara was devoted to her. How do you know Clara?"

Nate had wolfed down a good portion of his supper while Louise Wilson talked. "I don't know her exactly. The girl—Millie. That's who I know, and she mentioned Clara."

Louise nodded. "Heard all about that. Millie ran away and you took her in—bless you. Can't imagine what that child was going through, losing her mother and all. Now she's all alone. If that man hadn't fired Clara—over a silly candle, for heaven's sake!"

"Millie's back with her stepfather now and I'm a little worried about her. Seems to me Roger Fitzgerald has quite a temper."

Louise stepped closer to the cell and lowered her voice. "Word was he regularly hit the missus. Nobody ever saw it, of course, but that woman was a prisoner in the house. If it hadn't been for Clara and Gus…"

"Mrs. Wilson, I wonder if I could get a message to Mrs. Royce?"

"*Miss* Royce," she corrected. "No need for carrying messages. I'll have her deliver your breakfast and the two of you can talk."

"I wouldn't want to get you in trouble with Sheriff Wilson," Nate said.

Louise Wilson laughed. "Who do you think sent me over with your supper? Ted thought you might talk to me—said he couldn't get a word out of you. I can see why. You're not much for talking about yourself, are you?"

"Never saw the point of going on about something nobody needs to know."

She stoked the fire and added a couple of small logs. "Well, get through the night. I'll make sure Clara comes by first thing tomorrow, although I don't know what you think she can tell you."

"Just need to hear what she has to say—especially about Millie's mother," Nate said. "Thank you. That was a real good supper."

Louise Wilson frowned. "I wouldn't put too much hope in getting information from Clara. It's a small town and Roger Fitzgerald wields a lot of power. She won't want to draw his attention."

"I understand."

But as she picked up the tray and headed out the door, Louise didn't seem all that convinced. "Just tread lightly," she instructed as she pulled the outer door shut behind her. Nate heard the scratch of the key fitting into the lock and the following click. Then he heard Louise Wilson's footsteps fade and all was quiet.

He woke to darkness broken only by a handheld lantern as the sheriff and two other men crowded inside the jail. One man held the lantern while Wilson opened the cage door and then the door to the other small cell. "Come on, Harvey," he grunted as he half-carried a man into the cell. "Sleep it off. I'll let your folks know you'll be home by morning."

"No work," the man muttered.

"You had a job with that CCC outfit," Wilson argued. "You blew that off by showing up drunk and starting a fight. You think about that while you sober up— that was good money to care for your mom and pop, but you…"

He stopped mid-sentence and shook his head. "Talking to a wall," he muttered to the man holding the lantern. "Baker," he snapped, "be ready first thing. I'll be driving you over to Livingston for an appearance at the county courthouse."

"On what charge?" Nate just wanted to be sure Wilson hadn't changed his mind about not including kidnapping.

"You deaf or what? You're accused of assaulting another citizen. If that's not enough for you, I can probably come up with more."

"That'll do fine, Sheriff."

"Thought so." Wilson locked both cells and the outer cage, fed the fire and left—his deputy following close behind him. "Be ready at dawn. I'll have a thermos of coffee and some of my wife's biscuits in the car."

So much for Clara Royce bringing my breakfast, Nate thought.

In the next cell the drunk was already passed out and snoring so loud that Nate reckoned he wouldn't be getting much sleep. Wilson had mentioned the CCC and Nate recalled Benny talking excitedly about it.

"CCC stands for Civilian Conservation Corps," he'd told Nate one day. "President Roosevelt wants to do whatever he can to create jobs—jobs that aren't there now. The CCC is going to reforest the entire country—one tree at a time, according to Roosevelt." He showed Nate an article he'd clipped from the newspaper.

Nate recalled the article describing a program where able-bodied men who were out of work would be recruited to battle the devastation to the land and its resources, left in the wake of the dust storms and other natural disasters that had plagued the country.

Roosevelt had only been in office a little over a month when the program was not only proposed but put into action, and the state of Montana, along with Yellowstone, was already being targeted as a place this peacetime army could do some good. Benny was trying to figure a way he could apply without waiting for his eighteenth birthday.

Nate lay on his bunk, hands folded behind his head, and thought about the CCC. If he lost his job in the park, then working on one of the crews might be an option. Of course, the call had been for young, able-bodied men, but maybe they would appreciate his experience and overlook his age. Of course, the article had been pretty specific about who qualified—unmarried, physically fit, between the ages of 18 and 26.

"Three strikes and you're out, Baker," Nate muttered as he tried to find a comfortable position on the metal bunk.

Next door, the drunk mumbled in his sleep. Nate recalled all the nights he'd listened to his father muttering through the night while Nate and his mother and siblings huddled together in another room, consoling each other and tending to the wounds inflicted by Jacob Baker. Even when things were going good, Jacob found a way to cast doubt. And when things went sour, he blamed everyone but himself.

Nate stared into the black night surrounding him, heard the dry wood crackle and settle in the wood stove, smelled the stench left by men who'd spent time in this jail before him, and thought about Millie Chase. Truth was, in Millie he saw a lot of the kid he'd been at her age. Scared and at the same time resourceful. He wondered how Millie was handling being back under Roger Fitzgerald's roof—and control.

Millie
-25-

Millie overheard Gus tell Nan about Nate being in jail, so her first morning back when Gus drove her to school, she asked him what could happen to Nate.

He looked at her in the rearview mirror. "Now Millie…"

"He's my friend."

Gus sighed.

"My best guess is he'll be taken up to Livingston—the county seat—sometime today to appear before the judge. After that…" He shrugged.

She stared out the window, trying to figure out how she might ditch school and make her way to the courthouse in Livingston.

"Get that idea straight out of your head, Millie. There's no way you can get from here to there in time, even if I were of a mind to drive you—which I'm not."

He was right, but she didn't have to like it. She hugged her book bag and focused on the tips of her shoes. She could feel Gus watching her like he was maybe afraid she might leap from the moving car.

"Will there be witnesses?" She'd seen enough movies with courtroom scenes to know how things might go.

Gus frowned. "Maybe the ranger."

"Not Roger?"

"I drove him to the train station earlier. He's on his way to a meeting in Helena."

Suddenly Millie had an idea. She set her book bag on the seat beside her and took out a loose-leaf notebook and a pencil. "Pull over a minute," she instructed.

The car slowed but didn't stop. "Are you gonna be sick?"

"Just pull over, please." She balanced the notebook on her knees and started writing. It wasn't pretty but she figured the judge might understand. She finished scribbling the note, ripped the page from the binder loops and folded it. On the outside she wrote: *To the Judge,* before passing the note to Gus.

"After you leave me off at school, I want you to drive this up to that courthouse and hand it to the judge, okay?"

Gus sighed heavily and turned in his seat so he could look at her. "Millie, I can't. You know that. It would mean my job, and I've got…"

"How would Roger know? He's not even in town and…" She started crying.

Gus passed her his handkerchief. "I'll make you a bargain. I'll take this to Sheriff Wilson and ask him to give it to the judge, and in the meantime, you get to school and stay there until I come for you this afternoon."

"But…"

"Take it or leave it, Millie."

"Okay but promise me…."

"No promises. I'm sticking my neck way out here."

She knew he was right. "Thanks," she said. Gus nodded and drove the rest of the way to the school. He waited while she got out and watched until she was inside. The woman who worked in the office was waiting by the door.

"Welcome back, Millie," she said and when Millie started down the corridor to the single classroom for the upper grade students, the office lady walked right alongside her.

"I know the way," Millie said with a tight smile.

"Mr. Fitzgerald asked that we keep watch over you, Millie. You've had a lot to overcome since your mother died. He's quite worried."

I'll bet. She didn't say anything more, just kept walking, and once inside the classroom, she went to her desk and ignored the stares and whispers of the other students.

"Settle down, class," Miss Gibson said, clapping her hands together three times for emphasis.

Somehow Millie made it through the day. Thankfully, the couple of girls she considered friends were more interested in catching her up on school gossip—who liked who and who had thrown who over for someone new and whose birthday party had been a complete disaster— than they were in where she had been or what she had done. Apparently, most of the kids thought she had simply been at Roger's house trying to get over her mother's death.

When the final bell rang, she bolted from the building, her eyes scanning the street for Gus and the black monster car. He was standing by the driver's side, smoking. The minute he saw her, he dropped the cigarette, ground it in the dirty snow with his shoe and opened the rear door for her.

"Did you give the sheriff my note?" she asked even before the door closed.

"I did."

"Did you see Nate? Was he all right?"

"No, I didn't see him but I'm sure he's fine. And that is all we're going to say about that. How was school?"

Millie scowled at him—a look he caught as he glanced at her in the mirror. He put the car in gear and drove away.

On the way back to Roger's—she refused to call it "home"—they passed the railway station, and she thought about Ginny. *Did she know what had happened to Nate?*

Would she blame Millie for getting him in trouble? And if she did, would she want any part of Millie even if Momma's will said she had custody? Wouldn't she first think about Nate and her life—and their baby? Millie was trouble, and why would she want that?

She felt her chest tighten and her breath quicken, as if she'd run a race or something.

"You okay, Millie?"

She nodded, but the truth was she figured she might never be okay again.

Sheila Glover was the last person—other than Roger—she wanted to see, but there she was the minute Millie entered the house.

"I thought we might have a cup of tea and some of these delicious cookies Nan made for us," she said, as she watched Millie take off her coat and scarf and hang them on the hall tree in the foyer.

The last thing Millie was in the mood for was a tea party with this stranger. The second last thing she wanted was any of Nan's baking. Nan was pretty good at a lot of things, but cooking wasn't one of them. "I have homework," she muttered and made a beeline for the stairs.

"We'll talk over supper then," Sheila said brightly. "Your father won't be home until…"

Millie froze three steps up and turned slowly to face Mrs. Glover. "He is not my father, and this is not home," she said before adding, "and you are never going to be my mother." She ran the rest of the way up to Momma's room, slammed the door and threw herself on the bed.

She cried herself to sleep and was awakened by a light tapping at the door. Sitting up, she scrubbed away the remains of tears and sleep with the back of her hand. "Come in." She knew she sounded resigned, as if whoever might come through that door could not possibly surprise her.

She was so wrong.

Clara stuck her head around the half-open door and smiled. "Hello, Millie." She carried a tray and the smells of Millie's favorite dishes drifted across the room. Clara set the tray on the table closest to the door and held out her arms to Millie.

Millie ran to her and hugged her hard. "You're back?"

"At least for the time being." Clara wrapped her arms around Millie and patted her back. Millie realized she was a little taller than the housekeeper was when a tendril of Clara's gray hair that had escaped the neat bun at the base of her neck tickled Millie's cheek. Clara smelled of lavender.

"How?"

"Mrs. Glover apparently does not care for Nan's cooking. She persuaded Mr. Fitzgerald that if he was going to entertain business associates, he needed to provide them with a decent meal. It's a small town and there aren't a lot of choices, so here I am."

"What did Roger say to you?"

She smiled. "Oh, we have yet to come face to face. Today is my first day back, and he's still in Helena. But according to Mrs. Glover, his response to her insistence on bringing me back was something about 'better the devil you know.'" She stepped away, but still rested her hands on Millie's shoulders. "Now, getting down to business, how are you?"

Millie would have thought she was all cried out, but she realized tears were leaking down her cheeks. Clara wiped them away with her thumb before picking up the tray of food and carrying it to the chaise. "Have your supper, Millie, while you tell me everything that's happened. This may be our only chance to speak openly."

Millie glanced toward the door. "What about Mrs. Glover?"

"She is taking her supper in her room." Clara frowned. "I'm just a simple woman, Millie, but something tells me she wants to make things work with you."

"Why?"

"She's enamored of Mr. Fitzgerald and no doubt believes you are part of that deal. For that reason, she's going to do whatever she can to win your favor because she believes that's important to Mr. Fitzgerald."

"She's wrong. If it wasn't for Momma's money Roger would as soon leave me in the street as look at me."

Clara smiled as she set aside the covers on the food and handed Millie a napkin. "So, tell me about your grand adventure in Yellowstone."

Between bites Millie told her all about hiding out in the hotel, seeing Roger talking to Nate and the ranger, and being rescued by Nate. Then she told her all about how Ginny had been in Chicago because her sister's husband had killed himself and Nate took care of her while they waited for Ginny to come back. "He did nothing wrong at all," Millie insisted. "But now Ginny is pregnant, and Nate is in jail and they'll probably lose everything and it's all my fault."

"That's simply not true. Mr. and Mrs. Baker are adults and they made their own choices. Mr. Baker could have found you and immediately called the authorities, but he chose otherwise. And he knew the risk he was taking, especially as time went on."

"I guess maybe that's right." Millie broke off a piece of a biscuit and stuffed it in her mouth.

"Why did you go to Yellowstone, Millie? Why not take a train somewhere or…"?

Millie told her about overhearing Roger and the lawyer and remembering the Christmas card. "And when I tried to close the nightstand drawer, it stuck and look, Clara."

She pulled the drawer all the way out and dumped the contents on the bed, figuring this was her room now and she didn't have to worry about somebody saying she was snooping. "Look." She showed Clara the outline where the tape had been. "Momma must have hidden something here she didn't want Roger to find, but now it's gone."

It was a moment before Millie realized Clara had gotten really quiet. She was not looking at the bottom of the drawer. She was looking down at her folded hands and biting her lower lip. "What do you think, Clara?"

The housekeeper stood and smiled as she started gathering up the dishes. "I think you've got enough to sort through without looking for additional problems. Now it's time you got started on your homework. You slept the afternoon away." She headed for the door.

"Are you going to lock me in again?" Millie asked suddenly, wondering if Clara might be one more person she couldn't really trust.

"Lock you in? No. Of course not. I'll see you at breakfast, all right?"

Millie nodded but didn't look at her, and later, as she sat at Momma's dressing table doing her math homework, she heard the turn of a key. Just after that she heard Sheila talking to Roger as the two of them climbed the stairs. He was back, and as they passed Momma's room someone—and she didn't think it was Sheila--checked the door to be sure it was locked.

Ginny

-26-

Early the next morning, Ginny had just finished dressing when she heard a light knock on the cabin door.

She opened it to see James grinning at her. "Phone is working, Mrs. Baker," he said.

"Thank you." She followed the porter down the narrow hall to the lounge where he indicated a small table and the telephone.

When she was unable to reach Nate, she called Dan Atwood.

"He's been arrested, Ginny."

She stared out the train window at the passing scenery and saw nothing but her husband sitting in jail.

"How? Why?"

Dan gave her the short version of what had happened.

"You turned him in?" She felt like screaming the words but kept her voice down as another passenger walked by.

"Nate understood," Dan replied, his tone defensive.

"What about the cabin? Do we still live there?"

"Ginny, Nate hasn't been fired…yet. No one has touched your things."

Not that she cared. All she wanted was Nate—to see him and hold him and hear him assure her they would find their way through this mess. She tried to concentrate on what Dan was telling her—something about how Nate had been taken to Livingston for a court appearance and should be back in the afternoon.

"Back to the jail?"

Dan hesitated. "That depends on what the judge decides. Right now, he's only accused of going after Fitzgerald—things could be worse."

"How?"

"Fitzgerald also accused him of kidnapping Millie. The sheriff, though, just charged Nate with the assault."

Ginny studied her wristwatch, trying to calculate time. "The train will arrive later this morning. Can you get in touch with Benny and have him meet me at the station?"

"Sure. He's right here. It'll do you good to get home and rest a bit before--"

"I need him to drive me to wherever they've taken Nate."

"That's a really bad idea, Ginny."

"I'll decide what's a good or bad idea, Dan. Just have Benny meet the train." She hung up before he could say anything more. Her hands were shaking and the porter from the night before stopped on his way between cars.

"Are you all right, ma'am?"

Ginny nodded. She saw Helen headed her way, so she tried to stand, but a wave of dizziness and nausea overcame her and the next thing she knew she was back in the compartment lying on Gert's unmade berth. Her sister fanned her with a magazine while Helen was saying something to the porter about checking the passenger list to see if there might be a doctor on board.

"I'm fine." She tried to sit up, but Gert gently pressed her back onto the pillows.

"You're not fine, so just this once, humor me and stay put."

"Nate's been arrested," Ginny whispered, tears filling her eyes.

"For what?"

"He fought with Roger Fitzgerald and Roger brought charges."

"Nate? That man is the walking illustration for 'wouldn't harm a fly.' There has to be some reason."

Ginny was touched by Gert's outrage. "Roger struck Millie and Nate apparently thought that was out of line."

"Well, I should say so. He actually hit the child?"

Ginny nodded. This time when she pushed herself to a sitting position, Gert didn't try and stop her. Instead she poured a glass of water and handed it to her. "Thanks. How long was I out?"

"Couple of minutes was all. How are you now?"

"Better. Someone is meeting me at the station to drive me to Livingston."

"Because?" Gert drew out the word and Ginny knew her sister would agree with Dan that this was a bad idea.

"Because that's the county seat and, if Nate is not at the jail then, I expect that's where the sheriff took him to stand before a judge, and Nate doesn't have a lawyer to represent him, I'm sure of that, so I need to be there."

"You're not a lawyer."

Ginny decided to ignore that comment. "Perhaps you could go home with Helen and see if the house she's rented will work out."

"And if it doesn't?"

"Then there's a boarding house in town or you can come back to the cabin with me." Gert's expression of horror almost made Ginny laugh. "Relax. I'm sure Helen's rented house will be fine."

"Of course, it will," Helen said as she stood in the doorway to their compartment with a man Ginny recognized from the dining car the evening before. "Allow me to introduce Dr. Samuel Rockwell. He's on his way to set up his practice in Gardiner—how serendipitous is that?"

The doctor was probably somewhere in his mid- to late- forties-- old to be starting out. *Or maybe like everyone these days, he was starting over,* Ginny thought, and placed a protective hand on her tummy. "I'm fine," she assured him. "I had some upsetting news and got a little lightheaded. Thank you for stopping by."

The man glanced at Helen who shrugged. "You should see your doctor for regular check-ups, Mrs. Baker," he said.

"I'll do that," Ginny promised. "Now please, if everyone could just let me rest." She started to stand, but the compartment suddenly felt bereft of air.

"Uh-oh, here she goes again," she heard Gert say. And then she heard nothing.

This time when she came to, the doctor was perched on the seat opposite her, checking her pulse. "Have you eaten anything today?" he asked.

"I was on my way to breakfast when…"

"I'll get her something," Helen said and hurried off.

There was no use arguing, Ginny decided. Between Gert, Helen and the doctor, she was outnumbered. She picked at the toast and tea Helen brought her and listened to Gert question the good doctor about his credentials— schooling, past positions, and why he'd chosen Gardiner, of all places.

Dr. Rockwell answered every question—Harvard Medical School, Chicago's Rush Hospital, and, "I was ready for a change."

"What does your wife think of this move?" Gert had never been subtle when she wanted information.

"I'm not married," Dr. Rockwell replied. "Between school and my patients, I never found much time for socializing."

Gert could not hide her pleasure at this news. "Well, we'll just have to make sure you find time once we're all settled in Gardiner, won't we, Helen?"

Ginny drank the last of her tea and set the cup on the tray. "Thank you, doctor."

"You need to stay put for now—can't have you fainting again."

"I'll have James bring our breakfast here," Helen volunteered. "You'll join us, Dr. Rockwell?"

"My pleasure," he replied.

Ginny realized there was no point arguing, and by the time they had all been served and Gert had found out as much as she could about the doctor, Ginny was feeling quite a bit better. She glanced out the window.

"We're almost home," she said softly.

"We're here?" Gert bent to peer out the window. From her expression, Ginny realized her sister had been unprepared for just how great the change from Chicago would be.

The doctor leaned forward and took hold of Ginny's wrist. "Your pulse is still a little fast," he said.

"Oh, for heaven's sake. I'm pregnant and I just found out my husband has been arrested. In those circumstances I expect your heart might speed up a bit as well. Now, please let me stand and get my bearings. I have to see my husband." The doctor offered her his hand and she took it. "Thank you."

Outside the window she saw Benny hurrying down the platform. She stepped to the window, lowered it and called out to him. "Benny, over here. We're going to need some help with the luggage."

He nodded and a moment later he had joined the group crowded into their compartment. He took one look at Helen and blushed scarlet.

"Well, aren't you a good-looking cowboy," she teased, and his color deepened.

"Benny, we need to load everything on your truck and take most of it to…" She looked at Helen for the address.

"The Douglass house," she said. "I have the address here somewhere." She began rummaging through her purse.

"I know it," Benny muttered. "I'll get the stuff you checked, then take you there."

"First, I need you to take me to the jailhouse," Ginny said.

"Okay. I'll get the luggage and then meet you at the truck." He was gone as quickly as he'd come.

Ginny started gathering the items they'd brought on board with them, handing Gert her things. "Come on, Gert, help me."

Helen stepped forward and placed her hand on Ginny's arm. "Ginny, you go ahead. Gert and I can manage."

Ginny let out a breath of pure relief. "Thank you." Hastily she put on her coat and hat, picked up her purse and stepped into the corridor. "If Nate's at the jail, Benny can drop me off and come back for you. I'll come to the house as soon as I've made sure Nate is all right," she told Gert. "You go ahead and get settled in—at least for a few days. And remember, Gert, you have options now. If Montana isn't your cup of tea, you have your return ticket for Chicago."

"I'll make sure Gert is fine," Helen assured her. "We'll see you at the house."

The doctor was unintentionally blocking her way. They did a little dance of dodging from side to side and then he pressed himself to the corridor wall and allowed her to pass. "Make an appointment," he said.

"Yes sir," she replied, giving him a little salute. "Thanks," she added.

Once on the platform, she took a minute to gulp in fresh air and revel in the fact that she was nearly home. Gardiner was less than five hundred souls, and it looked like most of them were elsewhere. Benny's rusty truck was the only vehicle parked next to the station. He was putting the luggage in the back and hurried forward so he could help her climb up to the passenger seat. Cold air seeped up through the floor. Ginny shivered and pulled her coat tighter around her.

"Where to?" Benny asked as he pumped the clutch and turned the key.

"The jail."

Benny rested his hands on the steering wheel and stared at the nearly deserted street. "He's not there, Mrs. Baker. Him and the sheriff left early this morning. They've gone up to Livingston to see the judge."

"Then take me to Livingston."

Benny pursed his lips and blew out a stream of air that steamed the windshield.

"Well?" Ginny's patience was gone.

"I'll do what you want, Miz Baker, but they left here more than two hours ago. What if we go all the way up there and the mister is already on his way back here?"

He had a point. "All right. I'll wait at the jail. Just go, please."

Again, Benny hesitated. "None of my business, ma'am, but maybe you might wait at the diner? Warmer there and you could have a cup of coffee or something."

Everyone was trying to be nice—to take care of her, even this awkward teenager. She let out a breath and smiled at him. "That sounds like a good idea. Thank you, Benny."

He blushed and shifted the truck into gear. "If you like, I can wait with you."

"No. You'll need to go back for the others and get all that luggage over to the Douglass place. I'll be fine. Once you've done all that, I'd appreciate it if you could come back for Mr. Baker and me. I expect we'll need a ride home."

"Yes, ma'am." It was obvious he had his doubts Nate would be free to go home with her, but he was too polite to say so. He pulled to the curb in front of the *Cuppa Joe Diner*. "I won't be long," he promised, as Ginny opened the door and stepped out into slush that covered her shoe.

"See you soon," she said, and stepped gingerly onto the sidewalk.

The diner windows were all steamed over, and the minute Ginny opened the door, she felt a welcome wave of warm air surround her. She chose a booth near the window and settled in.

"Ginny Baker!"

She looked up as the diner's owner, Thelma Gauss, set a cup and saucer and a steaming pot of hot water on the table.

"How are you, Thelma?"

"Better than you and Nate, from the sound of things." She slid into the seat facing Ginny. "What was Nate thinking, getting mixed up with Roger Fitzgerald?"

Ginny opened the paper envelope that held the tea bag and set it in the cup, then poured hot water to cover it. "Long story," she admitted.

"I got time. Lunch rush won't start for another hour—not that there's much of a rush these days." She glanced around the nearly deserted diner. A man sat alone at the counter. "Paper keeps saying better days ahead. I just hope I can hold on that long."

"Nate's probably going to lose his job," Ginny blurted. "That is, if that man gets the contract to run things in the park...."

Thelma slid the sugar closer. "Hasn't happened yet," she offered.

Ginny poured sugar into her tea and stirred it slowly. "My sister might be moving here."

Thelma snorted. "Who in their right mind would make a move like that?"

Ginny smiled and sipped her tea. "Somebody with few other options?"

"Guess she may as well join the parade then. Town is full of people like that." She waited for Ginny to take another swallow of tea. "You want something with that? Made a lemon meringue pie this morning."

"My favorite—especially yours."

"Coming right up."

While Thelma was getting the pie and refilling coffee for the man at the counter, Ginny stared out the window, making out the shapes of passing cars and a few pedestrians through the film of steam. She would know when Benny returned. His truck had a distinctive rattle. She leaned back and closed her eyes, trying to imagine Nate in court.

He'd stand there, tall and strong, looking up at the judge. There was nothing subservient about Nate Baker. He would answer the judge's questions with as few words as possible, figuring that was the best course of action, even if it wasn't. According to Dan, Nate had struck Roger after Roger slapped Millie. Millie might have been a stranger to Nate, and he would not have stood for that.

So, what are we gonna do, Nate?

Thelma set the pie in front of her and Ginny opened her eyes. The man from the counter was standing next to Thelma. He wore a suit and tie. He looked prosperous in the same way Milt and his partners had. But Ginny knew better than most how deceiving looks could be.

"This is Alvin Stoner, Ginny. He's Roger Fitzgerald's lawyer." She frowned and stood her ground, clearly seeing the need to protect Ginny.

Ginny stared at the man. "My husband is a good man," she announced, as if he'd accused Nate of something.

"I agree. I've had the pleasure of meeting your husband—briefly." He nodded toward the seat opposite Ginny. "May I?"

Why she agreed to have him join her, Ginny would never know. Maybe it was something in his manner—courtly and a little shy.

"I also had the pleasure of serving Mrs. Fitzgerald," he said, as Thelma placed his coffee and a piece of pie in front of him. With a worried look at Ginny, she moved back to the counter to wait on a man just entering the diner.

Mr. Stoner picked up the fork and cut through the pie. *"Bon Appetit,"* he said before popping the bite into his mouth.

Ginny started with the meringue. She liked eating Thelma's pie in layers--savoring each flavor. "Best pie this side of the Mississippi," she said.

They ate in silence—Ginny trying to find shape and words for the questions that crowded her mind. "You knew Lavinia?"

Mr. Stoner's eyes softened. "It was my honor," he said softly. "She was quite an incredible woman." He took a swallow of his coffee. "She spoke highly of you."

"We had a falling out. If only I'd known she was here in Gardiner—practically in my backyard. We could have…" Ginny shook her head and pushed her pie away as she leaned closer. "Mr. Stoner, what exactly is your client's plan regarding my godchild?"

Stoner cleared his throat. "You are an educated woman, Mrs. Baker, and as such I am sure you understand I cannot discuss a client with you."

"Millie is not your client."

"However, Roger Fitzgerald is."

"He struck a child. There were witnesses. *You* were a witness. Tell me it's not true." She saw Thelma glance their way and realized she'd raised her voice.

"And your husband struck back. It might interest you to know that I was able to keep the charges to simple assault."

"Thank you," Ginny said, sarcasm dripping from each word. She reached for her pocketbook and took out her coin purse. "I have to go."

"Please allow me to pay your bill, Mrs. Baker."

She eyed him suspiciously. "What is it you want?"

"I have three daughters, Mrs. Baker. The youngest is only a little older than Millie is. I know Roger Fitzgerald—I know what he wants and what he doesn't. He doesn't want Millie."

Ginny felt poised on the edge of something she didn't yet understand. "Then why not leave her with us?"

"Come now, Mrs. Baker, surely I don't need to answer that question."

"It's the money—Lavinia's fortune." In her mind, lightbulbs came on like spotlights in a theater. "That's why you came over to speak to me? You want me to make some kind of a deal—Millie for the money that's rightfully hers—assuming there is any money?"

"Mrs. Baker, I assure you, I…"

This time she did not hesitate. She rummaged through her purse and slammed several coins down on the table before buttoning her coat and walking away. "Pie was delicious, Thelma," she called out as she reached the door. "Just lost my appetite is all."

The cold hit like a slap in the face. The wind had picked up and was blowing loose snow around, blinding her as she walked quickly up the street. She had no real destination in mind. All she knew was that she had to get out of that booth and away from that man. She saw it all clearly now. He thought he knew how to make this work for all concerned. She believed his concern for Millie was genuine, and so he had crafted this plan—Millie for the money. Everybody wins.

Not so bloody fast, she thought, as she stepped into the street and was nearly sideswiped by a car. She leapt back in the nick of time. The driver leaned on the car's horn and gestured angrily at her as he sped away. She held onto the pole of a streetlamp while she caught her breath and felt her stomach clench. She wondered if that was the first movement of her baby—a thought that brought her joy and renewed determination. They would work this all out— she and Nate together.

She heard rather than saw Benny's truck, flagged him down and got in. "Did you get my sister and her friend settled?"

"Yes, ma'am. Your sister seemed right pleased with how big the house was."

"She needs a lot of space," Ginny commented.

"I saw Sheriff Wilson's car on my way here—must mean him and Nate are back."

Of course. If the lawyer was back that meant Nate was as well.

"Let's go," Ginny said.

Nate—five minutes tops and they would finally be back together.

Nate

-27-

When Sheriff Wilson had driven up to the courthouse—a two-story red brick structure with arched windows outlined in granite, Nate's attention had been drawn to the steepled roof that featured an impressive clock tower. As they walked to the entrance, Nate had found himself thinking through what might be involved in getting snow off that nearly vertical clock tower roof.

"Through here," Wilson instructed as he'd held the outer door open and waited for Nate to enter.

Nate had scrubbed the soles of his boots on a brush intended for just such a purpose outside the door and then walked inside. He snatched off his cap and shoved it into the pocket of his jacket. The hall leading to various rooms and offices was busy—men in suits, women clutching files and papers to their chests, their high heels clicking on the marble floor, and everyone rushing. It reminded him of the first time he'd gone to Chicago with Ginny and how everybody seemed to be in such a hurry.

Wilson stopped at a desk, said something to the uniformed man seated there and then motioned for Nate to follow him down a side hall and up a flight of stairs. "Judge Krauss will see us in his chambers."

"I thought there was to be a hearing."

"In chambers. Don't buck the system, Baker."

They entered an office and Wilson handed the woman at the desk some paperwork. She disappeared into a connecting office while Wilson hung his wide-brimmed hat on a hall tree and waited for Nate to do the same with his jacket. Nate smoothed his shirt and ran his hands through his hair. He could use a shave. He must look like a bum.

"This way, gentlemen," the woman said as she stood aside and ushered them into a large, paneled office. A floor-to-ceiling bookcase lined one wall. The judge sat behind an impressive desk with carved decorations on the front panel. There were three chairs in front of the desk. The lawyer, Stoner, sat in one.

"Judge Krauss, this is Nate Baker."

Nate was unsure of what he should do—offer a handshake? Nod? Bow?

Without getting up, the judge indicated the two empty chairs, so Nate sat and waited while the judge reviewed a stack of papers. Then the man leaned back and closed his eyes a minute before looking directly at Nate.

"Well," he said finally, "it says here that you attacked one Roger Fitzgerald. What's your side of this, Mr. Baker? Did you strike Mr. Fitzgerald?"

"Yes, sir."

The judge arched his heavy gray eyebrows. "But?"

"He hit Millie. You don't hit a child—especially a female child and definitely not a child who isn't yours."

"So, you acted in defense of the child—Miss Mildred Chase?"

Nate had never thought of it that way. "I suppose that's one way to look at it," he replied. He kept expecting Stoner to say something. After all, wasn't he there to represent Roger?

Judge Krauss sorted through the papers. "I see that among the documents you brought with you, Sheriff Wilson, there is a note from Miss Chase. How did you come by this note?"

"Mr. Fitzgerald's driver brought it to me," Wilson replied.

The judge passed Millie's note to Stoner. "Have you seen this, Mr. Stoner?"

"No, your honor. Nor has my client."

"And where is your client, sir?"

"He had business in Helena."

The judge frowned. "I see. Business that he deemed more important than pressing charges against Mr. Baker?"

"He's a busy man, your honor."

"So am I," the judge thundered as he stood. "Mr. Baker, in light of the evidence before me—especially given the child's written testimony that you were only protecting her, I am going to fine you the sum of one dollar and admonish you to find other means in future for offering your protection to those in harm's way. Do we understand one another?"

Nate stood. "We do, your honor. Thank you, sir." His heart was beating so fast he thought for a minute he might pass out. Beside him, the sheriff and Stoner were shaking hands and Stoner didn't seem the least bit angry or upset with the judge's decision.

"Let's go, Baker," Wilson said. "If we make tracks now you just might get back in time to meet that train." He looked at the judge. "Mr. Baker's wife is returning home today after some time in Chicago to care for her sister."

Ginny.

Nate smiled. He suspected Wilson's wife had somehow gotten this news and passed it along to her husband. "Thank you again, sir," Nate said and this time he did offer the judge his hand. Krauss shook it and then stepped around his desk. "If we're all done here, gentlemen, I'm due in court. Mr. Stoner, walk with me. We can discuss that other matter on your way out."

Stoner nodded to Nate and followed the judge from his chambers. The secretary waited by the door. She was holding Nate's jacket and Wilson's hat.

On the drive back to Gardiner, Nate decided to see what he could find out about Fitzgerald's housekeeper. "When Mrs. Wilson brought my supper last night, she mentioned breakfast would be delivered by Clara Royce, but we left before that could happen."

"I thought it best to get on our way. Besides, my missus didn't know Clara's gone back to work."

"I'm glad for her. Millie mentioned her while she was staying with me—said Fitzgerald fired her."

"They must have worked out their differences, 'cuz she's back there doing the cooking and such." Wilson drove with one hand on the steering wheel and the other holding a cigarette between a thumb and forefinger. Clearly, he was in no hurry.

Nate thought through everything he'd seen and heard about Roger. The idea that he might forgive and forget did not fit the picture. "Really? I wouldn't have thought…"

"Sheila Glover is staying over there while work is being done on her house. She's divorced. My wife suspects she's got her eye on Fitzgerald as a candidate for husband number two." He took one last draw on the cigarette and flicked it out the window. "My wife says Sheila convinced Fitzgerald to bring Clara back once she realized the girl would be moving back in. Sheila is not exactly the motherly sort."

Nate wasn't used to gossip. At the same time, he was anxious to find out whatever he could about Millie's situation. "So, Millie's got somebody in the house she can trust," he offered. "That's good."

Wilson snorted. "Don't be so sure. Clara is a good woman, but she's a woman who's alone and getting up in years. She'll stand with whoever is most likely to keep a roof over her head and food in her belly. That ain't likely to be the kid."

Nate recalled Millie saying how she'd called out to Clara the night the housekeeper was fired. Clara had kept walking. Wilson had a point.

"You want me to drop you at the station, Baker?"

Nate reached for his pocket watch, thinking to check the time, but realized his personal effects were still locked up in the sheriff's office. "How about I get my stuff and then I can walk over?"

Wilson nodded. They rode for several miles in silence. A car passed them and tooted.

"That's Stoner," Wilson muttered. "Man drives like a kid. He's testing me, guessing I won't pull him over while I've got you in the car."

Nate watched the sedan disappear around a sharp curve.

"You got kids, Baker?"

"One on the way."

The sheriff glanced at him and it was clear he was measuring Nate's age. "Kinda long in the tooth for starting with a baby, aren't you?" He grinned.

Nate chuckled. "You might say that."

"Want some advice?"

"Have I got a choice?"

"Nope, but it's free so here it is: you've done a lot for that girl, but now you've got your own kid to consider. The one thing I know about Roger Fitzgerald is that if you cross him again, you won't get off so easy. It was Stoner who set things up for you with me and the judge this time. Fitzgerald won't let him get away with it again. Keep your distance. The kid's got Stoner and the driver and Clara Royce watching out for her. She'll be okay."

Nate thought about telling the sheriff about Lavinia's will and Ginny's part in all this, but they were approaching Gardiner and he decided there wasn't time to do the story justice. Besides, clearly Wilson was given to gossip, and Nate was a private man. He didn't like the idea of his business—and Ginny's—being discussed with strangers.

"I'll think about that," he said.

Wilson grunted and they said no more, even after Wilson turned the corner that led to the jail and his office.

Nate was barely out of the car when he heard the familiar rumble of Benny Helton's truck. He turned just as the truck pulled to the curb and Ginny leapt out. "Nate!"

He caught her and hugged her tight. "You okay?" he murmured as he smoothed back her hair and studied her face. It felt as if it had been forever, but here she was—his Ginny.

"I'll get your stuff, Baker," the sheriff said, as he tipped his hat to Ginny and stepped inside the office.

Benny cleared his throat. "If it's okay with you folks, I told the ladies I'd come back to make sure the furnace was working."

"Of course. Thanks, Benny," Ginny said.

Nate shook the younger man's hand and Benny loped back to his truck and drove away. Then he tightened his hold on Ginny. "Can't believe you're here," he said. "You're sure you're okay?"

"I'm fine. What happened in court?"

Nate frowned and shook his head. "Cost me a whole dollar and a promise to behave myself." Then he grinned and added, "It's all over, Ginny."

She slapped his chest with her gloved hand. "This is nothing to kid around about, Nate Baker. That man had you arrested and thrown in jail."

"It's all in the past. No harm done." He stepped away when he saw Sheriff Wilson approach. Wilson handed him the envelope that held his billfold, pocket watch and other things, then held out a clipboard and pointed to the paper on it. "Sign here," he said.

Nate scratched out his name, then accepted the handshake Wilson offered. "Remember what I said, Baker."

"Yes, sir. Thank you."

Wilson nodded. "Ma'am," he muttered, as he headed back to the office.

Nate wrapped his arm around Ginny. "How about some lunch? I'm famished."

As they walked together to the diner, Ginny told him all about Gert and Helen Matthews. "She's been a lifesaver, Nate."

"I look forward to meeting her." Nate could see that Ginny was taken with the stranger, but the last several days had taught him not to be quite so trusting. He couldn't help wondering what might be in this for the photographer.

They ordered grilled cheese sandwiches and tomato soup. "Welcome back, Nate," Thelma said as she delivered the food.

"Thanks." He waited for Thelma to return to the counter, where three other customers were nursing cups of coffee. "The housekeeper Fitzgerald fired is back working in the house."

"That's good, right?"

"Maybe. Sheriff Wilson told me she—and anybody else who works for Roger—are likely to stand with him in the face of trouble. They need those jobs."

"Nate, we have to get our hands on a copy of Lavinia's will. I went through everything Milt left behind and there was no trace of it. It's our only possibility for getting Millie away from that man."

Nate recalled the sheriff's advice. As much as he wanted to be sure Millie was safe—and more than safe, happy—he had a duty to his wife and child to consider. "Ginny, maybe we should leave things alone. I mean, we have a baby coming and we don't know how long I'll have a job and--"

"We are not abandoning that girl, Nate."

He should have known better than to think he might talk Ginny out of trying to help Millie. "Just so you know, you and the baby come first—no argument." He took a bite of his sandwich and the cheese oozed over his fingers. He licked them as Ginny shook her head.

"Can't take you anywhere," she teased, passing him extra napkins.

And he knew somehow the two of them would deal with whatever life threw in their path—a baby at their ages, Gert, Millie, even Roger Fitzgerald. "I love you, Ginny," he said softly, and smiled when she blushed exactly the way she had years earlier, when he'd said those words to her the first time.

Once they'd finished their lunch, they walked to the Douglass house. "It's only a block or so. Benny pointed it out when he drove me to the jail. I want you to meet Helen," Ginny said, "and of course you have to welcome Gert."

"Have to?"

"Come on, Nate. She's been through a lot."

"I know. Thing is you've been right there with her every step of the way. I'm sorry for her troubles, but I won't have her taking advantage, Ginny. Not in your condition."

"My so-called condition is as normal as breathing, Nate. I feel fine—better than fine." She stopped walking and faced him, cupping his face in her hands, her mittens soft on his skin. "Nate, we're going to have a baby," she whispered. "I know you have doubts and fears—so do I. But aren't you just a little bit pleased?"

He tucked a strand of her hair under the edge of her knit hat. "Pleased? I'm a little surprised at how much I want this. I just want to be sure…"

"I'm fine. We're fine. Now stop worrying and come meet Helen." She took hold of his hand and started down a side street leading to a rambling frame house that had seen better days. "This is it," she said, pointing to a mailbox where the 'o' and the 'a' in Douglass had worn away.

"Place could use some work," Nate muttered, testing a loose handrail as they mounted the steps to the front porch. "Don't see your sister taking to anything like this."

But Gert opened the door before Ginny could press the doorbell buzzer. "It's fabulous," she gushed.

Nate had never gotten used to the way his sister-in-law seemed to always begin conversations in the middle. He stiffened with surprise when Gert stood on tiptoe and hugged him. In all the years he and Ginny had been married, he could not recall a single time his sister-in-law had done that. Even at their wedding, the closest she'd come to contact was when she pressed his hand between both of hers and murmured, "Be good to my sister."

"Welcome to Montana, Gert," he said, awkwardly patting her shoulder. "Sorry to hear about Milt's passing," he added as he gently disengaged himself.

"And this is Helen," Ginny announced.

A tall woman with short-cropped white-blonde hair came rushing down the hall from what Nate assumed was the kitchen. She wiped her hands on a towel before offering Nate a firm handshake. "Really glad to see you," she said. "Ginny was worried."

"We're fine," Ginny assured her. She unbuttoned her coat. "Now what can Nate and I do to get the two of you settled before we head for home?"

"I just sent Benny off to the store with a list," Helen said. "That boy is a gem. He's already hauled my photography stuff up to the loft over the garage and taken Gert's trunks upstairs. Gert's been poking around, and she's found linens for the beds and bath." She ticked things off on her fingers. "Food, shelter, a bed and bath? What more could we want?"

Nate decided he liked her. "If you've found some tools, I could tighten that railing outside. Or we can wait 'til Benny gets back. He carries a toolbox in his truck."

Helen grinned at Ginny. "This one's a real find, Gin." Then she started back down the hall. "Follow me,

Nate. There's bound to be something you can work with out in the garage."

"But…I thought…" Gert stared at Ginny. "You're not staying?"

"Nate has to be at work tomorrow, Gert."

"But you don't," she whined.

"It's all right, Ginny," he said.

"No, it isn't. Gert, Nate and I will stay through supper and do what we can to get you and Helen settled in, but then we are going home—to the park."

Gert's lower lip quivered. "But…"

Helen stepped forward and wrapped her arm around Gert's shoulders. "Sounds like a plan to me," she said. "What do you say, Gertie?"

Nate turned away to hide a smile. In all the years he'd known her, no one had ever dared call his sister-in-law "Gertie."

Millie

-28-

Millie had been back in Roger's house a little over a week. Gus had told her all about Nate being let off with a small fine and a warning, and about Ginny coming back with her sister, who was living in town. While Millie had spent a lot of that week trying to figure out how to make contact with Nate or Ginny, Roger had made sure she was never alone, and neither Gus nor Clara—nor Sheila for that matter—would dare cross him.

Sounds from the party Roger and Sheila were hosting floated upstairs to her room. She tried to concentrate on her homework, but her mind kept drifting. In the time she'd been back, she'd already gone through everything in Momma's room. A lot of stuff had been packed up and moved to the attic —another place off limits to her, since a padlock blocked her way. Sheila was wearing Momma's fur coat these days—along with Momma's bracelet. Millie still hadn't found the ring.

Clara had talked Sheila into convincing Roger there was no need to lock Millie in her room with so many people around to watch over her. Millie had heard Nan and Clara whispering about how probably summer wouldn't be far along before Roger and Sheila married. Clara bit her lip and shook her head, grumbling about Millie's mother not yet cold in her grave.

Downstairs at the party somebody was playing Momma's piano and Sheila was singing—sort of. Truth was, it sounded more like chickens squawking. Millie slipped out into the hall and sat on the stairs leading to the third floor. Through the railing that ran along the second-floor hall, she could see people starting to leave, the men shaking Roger's hand while Clara and Nan held coats for the women. Most of the guests were from out of town—

businessmen and their wives from Helena. Clara had told Millie some of the men worked for the government and Roger wanted to impress them because they could help him be approved for the government contract. Millie didn't see anybody she recognized.

What she did see was guests hurrying from the parlor, bidding a hasty farewell to Roger and going. It was like when a thaw comes and there's a crack in the ice on the creek and then suddenly the water breaks through and gushes forward. The flow of guests leaving reminded her of that. The piano went quiet and Sheila rushed into the hall.

"But it's so early," she protested.

The guests all smiled and made comments about the long drive or a busy day to come. It seemed to Millie as if they couldn't wait to get out of there, and when Roger closed the door after seeing the last guest out, he stood there for a long moment. And then, in that voice she knew too well, he said, "Well, my dear, you put on quite a show tonight."

Sheila giggled even as Millie braced herself. And when the slap came, it cut Sheila's laughter to a choked cry of pain.

"Roger!"

He hit her again. The second blow sent her to her knees, cowering as she tried to protect her face with her arms.

Roger stepped around her, went into his study and closed the door.

Millie made her way down the stairs. "Come on," she whispered, offering Sheila her hand. She looked up at Millie, her cheek and eye already showing the effects of Roger's blows. "Millie?"

"Come on," Millie said, "before he comes back."

She guided Sheila up the stairs and down the hall. She smelled of too much perfume and the way she leaned on Millie, she expected Sheila was more than a little drunk, so Millie helped the older woman to sit on the stool in front of the dressing table covered with bottles and jars of make-up, perfume and face creams and then knelt to unfasten the straps of her shoes.

"He hit me," Sheila murmured, as if she couldn't quite believe it.

Millie set her shoes aside and stood. "I'll ask Nan to come up," she said, and slipped out of the room. The door to Roger's study was still closed, so she hurried down the back stairs to the kitchen.

"Mrs. Glover needs you," she announced, when Nan and Clara glanced up from washing the dishes.

Not waiting to see what they would do, she hurried back up the stairs and into her room. This time she was the one to lock the door.

The next morning, Millie grabbed her book bag and again used the back stairs to the kitchen. Nan was preparing a tray. Sheila always took breakfast in her room, declaring she simply was not presentable until after ten. Once or twice, Millie had heard the deep rumble of Roger's laughter coming from Sheila's room while her breakfast tray sat outside the door. But on this morning, she heard Roger clear his throat and rattle his newspaper as she passed by the swinging door that led from the kitchen into the dining room.

She waited for Nan to take the tray upstairs, then grabbed a biscuit from the pan on top of the stove. She slathered it with butter—remembering how when she was at Nate's, real butter was not something they had. As she poured a glass of milk—not the powdered stuff she'd had at Nate's—she wondered how it was with these hard times affecting most everybody, that Roger seemed to have whatever he wanted. It just didn't seem fair.

Clara arrived, bringing a blast of cold air with her. After removing her outer garments and leaving them on a hook in the back hall, she entered the kitchen, tying on her apron as she walked. She seemed surprised to see Millie still there. "Gus is waiting," she said. "You'll be late."

Millie shrugged, stuffed the last bite of the biscuit into her mouth, licked the butter off her fingers and then drank the rest of the milk. All the while, she kept her eyes on Clara, waiting for her to say something about Sheila and what had happened.

"Scoot," Clara said, taking the glass from Millie and handing her the book bag.

Millie already had her coat on, so she buttoned it and walked to the door. "Do you think she'll stay?" she asked with a nod toward upstairs.

"Not our business," Clara said, pulling Millie's stocking cap down over her ears. "Now go."

Gus had the car all warmed up. Most days Roger was already in the car. Gus would take Roger to his office and then drop Millie at school. Maybe because it was just the two of them for once, Gus seemed to be in an especially good mood. "My lady," he said, opening the door and bowing to her as she climbed in.

"Where's Mr. Fitzgerald?" she asked, even though she knew he was sitting in the dining room.

"He said he had some business at home to attend, so it's just you and me, kiddo." Gus was whistling as he put the car in gear and started down the drive.

"You're awfully happy," Millie said.

He winked at her in the rearview mirror. "Met a special lady last night."

Gus would have had the night off because of the party. "Where?" Millie put last night's ruckus out of her mind. She'd never really thought about Gus being with somebody—he was just Gus, the driver, who lived over the garage.

"I stopped by Ma's for supper and she just came walking up onto the porch and knocked on the door. She's a photographer from Helena and she's rented the old

Douglass place across the street. Seems the hot water wasn't working, and she wanted to use Ma's phone, since hers wasn't hooked up yet. I told her I could take a look."

This was more than Gus had ever said at one time in all the time Millie had known him. "And you fixed it?"

"Nope. But the good news is that means after I pick up a couple of parts at the hardware, I'll be going back once I finish work today."

Millie pictured the Douglass place—a house that looked like it might be about to fall in on itself, the windows shuttered and the paint peeling. Right after she and Momma came to live in Gardiner, Momma had taken her and a couple of girls she'd met at school trick or treating.

"That house is haunted," one of the girls had whispered. "We don't go there—ever." Momma hadn't laughed or anything, just nodded and crossed the street.

Gus was pulling up to the school. "She lives in that big ol' house by herself?"

"No. There's another lady." He frowned. "I got the impression that one wasn't all that happy to be there—especially with no hot water."

"Or maybe it's because the place is haunted," Millie said with authority as she climbed out of the car. "See you this afternoon," she called, hurrying up the walk, trying to beat the final bell.

Sheila didn't stay. When Millie got home that afternoon, she passed Sheila's room on her way to her own. The door was open, and everything was in place the way it had been before Sheila came there to stay. "She left?" Millie asked, after dropping her book bag and coat in her room and heading back down to the kitchen. Clara and Nan exchanged a glance.

"Her house was ready for her to move back," Nan said, a nervous catch in her voice.

Sheila's house had been ready for a couple of weeks from what Millie had overheard, so this wasn't about the house. "What did Roger say?"

"Mr. Fitzgerald has been at his office all day," Clara said.

"So, he doesn't know." Millie sighed. Whatever she might have thought about Sheila, she had come to count on her to keep Roger entertained at dinner. Tonight, for the first time since Millie had come back to the house, she and Roger would dine alone. She shuddered. "I think I might be getting sick," she said.

Clara laid the back of her hand on Millie's forehead and cheeks. "Might as well face the music, Millie. Get it over with. Just eat your supper, mind your manners and speak only when asked a direct question."

Millie thought about the suppers she and Nate had shared—how they'd be talking about something and he'd suddenly go to the bookcase and bring back some book with a picture to show her what he meant. She recalled one time they had talked seriously about Momma and dying and stuff like that. She couldn't imagine ever having talks like that with Roger.

Clara patted her cheek. "Now go wash your face and hands, change your clothes and get started on your homework until it's time."

Millie trudged up the stairs, shut the door to her room and lay down on the bed. She felt the cool, silky satin of the bedspread on her face and wondered how many times Momma had felt the way she was feeling—like a prisoner in the world's most luxurious jail.

Jail.

They'd taken Nate to jail and all she'd been able to learn was that they'd let him off. So, was he back home in the park with Ginny? And what about the baby? If Nate lost his job, how would they all survive?

Her mind raced with questions that had no answers and no way of gathering the information she wanted. She washed up and changed and then sat at the dressing table making a list. Gus would be able to find out what she wanted to know, but how to get him the list? Roger would never stand for her going out to Gus's quarters above the garage. Clara was off for the night and she didn't really trust Nan to get him the message.

She glanced around the room, wondering what Nancy Drew would do. Of course, she lived in books so she could do about anything she wanted. This was real life and Millie needed to come up with something that would work without raising Roger's suspicions. She'd kicked off the Oxford shoes she wore to school. She hated those shoes. She picked one up. The tip of the sole was just beginning to come loose so she helped it along. Then she pulled out the inner lining and stuffed her list inside before replacing the liner. It was a gamble as to whether or not Gus would find the paper, much less read it, but this was the best she could come up with for now.

She heard the clock at the foot of the stairs strike quarter to six, checked her hair in the mirror, grabbed the shoe and hurried downstairs.

"Stop running," Roger ordered as he led the way to the dining room.

"Uh, Roger, could I ask you something?"

He paused and slowly turned, focusing on the shoe in her hand. "What?"

"My shoe is coming apart and I thought maybe Gus might be able to glue it back together tonight so I could wear it tomorrow. Of course, I could always wear my good Sunday shoes, but they say it's gonna rain…"

"Stop babbling. You're worse than she was," Roger muttered as he grabbed the shoe from her. "Nan!"

Nan hurried out from the kitchen. "Yes, sir?"

He handed her the shoe, holding it with two fingers as if it were a dead mouse or something. "Take this to Gus and have him repair it."

"Yes, sir."

Millie breathed a sigh of relief. Step one accomplished. She was close to smiling when Roger turned on her. "Well, go wash up," he ordered as he removed a handkerchief from his pocket and wiped his own hands. "This could have been handled earlier," he said as Millie hurried into the small guest powder room near the front door.

He was already seated at the large dining room table when she slid into the chair next to him.

Nan delivered their plates, already filled with chicken, mashed potatoes and slimy canned peas. Roger focused on cutting up his meat. When Millie reached for the salt and pepper, Roger's hand shot out and stopped her.

"How do you know you need seasoning when you haven't even tasted the food?"

She could have said that because Nan had made the dinner instead of Clara, she was pretty sure a little seasoning would be a big help. Instead she withdrew her hand and took a small taste of the potatoes.

"Well?" he asked.

She took a larger bite and Roger's eyebrows shot up in triumph as he returned to his own meal.

The one thing Millie had learned over the years she'd known Roger was that he liked to win—he liked to be right—whether he was or not. She swallowed the lumpy tasteless mass and tried not to make a face.

For once Roger was eating slowly, chewing each bite, putting down his fork in between and sipping his wine. Millie tried to pace herself, but without the aid of conversation she was in danger of finishing well before he did. So, she forgot all about Clara's advice and said, "I see Mrs. Glover has moved out."

Roger set down his fork and picked up his wine glass by the stem. He twirled it slowly. "Mrs. Glover was here as my guest," he said, and then he looked directly at her. "As are you."

Millie shrank back in her chair, waiting for the blow.

He raised his hand and then dropped it. "Never forget that."

Ginny

-29-

"Let's walk over to the cemetery," Ginny said as she and Nate left the Douglass house. "I want to pay my respects to Lavinia."

Nate nodded. "I'll ask Benny to wait." He shoved his hands into his jacket pockets and walked quickly across the street, where Benny waited in his truck. Ginny watched him go, saw him speak briefly with Benny and then come trotting back, dodging traffic along the way.

What would she ever do if something were to happen to Nate? She couldn't imagine life without him. During the days following Milt's suicide, as she tried to comfort her sister, she had found herself thinking more and more about the impact of unexpected—even expected—tragedy on those left behind. For nearly twenty years she and Nate had formed one complete person. What if half of that person were no longer there? She thought of Millie, who had had only Lavinia—Millie, who was far too young and inexperienced in life to know how to find her way alone.

As she walked beside Nate along the narrow paths of packed snow that divided the rows of graves—some bordered by rocks and stones, others ringed by a low wrought-iron fence--she continued to think about Millie. From what Ginny had been able to gather, Lavinia had been ill for some time—weeks, if not months. Had the doctor assured her during that time that she would recover? Had he reassured Millie that the illness would pass?

"Here it is," Nate said, stopping before a small, gray stone marker that listed Lavinia's name, date of birth and date of death. The remains of wreaths obviously sent at the time of the funeral lay forlornly on the sinking mound of earth. It seemed evident no one had visited the grave recently—perhaps not even since the funeral. Ginny's anger at Roger Fitzgerald quadrupled. Then, beneath a wreath of dead roses leaning against the marker, she found a small bouquet of snowbells, tied with a piece of twine and fresh as the blades of grass that had forced their way through the melting snow.

"Let's clear these away," she said, and set to work discarding those arrangements that were long past their prime. Nate carried everything she handed him to a pile of similar compost behind a small shed while Ginny knelt and brushed away dirt and slush from the marker. She ran her fingers over the letters of Lavinia's name, tears filling her eyes.

"Don't worry, my dear friend. Nate and I will see that Millie is all right—more than all right," she whispered.

"Ginny, we need to get going," Nate said. He was standing next to her, offering her a hand up. She took the bouquet of snowbells and placed it so that it covered the word "Fitzgerald" and then stood. "There," she said with a satisfied huff. She hooked her hand through the crook of Nate's elbow as they trudged over the uneven terrain of the cemetery, back to the road, where Benny waited.

Spotlighted by the dim headlights of Benny's truck, the cabin looked at first glimpse as forlorn as Lavinia's grave had—as if no one had been there for weeks instead of just a couple of days. Once inside, Ginny set to work. While Nate built a fire in the stove, she turned on every lamp, and prepared supper for the two of them. Outside, Nate shoveled the spring snow that had fallen during their absence, leaning on his shovel now and then and staring off toward the horizon, where the sun had set, leaving behind streaks of orange and purple fading to black across the sky.

She wondered if he was thinking of Millie, remembering the time they had shared. Or perhaps he was recalling the night he'd spent in jail. Nate was not used to being confined. That night had to have been torture for him, the closed-in walls, the uncertainty of when or if he would be released. She carried dishes and flatware to the greenhouse and set them on her worktable.

"What's all this?" She hadn't heard Nate come in, but he stood at the door to the greenhouse, grinning at her.

"A picnic," she announced. "All things considered, spring is finally on the way and we have a lot to celebrate." She pulled a low bench out and swept it free of dirt, then began setting places for the two of them on her work table.

Nate went back inside the cabin and returned with two folding chairs they kept for the rare occasions when they had company.

Ginny brought out cheese and salami. She pulled a small ripe carrot from the deep planter behind them and handed it to Nate to wash off and slice, then filled their glasses with water. "I'll make bread tomorrow," she said. "And a pie."

"Millie really liked your pecan pie," Nate told her as he pulled his chair closer to the bench and sat down. "So do I," he added with a smile.

"So that's a hint?"

He leaned back and looked at her. "It's so good to have you home, Ginny."

She reached over to take his hand. "Nate, what are we going to do?"

She had meant to hold off talking about the multiple complications of their life until they'd had a chance to enjoy their supper, but the Mulligan stew that was made up of the baby, Gert, Millie, and Nate's job had roiled to a boil and spilled over. It was time.

He sighed and stacked salami and cheese on his fork. "Where do you want to start? Seems to me we're doing all right—for the moment. And from what I could tell, Gert has found the support she might need in Helen, but Millie…"

"That child really got to you, didn't she?"

"She's smart and resourceful and impulsive—and there's the danger. She's so desperate to get shed of Fitzgerald, I'm afraid she might try something rash."

"Don't you think we need to first be sure your job is secure—that we have a roof over our heads and some way to provide for Millie, even assuming we can get custody?"

"Fitzgerald doesn't own the concessions yet," Nate mumbled around a mouth filled with food. "My guess is he needs Lavinia's money to finalize the deal, and until then there's no reason to waste time worrying about my job."

"Still…"

The phone rang. Nate wiped his mouth with his napkin and got up to answer, closing the door that separated the greenhouse from the living room. "Probably Dan," he said.

Ginny nibbled at her supper while she waited for Nate to return. She could hear only his side of the conversation and because Nate was a man of few words, that wasn't much help. Right away she figured out he wasn't speaking to Dan.

"I see," he said.

Then a long pause.

"No sir, I understand. I appreciate the call. Goodnight."

Through the glass panels of the door, Ginny saw Nate place the receiver back in its cradle, then stand there staring at it for a long moment. She went to him, stepping around him so that they were facing each other. "Nate?"

The sound that came from him was half choked cry and half laughter. "Seems I misjudged Roger Fitzgerald," he said. "That was my supervisor. He got a call from the company with orders to fire me."

"On what grounds?"

"Apparently Roger offered to increase the purchase price by several thousand dollars on the condition I be fired immediately—something about the current owners showing 'good faith' that things in the business were as they should be, with no loose ends."

"That's barbaric," Ginny fumed. "You mean immediately, as in right away."

Nate nodded.

"Where are we supposed to go?"

"The boss said he'd gotten me two weeks' severance pay." He wrapped his arms around her and pulled her close. "That and our savings should see us through for a while. I can look for work in town and…"

"But the park is your life, Nate. It isn't fair. You've done nothing wrong."

"We knew I'd have to look for something by the fall anyway, Ginny. Even I have to admit I'm getting too old to keep on as winterkeeper. Schedule just got moved up some."

"Yes, but…"

"Shh." Nate tightened his hold on her.

Ginny relaxed against him, but inside, the hatred she felt toward Roger Fitzgerald for what he'd done to Lavinia and Millie and now her beloved Nate hardened to a knot—a resolve that he would not defeat them.

The following morning, while Nate went off determined to complete the work he'd begun in Mammoth, making sure everything was ready for opening the park, Ginny began organizing and packing their belongings. Helen and Gert did not yet have a telephone, so Nate was going to ask Benny to stop by the Douglass house while in town picking up the mail and ask Gert to call Ginny from the neighbor's house.

Throughout a sleepless night, they had made their plans. If Helen agreed, they would move into the larger house with Gert for the time being. When not out looking for work, Nate could make the repairs he'd noticed, Ginny would prepare meals and they would offer to pay rent but hoped maybe the repairs and cooking might be enough. Nate had run through a list of things he'd noticed— patch-ups to the house that would hopefully help him adjust to life outside the park.

As she worked, Ginny felt a flutter some would say was simple stress, but she knew it was the baby. Every reminder of her pregnancy gave her pause. What would they be able to offer this child?

Love, she decided, which was a lot more than Millie Chase had at the moment. She'd made a promise to Lavinia as she knelt by her friend's grave, but was it a promise she could keep?

She was in the loft, collecting the linens stored there when the phone rang. She hurried to get it, nearly losing her balance on the second step so that when she grabbed the receiver, she was breathless. "Hello?"

"My stars, Ginny, you sound like you just ran a mile," Gert said. "What on earth is going on?"

"Where are you calling from?"

"I'm at a neighbor's house. Talk to me."

"Is Helen there?"

"Yes, we're both here," Gert replied. "Now, talk to me. Is it the baby? Shall we send help?" Her voice rose with panic.

"I'm fine—the baby's fine," Ginny assured her. In as few words as possible she told her sister what had happened. "Can you put Helen on?"

"I'm right here," Helen said. "I heard everything. Now you listen to me. You and Nate are welcome, and I won't have you paying rent. That's just ridiculous. We have the room, don't we, Gert?"

"Just come," Gert added.

"Thank you," Ginny whispered, feeling the lightness of relief flowing out through that breath.

"And don't you and Nate try moving furniture. Benny can help with that and there's plenty of stuff here to make do," Helen instructed. "Our neighbor's son has the day off tomorrow. Just have the things you prize packed up and ready and we'll be there."

"Helen, we are so very grateful and…"

"Shush," Helen interrupted. "We'll have the two—three—of you settled in no time."

"Ginny?" Gert apparently had taken the phone from Helen. "There's a crib in the attic—and a high chair. And there's plenty of room in the yard for a garden. Oh, this is going to be such fun."

Ginny couldn't help smiling. When Gert's world was falling apart, she was always certain there could not possibly be a silver lining. For every positive presented, she could name three negatives. Odd that when it was Ginny's world turned upside down, Gert was the one finding reasons to look on the bright side.

"It'll be good to be together," Ginny agreed. "I'd best go. There's a lot to do."

"We'll see you tomorrow then," Gert said, and in the background, Ginny heard Helen add, "Bright and early."

She hung up and stood at the window for a long moment, watching a magpie flit from tree to tree, realizing that Nate was not the only one who was going to miss life in the park.

The next day Ginny and Nate had barely finished their breakfast when they heard Benny's truck stop outside the cabin. Another vehicle—an old model car—pulled in behind him. Gert and Helen climbed out of the car—Gert almost taking a tumble in the melting snow that had formed a crust of ice overnight.

Nate and Benny hurried to her aid, each taking one of her arms and guiding her down the path. The driver of the car got out and walked with Helen. He was dark and good-looking, and Ginny smiled as she stood at the sink watching them come. Maybe Helen would find romance and stay on in Gardiner.

She wiped her hands on a towel and opened the front door. "Welcome," she said as the five of them crowded inside.

"You steady?" Nate asked Gert, refusing to let her go until she reassured him.

"I need proper shoes," she replied, then looked at Ginny. "We'll go shopping as soon as we get the two of you settled."

"Nate…Ginny," Helen said as she stepped forward, "this is Gus Olinger—our neighbor's son."

Ginny was just reaching out to shake the man's hand when she noticed Nate. Her husband stood as still as a statue, staring at the stranger.

Gus snatched his hat off his head and faced Nate. "Hello, Mr. Baker," he said as he nervously turned the hat with both hands.

"Gus," Nate said, his voice barely audible.

"You two know each other?" Helen glanced from one to the other, clearly aware something was not quite right here.

"We've met," Nate said before turning to a stack of boxes by the stairs to the loft. "Come on, Benny. Let's get these loaded. Then you can help me take the bed apart."

"We have beds, Nate," Helen protested.

Nate smiled at her. "Call me sentimental," he said, as he hefted the first of the boxes and headed for the door.

"How about I put those boxes in the trunk of my car while you guys take the bed apart?" Gus suggested. He held out his arms for the box Nate carried.

"Sure."

"Nate, could I see you a moment in the bedroom?" Ginny turned to the others. "Just want to show him a couple of things. Benny, why don't you help Mr. Olinger with those boxes?"

"It's just Gus, ma'am."

Nate had already headed for their bedroom, so Ginny just nodded. "Helen, maybe you and Gert could finish washing up our breakfast things?"

"Okay." Helen frowned as she watched Nate and Gus head in opposite directions. Gert, on the other hand, was oblivious to the tension filling the room.

"There are just two plates and glasses, Ginny. Surely that can wait."

"We'll just get them washed and put away—for the next occupant," Helen said, handing Gert a towel.

Nate was sitting on the bed when Ginny entered the room and closed the door. "What on earth, Nate? You look like you've seen a ghost, or maybe the devil or both."

"Gus Olinger is Roger's driver," he said.

"Oh." Ginny sat next to him and heard the familiar squeak of the bed springs—the only sound in the room aside from Nate's steady breathing. "Well, we can hardly blame him for that. A job's a job—especially in these times. He seems like a decent sort. Helen likes him and I see her as a good judge of character. Perhaps…"

"He may be a decent sort, but he works for Roger and that means Roger will now know our business—where we are, what we do."

"But then so will Millie, and maybe he can help us get a message to her or her get a message to us. He could be the link we need, Nate."

"Or not," Nate said and pushed himself to his feet. "He's here and if he wants to help, I don't see a choice. Just watch what you say around him, Ginny."

He pulled pliers from his back pocket and began dismantling the bed. Ginny folded the bedspread and other linens. They worked in silence for a couple of minutes and then she said, "Nate, we have to trust somebody."

"Yeah, we do. But just be careful who you choose, okay?"

Someone knocked on the door. "Ginny?"

"Come in, Helen."

Helen opened the door. "Benny and Gus have finished loading the boxes. Want to come show them what other furniture goes?"

"Be right there." She picked up the pile of bedding and as she passed Nate, stood on tiptoe to kiss his weathered cheek. "I'll send Benny to help you with this, okay?"

Nate stopped what he was doing and stroked her cheek with the back of his fingers. "Send Gus. Let Benny load the chairs and the radio."

Nate

-30-

Gus stepped into the room and hesitated. "You need a hand?"

Nate continued loosening the clamp holding the headboard to the bed frame. "How's Millie holding up?"

"Okay, I guess."

Nate's fingers tightened on the pliers. "You guess? I thought you cared about her."

"I do. I try."

Nate set the screw on the window ledge while Gus reached over and steadied the headboard as it started to tilt. "You take her to and from school every day. She must talk to you."

"Sometimes."

Nate shot him a look as the headboard came free. "Is she planning to run again?"

"Not so I can tell," Gus replied. He lifted the headboard and set it against the wall.

"Has Fitzgerald hit her again?"

"I don't think so." Gus hesitated, his eyes on Nate, as if trying to decide whether to say more.

"What?" Nate demanded.

"Millie got a note to me." He smiled and shook his head. "Hid it in a shoe I'm pretty sure she deliberately ripped and then talked Fitzgerald into letting me repair for her."

"What did the note say?"

"She was worried about you and your wife."

"She's a good kid."

"I followed her lead and sent a note back, letting her know your wife was back and you were out of jail with both of you back home here. Do you want her to know you're going to be living right down the road from her?"

Nate thought about that. "Not yet. How come you two sent notes back and forth? Isn't she in the car with you twice a day?"

"This was a Friday and we wouldn't see each other without Roger being around until Monday so…"

Nate nodded. "Just keep a close eye, okay?"

"Don't worry."

They finished dismantling the bed. Nate knew Gus was waiting for him to keep talking. "Your mother lives across from where my sister-in-law is staying?"

"That's right. Helen—Miss Matthews—came by to use the phone and we got to talking…"

The man was blushing. "So, you coming here today is because you wanted to impress Miss Matthews?"

Gus chuckled and looked at his hands. "You know how it is—you meet a woman…"

"Yeah, I remember."

Gus glanced at him and his eyebrows shot up in surprise. "You didn't think I came here because…I mean, you don't think I'm trying to spy on you or get you and Mrs. Baker in any trouble?" He shifted from one foot to the other. "Because I would never—you probably saved Millie's life …"

"All right. Just needed to understand where things stood here. You've got to admit it was pretty strange seeing you come walking up to the cabin when your boss had just made sure Ginny and me had to leave." He handed Gus a pile of bed slats. "Could you get these loaded on Benny's truck?" he asked. "Benny can help you load the head and foot boards and mattress."

Once Gus left, Nate stood with his back to the window and looked around the room—a room that suddenly looked smaller when it probably should have seemed much larger. He and Ginny had spent their whole married life in this cabin—this room. He was too old to start over. More to the point, he didn't want to start over. The park wasn't just where he worked. It was his home.

"Nate?"

Ginny knocked lightly on the door and opened it. "You okay?"

Nate shrugged. "Big part of our life, Ginny," he muttered.

She crossed the scarred, uneven wooden floor and wrapped her arm around his waist as she stood next to him, taking in the empty space. "Lot of memories," she agreed. Then she took his hand and placed it on the slight bump of her tummy. "More to come," she said softly.

He smiled. "Yeah." He pulled her close and kissed her. "You're going to be a terrific mom, Ginny."

"Hey, we're in this together, buster. Don't try to sweet-talk me." She tweaked his nose and pushed herself away from the window. "Come on. Let's get this party started."

"Some party," Nate muttered, but he followed her from the room.

Benny's truck was loaded, and Gus was just shutting the trunk of his car. "I'll ride with Benny," Nate said. "You go ahead with Gert and the others."

He saw Ginny hesitate, but then she slid into the back seat with Gert. He waved to her as Gus drove away, then climbed into the cab of Benny's truck. "Everything tied down?" he asked, with a jerk of his head toward the load in the back.

"Yes, sir. I checked it twice."

"Good man."

As Benny drove, Nate gazed out the window, taking in the passing scenery. Wildlife was awakening even as the land itself came out from hibernation. Creeks tumbled over rocks into rivers, where the flow of water was visible beneath the coat of thin ice, and snow melt trickled down the face of cliffs. Shoots of greenery poked through the snow that still covered much of the land.

An eagle soared high overhead, headed for the landmark rock formation named in its honor. Nate wondered if this particular bird was returning to its home on Eagle Nest Rock. He rolled down the window so he could stick his head out and follow the massive bird's journey. He'd always felt a connection to these majestic creatures. Like him, eagles were loners who kept their distance from people. Like him, they mated for life. It remained to be seen if he—like an eagle—would be a good parent.

Next to him, Benny blew on his bare hands to warm them, so in spite of enjoying the cold, fresh air on his face, Nate rolled the window up and sat back against the cracked leather of the seat. "Hard to leave home, Benny," he said.

"I reckon so for you and Miz Baker," Benny replied. "For somebody like me or that runaway girl you found…" He let his words trail off as he concentrated on driving.

Nate decided talking about his own unhappy childhood would do nothing to ease Benny's misery, so he turned the conversation to Millie. "That girl needs to find her way," he said.

"Hard to do when, from what I've heard, she's pretty much a prisoner in that rich man's house."

Benny was someone who knew a lot of people. He busied himself in the area, doing odd jobs, and he was privy to a lot of information people tended to either share with him or simply divulge in conversation without realizing Benny was within earshot. "You heard something?"

Benny shrugged. "Overheard is more like it."

"Okay, what have you overheard?"

"Gus Olinger takes her to school every day and picks her up again. Other than that, nobody's seen her. She used to show up with Clara Royce in the grocery store or drugstore before her mother died, but nobody's seen her." He chewed on his lower lip. "Some say he's got her locked up her room. He had me come over a couple of weeks ago and nail windows shut in a second story room—Clara said it was the room where Millie's mom died, so I figured maybe in his grief…"

Nate snorted a derisive laugh. "Not sure that man knows the meaning of the word."

"Heard Millie is in that room since she came back." Benny chewed his lower lip, then said, "Gonna be hard to keep her from finding out you and Mrs. Baker are living in town. Small town like this? Nan or even Clara is bound to let something slip, or she might see one of you on her way to or from school. Gus drives right past the Douglass house going to and from."

"Not to mention his mother lives across the street," Nate added. Knowing Millie, once somebody let her know he and Ginny were back in town, she would not be content to just wait for something to happen. More and more, he was coming to understand that it was up to him to make sure Millie found a way out from under Roger's control.

They were passing through the village of Mammoth. Automatically, he surveyed the buildings to be sure he hadn't missed anything. The roof of the hotel was covered with a thin layer of snow, but in another week or so that would melt. The hotel staff would come back to start the process of cleaning and getting the place ready for tourist season. He recalled the day he'd first seen Millie, her hands pressed against the glass, her face contorted with desperation. Had only a couple of weeks passed? He thought about the bond they had formed in that short time. He sure had spent a lot of time worrying about her and thinking of ways he might protect her and provide her with a better life. And he had to admit that just because he and

Ginny were expecting a child of their own, he couldn't accept that Millie was no longer his concern.

He was pretty sure Ginny felt the same.

Outside the window, the scenery flashed by as they drove the final five miles from the park to Gardiner. They were following the so-called "boiling" river, steam rising from the water that ran free over rocks sprinkled along the bed. He recalled a night shortly after they were married when he and Ginny went skinny-dipping there, only to be discovered by Dan Atwood, out on patrol. The ranger had beamed his flashlight over them and shouted that they were trespassing.

Nate had immediately raised his hand, signaling they were leaving, but Ginny had stood her ground. "We're the Bakers. We live here," she'd shouted up to where Dan stood on the road above the river. "Plus, our shower is broken."

He recalled how Dan had lowered the light and called for them to get dressed.

"Or what?" Ginny had challenged.

"Or I'll be forced to strip down and come in to get you," Dan had called back.

Nate had chuckled and reached for Ginny's hand. "Come on. I've got to work with that guy."

By the time they dressed, Dan had worked his way down to the shore. "Come on," he called. "Bertha Conroy promised to drop off a blueberry cobbler and she's been wanting to meet you, Miz Baker."

And that had been the beginning of friendships they had treasured for nearly two decades. Nate wondered how that would change now. He was glad Ginny would have Gert, and certainly Helen Matthews seemed like someone who would be a good and loyal friend. Ginny would be fine.

As for him, as long as he had Ginny, he, too, would be fine.

Ginny

-31-

A few days after they had settled in town, Ginny received an envelope marked with the return address of Milt's office. She stood on the porch and ripped it open. Finally, Edith must have located Lavinia's will. Now she and Nate could go to Mr. Stoner and show him they had proof of Lavinia's final wishes, forcing his hand—and Roger's.

But the blue envelope inside the package was not the blue of a legal document. This was a letter to Milt from Lavinia—a letter that, according to the date stamp, had been mailed just a week earlier, which was of course impossible. A note paper-clipped to the unopened envelope read: *This arrived with Friday's mail.*

She slid her thumbnail under the flap and pulled out two sheets of stationery. The handwriting was unsteady and sometimes almost ran off the page, as if the letter's author had been in a hurry or perhaps unable to concentrate properly on the message. But there was no doubt it was Lavinia's handwriting.

She quickly scanned the message, and then in complete disbelief re-read the words slowly and carefully.

Dear Milt,

If you are reading this, I am no longer living. I have been ill for several weeks with no pain or real symptoms other than extreme fatigue and weakness that has the doctor mystified. He has prescribed a variety of tonics and other medications, but none of them has made a difference. Roger even brought in a specialist from Helena, but he had little to add. Malaise was his diagnosis, and bedrest with a nightly tonic was his prescription. And so, we have followed that routine.

Once I did suggest to Roger that I return to Chicago, but Roger said both doctors felt I might not survive the journey. It is only in the last few days I have been clear-minded enough to understand what is really happening.

I believe Roger is poisoning me—has been poisoning me for weeks. Unfortunately, I have now passed the point of fighting back. My concern is for Millie and so I have asked my housekeeper, Clara Royce, to mail this to you upon my death. You have my will and you need to take immediate action to get Millie to Ginny and her husband or she will also be in danger.

I am sending this to you rather than the local authorities because I don't know whom to trust. But here is the evidence you need to present: In February, Roger announced his intention to turn over a new leaf and suggested that we share a night cap before going to bed as we discussed our day. I was skeptical at first, but because the frequent abuse stopped, and he even seemed interested in what I had to say, I let down my guard. After two weeks of these night caps he prepared I experienced the first symptoms—fatigue and weakness. Even when I begged off sitting with him before going up to bed, he came to my room, insisting we continue to share this nightly ritual. When I could no longer stomach the liquor, he stopped for a bit, but then, after the doctor from Helena called on me, Roger began coming to my room nightly with what he called a tonic prescribed by that doctor.

Now I realize what a fool I was. The signs were there—the way he pressed me to finish the drinks and "tonic," his barely contained irritation when I refused— little things.

It's too late for me, Milt, but we must save Millie. Please, do not delay—I am counting on you—you and Ginny.

These last words trailed off the page and there were stains and smears that Ginny was sure were Lavinia's dried tears. She looked at the envelope again—the letter had been mailed a little over a week earlier. She calculated the time it took for it to arrive in Chicago and for Edith to send it to her…

"Nate!" She pulled her sweater closer to her suddenly chilled body—a chill that had nothing to do with the weather--and ran around the side of the house. Nate was repairing the garage door that led into Helen's studio and up to her apartment.

Clearly reacting to the panic in her voice, he dropped his tools and ran to her. "Is it the baby?"

She shook her head, suddenly unable to speak. She pressed the letter she clutched into his chest. "Read this," she said.

She watched as he read, knew the moment he'd realized what Lavinia was telling them, and saw the way his hand shook slightly as he finished and studied the envelope.

"Look at the date stamp, Nate. Lavinia was already dead at least two weeks when this was mailed. We need to get Millie out of that house today."

Nate placed the letter back in its envelope and put it in his jacket pocket. "You stay here. I'm taking this to the sheriff."

"I'm going over there this minute and demand to see her," Ginny insisted.

"Millie's in school so safe for now. Let's let the sheriff handle this, Ginny."

"But we should call Gus and have him bring her here when he picks her up from school." She was clutching at straws—the need to take immediate action causing her chest to tighten with anxiety.

Nate wrapped his arms around her. "We have to be careful, Gin. Let Sheriff Wilson handle this, okay?"

"But…"

He tightened his hold on her. "Promise?" he whispered, and she nodded, knowing she was lying but also figuring it was the only way to make sure Nate hurried off to find the sheriff and show him the letter.

Once she watched him turn the corner on his way to the sheriff's office, Ginny headed in the opposite direction.

When she reached the house Roger and Lavinia had shared, she stopped at the end of the driveway to catch her breath and decided to go to the back entrance. She was more likely to find Clara Royce there.

Sure enough, when she rang a buzzer by the back door, the curtain over the glass moved as someone peered out, but no one opened the door. "Clara Royce?" She pressed the buzzer again and this time the door opened a crack and a harried-looking woman peered out.

She put a finger to her lips and stepped outside, pulling the door shut behind her and then wrapping her hands and forearms in her apron. "What do you want?"

"You're Clara Royce?"

The woman nodded.

"Do you know who I am?" Ginny asked.

Again, Clara nodded.

"The letter Lavinia asked you to mail arrived today."

That clearly surprised her. "That letter was sent to a lawyer in Chicago."

"My brother-in-law died. His secretary sent it to me. Why did you wait so long to mail it?"

"I…" She glanced nervously back at the house. "Can we talk about this another time, Mrs. Baker? Mr. Fitzgerald is working at home today and if he finds me talking to you, I'll…"

Ginny ignored her plea. "Do you know what the letter said?" She didn't wait for a response. "Millie is in danger."

Clara relaxed slightly, letting out a breath of relief. "No, ma'am. Millie is just fine. I saw her off to school myself this morning."

Clearly Clara had not read the letter nor had Lavinia confided her suspicions about Roger in the older woman. So why the delay in sending it? "You held Lavinia's letter for some time before mailing it. Why?"

Clara's eyes narrowed. "That day while they were at the funeral, I put a candle in Miz Fitzgerald's room and then took the letter just like she asked and shoved it into my pocketbook. She'd had me tape it to the bottom of her nightstand drawer, so I knew where to find it."

"That still doesn't explain why you didn't do as she asked and mail it straight away."

"Once he got back from the cemetery the mister was in a rage—the way he gets sometimes. He wanted me out and all I could think about was that I had no job in these hard times, and I'm not so young anymore..." She sucked in a breath and sniffed back tears. "The truth is I went home and forgot all about it. I was so upset and scared," she whispered, then grasped Ginny's forearm. "But when Millie got back after running away, she showed me the drawer where her mother had hidden the letter, and that's when I remembered I'd taken it. I went straight to the mailbox and sent it. I swear."

The door behind her opened and a younger woman looked out. She stared at Ginny and then said, "He's wanting his lunch, Clara."

"Coming." Clara's eyes pleaded with Ginny.

"So, you refuse to let me even speak to Millie?" Ginny said, raising her voice for the other woman's benefit.

Clara caught on at once. "You've no business here, so please leave now or I'll call Mr. Fitzgerald to see that you do," she replied. She changed her stance to one of authority. "I mean what I say. You and your husband have done enough damage to that child."

Ginny turned and walked away. *Well,* she thought, *Clara Royce is not quite the coward I thought—at least when it comes to protecting herself.*

Nate was waiting for her when she returned. "Where were you?"

"I went to see why Clara Royce held onto that letter. Did you speak with Sheriff Wilson?"

"He's out of town—gone up to his son's ranch for a few days. He'll be back the day after tomorrow. Ginny, I thought we agreed you would leave this alone."

"I just needed to find out why Clara Royce waited so long to mail Lavinia's letter."

"And did you?"

Ginny told him what she'd learned from Clara and was surprised when he frowned.

"Seems like a pretty weak explanation, not to mention the fact she's back there working again. She may know a lot more than she's admitting."

"But Lavinia trusted her."

"Who was she going to trust? Who was around for her to trust? Ginny, she was trying to protect Millie."

"And now it's up to us."

"Yep."

"So, what can we do, Nate?"

Nate removed his cap and ran his fingers through his thick coarse hair—hair that was showing more gray than she remembered. "Gus Olinger said he'd come by later to help me get that old jalopy Helen bought running right. I think in a choice between Millie and Fitzgerald, he just might choose Millie."

"But…"

"It's the best we can do 'til the sheriff gets back, Ginny. Millie's a smart kid and she doesn't trust Roger any farther than she could throw the man, so I'm pretty sure she'll not fall for anything like a nightly tonic."

"You don't fool me for one minute, Nate Baker. You're just itching to go over there and punch the stuffing out of that man, and do not tell me otherwise," Ginny said, fuming.

"You're right, but all of a sudden I've got all these females in my life wanting me to be around and not in jail, so let's just hold on 'til I can talk to Gus, okay?"

"I want to be there when you do." She saw Nate about to disagree and held up her hand. "I have questions, Nate, and Lavinia left Millie in my care."

She knew by the softening of his expression that she'd won this round. She also knew that Millie had won a place in Nate's heart and he would do whatever necessary to make sure she was safe.

Millie

-32-

Millie had become pretty good at eavesdropping. At night after Clara and Nan both left, she told Roger she was going to do homework on the dining room table, where she could spread out her books and papers. He would grunt and head to his study and shut the door. Millie knew better than to try and leave again because Roger made a big deal of having Gus install alarms throughout the house once he found out Nate was out of jail and no longer facing charges. One night, Millie opened a window in the dining room so she could get some air. A shrill whistle sounded, making her back away from the window, as Roger came thundering out from his office.

"Mildred!"

"I'm right here," she assured him. "It's so hot in here that I'm falling asleep and I really need to study for my math test."

Unmoved by her plea, he pointed to the stairs. "Bed. Now," he ordered.

Millie gathered her papers and books in her arms. Her mistake was in not just going. Instead she muttered, "If I fail this test…"

Roger grabbed her so hard she dropped everything and twisted her arm the way she'd seen him twist Momma's arm that night. She bit her lip to keep from crying out, mostly because she thought making any sound would make him twist harder.

Leaning in close so that she could see spit on his lips, he said, "You should have thought about your grades before you decided to go running off. And let me tell you this, little girl. If you think that Baker fellow is going to come charging in here and rescue you, think again." He released her with a shove that left her on her knees as he stalked to the window, slammed it shut, reset the alarm and went back to his study without looking at her once.

She sat there for a minute, rubbing her arm, and then realized Roger was talking to somebody, so she edged closer to the door and listened. He was on the telephone, talking to his lawyer. It was pretty obvious the alarm she'd set off had interrupted his call.

"The kid is driving me nuts, Al."

Whatever Mr. Stoner was saying, Millie figured Roger didn't like because she could hear him try to interrupt a couple of times.

"I know all that. Just tell me you're getting closer to breaking Lavinia's will."

Silence. Then…

"Look. Al, I need that money and I need it tomorrow. I thought Sheila would come through with funds for the down payment, only to find out she's dead broke. I've put them off as long as I can, and either I give them a check by end of business Friday, or the deal is off. So, get it done, or I swear we'll do things my way." He banged down the phone and Millie hurried to grab her books and run up the stairs.

She needn't have worried, because Roger stayed in his office for a long time after. It was close to midnight when she heard him pass her room. With the alarms installed, he saw no reason to lock her in at night. What he didn't know was that she still locked him out.

The next morning—the Friday of the last week of March—Gus was awfully quiet as he drove Millie to school. She figured maybe he and Miss Matthews had had an argument or something.

"I heard Nan talking about a dance this weekend at the VFW hall," Millie said. "She got Roger to give her today off so she could get a perm and go shopping. You planning on going?"

He shrugged. "Maybe."

She had taken to riding up front unless Roger was in the car, so she noticed how Gus kept glancing over at her as if he had something on his mind. They were getting close to the school, so she figured he'd best spit it out if they were going to talk at all.

"Something wrong?" she asked, and then felt her heart start to hammer. What if Gus was trying to find a way to tell her something bad had happened to Nate or Ginny or the baby? "What?" she demanded.

"What time is your math test?"

"First thing after homeroom. Why?"

"Once the test is done, how would you feel about playing sick and getting the office to call Clara for me to come get you?"

"Because?"

"Clara and me and the Bakers need to talk to you, and with Nan off and Mr. Fitzgerald gone to Helena, this seems to be our chance."

All Millie got out of that was that Nate and Ginny wanted to see her and had found a way to do it. Her heart raced with pure joy and excitement. Ever since she'd found out they were only a couple of blocks away, she'd hoped maybe she might see them, but hours and days had gone by with no opportunities at all. They might as well have been back in Chicago.

"I can do that," she said. "Momma always said I was a pretty good little actress and, well, you just tell me how sick I need to be..."

"No need to go overboard—stomach upset, chills, something simple. Otherwise they'll insist on calling the boss or a doctor."

"Got it." She grabbed her book bag and climbed out of the car. "See you soon," she murmured and then walked slowly up the walk and down the hall to her classroom.

"Mildred, is everything all right?" Miss Gibson asked as Millie slowly made her way to the coatroom.

"I don't feel so great," she admitted. "But I'll be okay," she assured her.

Step one, she thought, and fought against the temptation to smile when she realized Miss Gibson had followed her to the coatroom.

Once she'd hung up her coat, Miss Gibson held the door for her, and Millie walked to her desk, opened her math book and pretended to study.

The class went through the usual morning rituals—pledge to the flag, reciting the twenty-third psalm and the Lord's prayer, and then they cleared their desktops of everything except clean sheets of paper and two sharpened pencils while Miss Gibson wrote the test problems on the board.

Millie's desk was about halfway back, and all around her the other students bent over their work. Millie copied every problem, then got to work. Math was not her best subject, but for some reason she had no trouble completing the test. Momma would say that was her father's spirit watching over her, making sure things went her way. The tears that threatened every time she thought about Momma gathered right on cue, and all of a sudden, she knew exactly how to get them to call Clara and have Gus come get her.

She stood and took her paper to Miss Gibson's desk. The teacher looked up and frowned. "Mildred?"

Millie laid her test paper on Miss Gibson's desk and leaned in close, making sure the teacher saw the tears. She wrapped her arms around her stomach. "I think I just got my period," she whispered. "My stomach hurts really bad and..."

Miss Gibson was on her feet at once, guiding Millie toward the door, her heavyset body shielding her from the curious stares of her classmates. Once they were in the hall, she aimed Millie toward the office and said, "You go right now and tell Mrs. Thornton I said you need to go home for the day." Then she turned Millie and looked down at the back of her skirt. "Do you have supplies? Did your mother…"

"Yes, ma'am," Millie assured her. "It's just the cramps are so bad. Momma always said a heating pad helps."

"Go along then." She glanced back at the classroom, where Jeremy Turner was already causing a ruckus that had the rest of the class snickering. "Jeremy!" she shouted, and the door closed behind her.

Millie practically ran down the hall but slowed her step when she saw Mrs. Thornton step into the hall. "Miss Gibson says I need to go home," she told her.

"Are you ill, Mildred?"

"Yes, ma'am. It's…I just got my period and my stomach hurts and Miss Gibson said you should call our housekeeper, Miss Royce right away."

Maybe this wasn't the first time Mrs. Thornton had been faced with a situation like this, because she nodded once before stepping back inside the office and picking up the phone.

"Your stepfather's driver is on his way. I'll get your coat, Mildred," she said. "You just sit here, all right?" She motioned toward a wooden bench outside the office.

Millie nodded and took a seat, making sure she wrapped her arms around her middle and bent forward, as if that helped ease the pain.

Gus must have been waiting just around the corner because before she knew it, he came running up the steps and into the hall. "Thank you, ma'am," he said as he shook Mrs. Thornton's hand.

"Perhaps we should contact Mr. Fitzgerald?"

"He's out of town on business," Gus said. "Miss Royce knows what to do and if things get any worse, she'll be sure to call the doctor."

That seemed to satisfy the secretary because she looked at Millie and said, "Feel better, Millie," before returning to the office.

As soon as they were in the car, Millie told Gus how she had finished the test and then out of the blue come up with the idea of saying she'd gotten her period. His cheeks turned red. Momma had always told her getting her period was just part of the cycle of life, so Millie wondered why it made everybody act like it was something she shouldn't talk about.

Instead of driving to the big house on the hill, Gus turned down a side street and pulled into a driveway. "This isn't the Douglass house," Millie said.

"No, this is my mom's house. We thought it best to meet here. It's not unusual for folks to see Mr. Fitzgerald's car parked in Ma's driveway."

Using the side door off the driveway, they entered a small room with coat hooks on the wall and three steps leading up to another door with a frosted glass window. As Millie took off her coat and Gus hung it on one of the hooks, she smelled cinnamon and apples.

The door with the frosted glass opened and a small, gray-haired lady dressed in a flowered dress covered by a bibbed apron smiled at her. "So, this is Millie," she said.

"Millie, this is my ma—Mrs. Olinger," Gus said.

Millie climbed the three steps and offered her hand for a shake, but then behind Gus' mother she saw Nate standing by the table and forgot all her manners as she ran to him.

"Nate!"

He wrapped his arms around her, and she could feel more than hear the rumble of his chuckle. She pressed her cheek to the soft flannel of his shirt and held on until he stepped back—his hand still on her back. "Got somebody you need to meet," he said.

The woman she'd seen in the framed photograph Nate kept on the side table next to his chair stood. "Hello, Millie. I'm Ginny."

She was a lot prettier than her picture. She had the most beautiful curly red hair Millie had ever seen, and her eyes were what storybooks would call "forest green." Suddenly shy, Millie fingered her own lank hair. "Hello," she mumbled.

"Let's sit," Mrs. Olinger said. She placed a slice of cinnamon coffeecake topped with dried apples in front of Millie.

Gus pulled out the chair and then sat next to her. "I do hope you're not too ill to enjoy this, Millie," he said.

Everyone laughed. While Gus's mom cut cake for everyone else, Clara served coffee. She made Millie a special cup that was mostly milk with a little coffee added. Once everyone was seated, Nate cleared his throat.

"Millie, the first thing you need to know is we are not going to let anything happen to you."

Her heart beat a little faster.

"Nate," Ginny said as she placed her hand on his. "You're scaring the child."

"No," Millie protested, then gave Nate her full attention. "What's going on?"

Nate explained that while they had letters showing what her mother had intended for her future, so far they had been unable to locate a copy of the will.

"But Mr. Stoner has a copy," Millie said. "He must because I heard him telling Roger what it said, and Roger got really mad…"

Ginny leaned forward. "Millie, has Roger done anything that makes you afraid of him? Clara tells us once he stopped locking you in overnight, you began locking your door from the inside."

She shrugged, deciding they didn't need to know what had happened last night. "I don't know. He hit

Momma and he hit me. He gets so mad sometimes, and after Clara and Nan leave and it's just him and me in the house…"

She frowned. "Has he ever suggested the two of you have a snack or something to drink before you go to bed?"

Millie laughed. "He can barely stand to sit with me at dinner," she said. "He goes into his office the minute…" She felt a chill. "What's going on?"

Nate cleared his throat. "Millie, we all know Roger does not agree with the terms of your mother's will."

Ginny interrupted. "You see, he needs that money to buy the concessions business in the park. He's already signed a contract, and if he fails to come up with the money he's promised, well, he could go to jail for breach of contract."

Gus let out a sigh. "Here's the thing, Millie. The boss is desperate. You know how he gets when things don't go his way—when somebody gets in his way."

"And right now," Nate said softly, "you're in his way, Millie."

Her hands began to shake. "He can have the money," she said, turning to Nate. "Tell him I'll give him the money if he'll just let you go back to work and you and Ginny go home and maybe I can live with you for a while …"

She saw Ginny's eyes fill with tears. "Oh, Nate," Ginny whispered, and suddenly Millie realized there was something they weren't telling her. She looked around the table. "You're the ones scaring me now," she said.

Nate turned to Ginny. "Show her the letter," he said. "She's going to find out what he did soon enough, and she needs to know what kind of danger she's in."

Millie saw Gus and Clara and Mrs. Olinger nod, and Ginny pulled a familiar blue envelope from her pocket and passed it to Nate. The envelope bore a Chicago address.

"This is what your mother had me tape to the bottom of her nightstand drawer, Millie," Clara said. Now she was crying. "If only I had…"

Nate removed the pages from the envelope and passed them to Millie. It was Momma's handwriting all right, although there were places where it was like she couldn't hold the pen steady and there were words blurred because they'd gotten wet at some point. The whole time Millie was reading the letter Nate kept his arm around her shoulders and no one spoke.

She read it once and then again. "I don't understand," she said, handing the letter back to Nate. "She's saying Roger poisoned her? Why didn't she say something?" She turned on Clara and Gus. "Why didn't you do something?" Then she was on her feet, jerking away from Nate's attempt to hold onto her. "You all knew, and Roger is still out there, and Momma is dead? Why?" She jerked the door open so violently the glass rattled, but she didn't care. "I hate you—all of you."

Not bothering to take her coat, she ran from the house. Behind her, she heard Ginny telling Nate to catch her and then Gus calling for her to stop. "Millie, you can't…"

Don't tell me I can't, she thought, and ran faster, heading for the woods that bordered the edge of town.

Nate

-33-

Unhampered by ice and deep snow, Millie was fast and sure-footed. Before Nate could reach the place where the street ended and the open field leading to the woods began, she was already halfway across the field.

"I'll go," Gus said, coming alongside him.

"No. Give her some time." By now Ginny had caught up to the two men. She was gasping for breath and holding her hand protectively over her pregnant stomach.

"Go back to the house," Nate said. "I'll handle this."

"But…"

"Ginny, please. If she's going to trust anyone, it'll be me."

"Come on, Mrs. Baker," Gus said and to Nate's relief Ginny agreed.

Nate walked slowly across the field, his eyes on the woods, as the memory of a time when he had been the one who believed he'd been betrayed by everyone crowded his mind. He'd just turned sixteen—a year when his body had filled out and for the first time in his life, he knew he had the power to stand up to his father. *No more*, he had vowed, as he waited for his father to sleep off yet another binge that had included drinking himself into a rage and taking that fury out on Nate's mother before collapsing onto the bed and passing out.

Nate had sat by that bed, his fists clenched, watching the old man sleep and letting his own hatred build like a geyser ready to erupt. The minute his father stirred Nate was on him, dragging him to his feet and pressing him against the wall, his forearm jammed against the man's throat. "Pa, if you ever lay a hand on Momma again," he'd hissed, "I will kill you."

He'd given the man one more shove to make his point and then released him, not caring what might happen next.

And then, from where he'd collapsed to the floor behind Nate, his father gasped, "I ain't your Pa, you bastard, and I'll do what I damn well please to you or that woman—the two of you always thinking you're better'n me. Well, you ain't nothing now and you never will be." He'd staggered to his feet and spit in Nate's face. "Get out of my house, boy, or I swear I'll make that woman wish I'd killed her already."

"Not this time," Nate had said as he wrapped his arm around his mother's thin shoulders and headed for the door.

But she pushed him away. "Just go," she whispered.

"Not without…"

Then she shoved free of him. "He's not lyin', Nate. You ain't his, so just go on now."

"I won't leave you…"

"It's not your choice," she'd said softly, as she smoothed his hair away from his forehead. "Your Daddy was a good man…"

The old man had stepped between them, shoving Nate's mother aside. "Your *Daddy* was my no-good brother, who thought he could steal my woman. Son-of-a-bitch shoulda learned how to swim."

Nate knew the story of his uncle's tragic death, when the two brothers went fishing, and only this man, spewing his hatred and evil in Nate's face, returned. Nate had been six or seven, and the abuse had started shortly after that.

Nate had left that day, lied about his age and volunteered for the army. By the time he'd finished his stint overseas and returned to Montana, his mother was dead, her husband in prison and his siblings had scattered with no forwarding addresses. The land and outbuildings that made up the farm had been abandoned and held far too many bad memories for Nate to care. Shortly after that, he'd taken the job in the park--and sworn he would neither marry nor father a child.

And then he met Ginny--and more recently, Millie.

From the day he'd rescued her and taken her back to the cabin, he'd acted purely on instinct. She was sick and cold, and he should have taken her straight to Dan's house just a couple of blocks away. Even with Dan away for the night, Nate knew the ranger didn't lock up. So why hadn't he?

Something about his first meeting with Roger had not sit right with him, and the minute he realized who Millie was, he felt something he'd only observed in bears and other animals. It had taken him two days to understand that what he'd felt was protective.

Ahead of him, Millie trudged determinedly up the hill. "Leave me alone, Nate," she shouted over her shoulder.

He did not reply, except to take longer strides. She kept looking back over her shoulder as she tried to move faster. "I mean it, Nate," she called out. "I'm leaving and you can't…"

Nate thrust his hand forward, knowing the distance was too great for him to break her fall as he watched her foot catch in a tree root. She went down hard. He started to run. "Millie!"

By the time he reached her she was sitting up and holding her ankle. "I think it's broken."

Nate sat next to her. The ground was cold and damp. "Let me see."

He bent to examine her ankle, which was already starting to swell. "I think it's a bad sprain. Come on," he said as he got to his feet and held out his hand to her.

"Climb on my back and let's get you home so we can get some ice on that."

She folded her arms and dropped her chin to her chest. "In case you haven't noticed, I don't have a home."

Nate sat on a log facing her. "Now you listen to me. You will always have a home with me and Ginny,"

She looked up at him, her eyes flaring with anger. "Then how come you and Ginny haven't done anything to get me away from Roger? How come you had to find out he probably poisoned Momma before you even cared?"

Her words stung, mostly because there was a grain of truth in them. How to explain they didn't have the money for lawyers to fight Roger or that they needed to wait for Sheriff Wilson to return before they could confront the man? How to explain they didn't have anything but an old letter to Milt saying what Lavinia wanted—should anything happen to her--was for Millie to live with them?

"Millie, we have to do this the right way—the legal way-- and right now we don't have a copy of your mother's will."

"I told you--Mr. Stoner has a copy. Ask him."

"Mr. Stoner works for Roger."

She stared at him for a long moment. And then her lower lip started to quiver, and her face turned red. She drew her knees up to her chest and rested her face on her knees. "How come bad stuff keeps happening to me, Nate?" she moaned.

Nate thought maybe that was the moment he knew that he would do just about anything to give Millie the happy life she deserved.

"Come on, kid," he said, as he turned and motioned for her to climb on his back. "We're going to get this worked out. You have my word on that. Whatever it takes, okay?"

He felt her arms come around his neck as she positioned herself for the ride back down the hillside.

"Nate," she said, when they had cleared the woods and were halfway across the field, "I know Momma wanted Ginny to take me in, but she didn't say anything about you."

"Ginny and I come as a package deal," he replied.

He stopped short of making promises he wasn't sure he could keep. Not that he didn't want to tell Millie he'd be honored to have her as his daughter, but he'd learned the world didn't always work the way he thought it should.

Ginny

-34-

Ginny waited with Clara and Gus for Nate to bring Millie back, and all the while she was thinking about what it might mean having Millie in their life day in and out, while they were also adjusting to being new parents. She knew all the reasons Nate had resisted becoming a father, how even when she had reminded him that the man who'd raised and abused him all those years was not his biological father, he worried. And yet when it came to Millie, he was different.

Maybe he felt a connection to her, both of them having endured heartbreaking childhoods. Maybe he understood Millie in a way Ginny thought she never could. Lavinia had been her dear friend, but it was Lavinia she had known—not Millie. Millie was the offspring not only of Lavinia, but of the young soldier who had died before Ginny could really know him.

When Nate reached the Olinger house, Gus eased Millie off his back and carried her inside.

"Pretty sure it's a sprain, not a break," Nate assured Clara, who followed Gus inside. He glanced at Ginny. "She's scared," he said softly, as if that explained anything.

Ginny nodded. "Sit and catch your breath. I'll see to her."

In the kitchen, Gus was kneeling next to Millie's chair, holding ice wrapped in a dish towel against her ankle. Clara was at the sink, drying the dishes Gus's mother was washing from their coffee and cake. Ginny pulled a chair close to Millie's and took the ice pack from Gus. "You and Nate need to come up with a plan," she said.

Gus nodded and went out to the back porch. Clara and Mrs. Olinger wiped their hands on towels and stood uncertainly by the sink. Ginny looked up at them and they got the message.

"Could I use your bathroom?" Clara asked. Gus's mother nodded and led the way down the hall, leaving Ginny alone with Millie.

"Does it hurt?" she asked, as she pressed the ice to the swelling.

Millie shrugged and took over holding the ice pack. "I've got it," she said.

Ginny sat back and saw Millie glance at the small mound Ginny could no longer disguise. "Baby's due in late summer," she said, as she ran her hands over her stomach.

Millie turned her attention to her foot.

Ginny waited and when the girl said nothing, she let out a long breath. "Millie, it's all going to work out." The words sounded weak even to her.

Millie let out a sound that was part laugh and part disgust. "That's what everybody keeps saying, but even a kid like me knows that's not true. You and Nate need a copy of Momma's will and we don't have that. But Roger does, and he can do anything he wants with that, can't he? He could say he lost it, or he could change it or..."

"We have your mother's letters, Millie."

She rocked back in the chair and glared at Ginny. "And one of those letters says Roger poisoned Momma, but he's still out there. He's still going to come back to that house after me because he still needs that money, doesn't he?"

"Yes, but..."

Ginny was taken aback at how much the child had absorbed of the seriousness of the situation. She was hardly prepared for what it would take to raise a newborn. Raising Millie would be a challenge beyond anything she could have imagined. When she'd read Lavinia's first letter, telling Milt she wanted Ginny to take Millie in, she saw now that her naivete had been laughable. Of course, they would, she had assured Nate. But she'd barely stopped to think what that might mean for Millie. She had assumed the child would be grateful. It had never occurred to her that Millie might see the idea of moving in with strangers—kind strangers, to be sure—merely as the lesser of two evils.

She decided to try a different tack. "Millie, I can't imagine what these last weeks and months have been like for you—no one could."

Millie bit her lower lip to stop it from quivering and giving away the tears Ginny knew she was struggling to conceal. "Look, I know you and Nate have troubles of your own. I'm not going to hold you to something you didn't even know Momma wanted from you. She had no right…"

Ginny placed her hand on Millie's. "She had every right. Your mother was my dearest friend. She was the only person who stood by me when I decided to marry Nate. She was the only one who stood up to my parents and sister and told them they, of all people, ought to know that real true love comes along once if you're lucky and you have no idea for how long. She was talking about her love for your father—a love they were robbed of far too soon. You are the product of that love, Millie Chase, and it would be my honor to take you into our home and my heart."

Her voice was shaking by the time she completed this soliloquy and it was now her lashes that were wet with tears. "So, I am asking you to allow us to help you walk away from this nightmare you find yourself living."

A half-smile tugged at the corners of the girl's lips. "Nate told me you were not somebody to mess with," she said.

"Does that mean you'll stop trying to run away and let us handle this?"

There was a long pause, during which the only sound in the kitchen was the faucet dripping. Then very softly, Millie said, "Okay."

Ginny felt a mix of relief and apprehension race through her, and she wasn't sure of her next move. She knew Millie was watching her—and waiting.

So, she did the thing that seemed most natural under the circumstances. She leaned over and wrapped her arms around Millie's shoulders and hugged her. And when she heard the ice pack hit the floor and felt Millie's arms snake around her waist, she felt for the first time since returning from Chicago that they could make this right—for Millie and for Lavinia.

Millie

-35-

The truth was that Millie felt as if she really knew Nate, but Ginny was somebody she'd gotten to know through Momma and Nate. She seemed really nice, but she was expecting a baby of her own. So, no matter how much she might care about doing something for Momma, how could Millie expect her to stick out her neck for somebody like her?

And because Nate was that baby's father, Ginny wouldn't want him getting into trouble either. She had to know he'd lost his job because of Millie. And then there was the fact that Millie's mother hadn't even told Ginny about that letter saying Millie should come live with her and Nate if something happened to Momma.

And to top it off, Roger might have killed Momma. The way she saw it, that ought to make Ginny think twice about either one of them getting any more mixed up in this mess than they already were.

So, when Ginny came into the kitchen and sent everybody else away, Millie figured this was it. She wouldn't be mean or anything, but she was going to explain why they couldn't do anything more.

She had pretended she was fine on her own and wouldn't hold Ginny to a promise she'd never made. And then Ginny made that speech about how Momma had helped her fight for Nate and their love and how she'd reminded them true love didn't last forever, and Millie began to understand that for Ginny, this was her chance to mend the break she and Momma had gone through when Momma married Roger—even if Momma was no longer here. And how dumb would it be to turn down her offer?

After they hugged, Ginny went to the back door and called for Nate and Gus to come inside, and then did the same to get Clara back. Gus's mother stayed away.

They all sat around the kitchen table and waited for Nate to lay out the plan.

"First, I'm going to call Sheriff Wilson and let him know about Lavinia's accusation against Roger. My guess is he'll be back tomorrow to look into that. Clara will stay with you, Millie, so everything will be fine since Roger isn't due back until Sunday. Meanwhile, Gus tells me Roger had him move several boxes of Lavinia's things to the attic, so while you and Clara have the house to yourselves after Nan leaves for the day, the two of you can look through those and see if maybe you can find a copy of the will."

"I'll help," Ginny said.

"No. I don't want you in that house. If Roger comes home early, Clara and Millie can make up a story, but no one could explain why you came to be there."

"Nate, I know what we're looking for and you said yourself there's no danger, so let's not debate this."

Everybody—including Millie—looked at Nate, who smiled and shook his head. "You'll be careful of the stairs and boxes and dust and all?"

Ginny laid her hand on his and he didn't say anything more.

"If Roger should come back unexpectedly," Ginny said, looking at Clara and then at Millie, "we'll have a signal, okay?"

Millie felt excited that finally they were going to be doing something. "You could beep the car horn," she suggested to Gus. "Or signal with a light—I read that once in a Nancy Drew story."

Gus smiled. "The horn's a good idea. Three short toots."

"Wouldn't he call for you to come get him?" Ginny asked. "You could let Clara know when you leave and that would give us time to put everything back in order ..."

Gus shook his head. "He's traveling with Mr. Stoner. Mr. Stoner's car is at the railroad station."

"And what if we don't find the will?" Millie asked.

"Roger's in enough trouble trying to answer the accusations your mother made in her letter, Millie," Nate said.

And that gave Millie an idea. She turned to Ginny. "We should also look for what he might have used in those tonics or maybe a glass that didn't get washed or..."

"Honey, it's been weeks," Clara said.

"Can't hurt to look," Ginny said. "Maybe the medicine cabinet in your mother's bathroom?"

"Or the one in Roger's," Millie added, which made all the adults frown. "I can do this," she assured them. "I'm really good at snooping." She turned to Clara. "How do you think I knew what was in every wrapped Christmas and birthday present before I even opened it?"

Nate let out a snort of laughter and Gus grinned, but Clara and Ginny just looked worried.

"We'll look together," Ginny murmured.

Gus checked the clock above the sink. "We should get going. Nan will wonder why you aren't home yet."

Millie stood and tested some weight on her ankle. "I can walk," she said, when Gus circled the table, ready to pick her up.

Ginny buttoned her coat and turned up the collar. "Just promise me you'll be careful," she whispered as she hugged her.

Millie nodded.

Clara collected the groceries she had told Nan she needed. They would tell Nan that Gus and Millie spotted Clara walking and picked her up. They had an answer for everything.

It seemed like forever before Nan left for the day. Millie could hardly wait to get started looking through those boxes in the attic. In the meantime, she went over everything in Momma's room, opening every drawer, climbing on a chair to check the top shelf in the closet, and even looking under the bed.

Nothing.

Of course, Nan had cleaned the room when Roger told her to get it ready for Millie's return, and who knew what she might have found and thrown away. Millie stood in front of the mirror, hands on her hips, and tried to think where else she might look. And then it hit her. Momma had hidden the letter for Clara to mail under a drawer. Just maybe she'd done the same with her will.

By the time Clara let Ginny in through the side door, Millie had pulled out every drawer in the room. She was breathing hard and coughing from the dust she'd raised in the process, so she didn't even hear Ginny open the door.

"What on earth?" she exclaimed, startling Millie so that she nearly tripped over a bureau drawer she'd set on the floor.

"Easy there." Instinctively, Ginny reached out to steady her. She smiled, "Don't want you spraining the other ankle."

"I'll get this cleaned up and then…"

Ginny picked up a drawer and slid it into place. "What were you looking for?"

Millie described her idea that maybe Momma had hidden the will the same way she had the letter. "But nothing," she said.

Ginny grinned. "Nate told me what a clever girl you are, and now I see he was right. Your mother was the same—always thinking up schemes for whatever adventure we wanted to try."

Millie really liked the way Ginny had these memories of Momma. "I wish she was here," she said, as she closed the final drawer and looked around to be sure everything was back in its proper place.

"So, do I." Ginny let out a long sigh, then said, "Now where is this attic?"

Millie led the way to the third floor, down a dim hallway, past her old room, to the door that led to the attic. Above the worn doorknob was a shiny new padlock.

"No," Millie whispered. She had forgotten the door was locked, and it felt as if once again Roger had won.

But Ginny just grinned. Digging deep in the pocket of her dress, produced a key. "Ta da!"

"Where did you get that?"

She shrugged. "Roger had Gus install the padlock and, bless him, Gus decided to keep an extra key with the other keys he has for the property." She opened the lock, returned the key to her pocket and hung the open padlock on the outside of the door.

Millie found the light switch and led the way up a short flight of steps to where cardboard boxes were stacked in neat rows down one side of the space. The boxes were sealed with paper tape and labeled: *Clothing; purses and shoes; books; knickknacks and miscellaneous.*

"Let's start with this one," Ginny said as she ripped the tape from the box labeled *miscellaneous*.

"Wait!" But it was too late. She had already ruined the opening. Roger would know immediately someone had been snooping.

"It's okay," Ginny said when she saw Millie's expression. "By the time Roger finds out we were up here, it will be too late for him to do anything. Now come on, help me sort through these items—and if you come across something you want, leave it out. You should have anything you want of what's here—it all belongs to you, not Roger."

She sat on a wooden crate and began removing items from the box. She opened something wrapped in layers of tissue paper and held up a baby's blanket. "Was this yours, Millie?"

Millie nodded. It had been so long since she'd seen the pale-yellow blanket Momma had told her she'd wrapped her in to bring her home from the hospital. "Do you want it for your baby?" she asked. "I think Momma would like that. I mean, she would have gotten you a present—probably a whole bunch of presents. Of course, if it's too old and ratty…"

Ginny clutched the blanket to her chest, caressing her cheek with a corner of the fabric. "Oh, Millie, are you sure? I would love it, but if…"

"I'm sure," Millie said, and started taking other tissue-wrapped bundles from the box. "She saved all this stuff, so whatever you and Nate want…" The truth was she couldn't believe that finally, after everything she and Nate had done for her, Millie could do something for them— something that seemed to make Ginny so happy.

As it turned out, the entire carton marked *miscellaneous* was filled with baby things—clothes, toys, more blankets, and a Teddy bear that brought Ginny to tears. "I gave your mother this when you were born—Nate and me," she said softly.

Millie could see one of the bear's ears was frayed. Momma had told her that when she was teething, she'd chewed on Teddy's ear. "Maybe I could keep that," she said. "I mean, you really gave it to me, didn't you?"

"We did. Do you want it?"

"Yeah."

She nodded and handed Millie the bear. It smelled of baby powder and the moth balls Clara must have added to the boxes as she packed them. "Thanks."

Ginny stood, set the blanket aside to take with her, and put everything else back in the carton, then closed it by folding the flaps in that special way Millie could never figure out. "Thank you, Millie. If it's okay with you, I'll ask Gus to bring this to me later. Let's move on," she said, wiping her eyes with the knuckles of one hand.

They went through the boxes one by one. Outside the small window covered with cobwebs, Millie saw that it had gotten dark. They'd been at it for a couple of hours without finding the will or anything else that might help make the case against Roger. The last box contained shoes, which reminded Millie how she'd hidden the note to Gus under the lining of her shoe.

Ginny had been coughing off and on as they worked, blaming it on the dust, but determined to keep going. Millie could tell that she was really tired.

"It's getting late and Nate's bound to worry. This is the last box," Millie told her. "You go on and if I find anything, I'll have Gus bring it to you right away."

"Millie..."

"Please," she begged. "I want to know what the sheriff said, so please let Gus take you home and then he can come back with whatever news Nate's gotten."

She stretched her back and glanced around. "You promise you'll check this one last carton and then leave anything else for tomorrow? No checking out Roger's room or bath on your own?"

Millie hesitated.

"Millie, I will not leave if I think I can't trust you."

"Promise," she said. "I'll just check the shoes, then lock up here and wait for tomorrow."

Ginny kissed the top of Millie's head. "That's my girl. I'll have Clara warm your supper, so don't stay up here too long." She picked up the tissue-wrapped baby blanket and started down the steps. At the door, she hesitated and looked back.

"Go," Millie said, knowing what she was really doing was reminding her Clara would check on her. "Nate's gonna be worried."

She waved, and Millie heard her walk down the hall and on down to the second floor. Glancing out the window that overlooked the garage, Millie saw Ginny hurry out a few minutes later, buttoning her coat-- that didn't quite close over her hips and tummy-- and saying something to Clara. Then Gus helped her into the car, and they drove away.

Millie's mother had had a lot of shoes and pulling the lining free in each one took time, but Millie was determined to go through them all, so really didn't pay attention to anything else. After a while she heard the car on the drive, and assuming it was Gus returning, she began to rush so she could get downstairs to see what Nate had learned.

She was nearing the bottom of the box when she heard the voices of a man and a woman approaching from downstairs and figured Clara and Gus were on their way up to get her.

Then she heard a thump that sounded like something heavy falling and had just replaced the carton and started for the attic door when she saw Roger coming toward her.

She backed away, putting the cardboard cartons between them, fearful of the beating she knew was coming. But he stopped at the top of the short flight of steps, took out the lighter he used for those smelly cigars Momma always hated, and started clicking it on and off.

"You think you can beat me?" he said. "A kid and a janitor?" He laughed as he stepped into the attic and pulled open the box closest to him. Then, looking her straight in the eyes, he flicked the lighter on and lit the edge of the packing paper.

Millie stood frozen, watching the fire catch and flame and the smoke start to fill the cramped space. "Clara!" she screamed. "Get help now!"

Roger laughed. "Save your breath, kid. It's over." He opened another box, flicked the lighter on and threw it inside the carton. "Such a tragic accident…" he muttered as he turned away.

Then he made his way down the attic steps as the smoke and flames flared. The door slammed and Millie heard the padlock click into place.

Nate

-36-

The minute Nate heard the rumble of Fitzgerald's black car, he hurried to the door. He'd been sitting in the front room with Gert and Helen, filling them in on the meeting they'd missed with Millie earlier that day, because once Nate and Gus got the car Helen had bought running, she and Gert had driven to her family's ranch to collect the rest of Helen's clothes and photography equipment.

Gert was close on his heels as Nate opened the door, saw Gus help Ginny out of the car and watched her come up the front walk.

"What were you thinking?" Gert demanded, pushing past him to face her sister. "In that attic, in your condition! Are you trying to lose this baby?"

Ginny kissed Nate's cheek, set a bundle wrapped in tissue paper on the steps leading up to the bedrooms, and let him help her remove her coat. "Hello, Gert. How was your day?"

She accepted the cup of tea Helen brought to her and collapsed on the sofa. Gus hovered just inside the door.

"Any news?" he asked.

Nate nodded. "I spoke to Sheriff Wilson. He wants me to bring Lavinia's letter to Livingston and meet him there so he can use that evidence to get a warrant to search Roger's property. Can you drive me there?"

"I'll take it. You stay here," Gus volunteered.

"I'll go with you," Helen offered as she grabbed her coat from the hall tree, pocketed the letter Nate handed her, and followed Gus out to the car.

"Did you find anything?" Nate asked, sitting next to Ginny and putting his arm around her shoulders.

She shook her head and took a sip of her tea. Then she added, "Well, at least not what we were hoping to find, but Nate, we found all of Millie's baby clothes and toys that Lavinia had kept, and Millie wants us to have them for the baby. Isn't that incredibly sweet?"

Gert made a strangled sound accompanied by a look of disgust. "Surely we are not so down on our luck we can't afford a proper layette for the child," she said.

"That's not the point," Ginny said. "If things go the way we all hope, Millie will be living with us and this is a connection to Lavinia—for her and for us."

Nate wanted nothing so much as a moment alone with his wife. "Gert, Ginny hasn't had anything to eat. Could you maybe fix her a sandwich or some eggs or…"?

Ginny giggled. "Honey, Gert doesn't cook."

"I'm not asking her to cook—a cheese sandwich…"

Ginny looked at her sister. "Two slices of bread, mustard, maybe some pickles if there are any and, of course, cheese."

Gert nodded and went to the kitchen, ticking off the ingredients on her fingers.

"You're kidding," Nate said.

"Nope. Now tell me. Are you saying the sheriff believed you?"

"Not at first, but it seems he remembered his wife talking about how Lavinia was practically a prisoner in that house. And the truth is, Roger hasn't done much to make himself part of the community here. Folks in small towns tend to notice things like that."

"So, the sheriff gets the warrant and gets back when?"

"Maybe tonight, if Gus makes good time." He tightened his embrace. "We're getting close to this being over, Ginny—for us and for Millie."

Gert appeared, carrying two plates, each with a sandwich stacked with layers of pickles and cheese held together with bread minus the crusts and oozing mustard. "It occurred to me you haven't eaten either," she said, handing Nate one plate and Ginny the other.

"And you said your sister couldn't cook," Nate murmured, biting into the sandwich Gert had cut into quarters.

"It's not really cooking," Gert said, blushing with pleasure.

"Hits the spot," Nate assured her.

Once they'd finished eating and Nate had persuaded Ginny to lie down on the sofa and rest, they heard the clang of the volunteer fire engine bell as it raced past.

"Seems like everybody's got trouble," Ginny remarked wearily, caressing Nate's whiskered cheek. She closed her eyes then, so Nate went back to the kitchen, picked up a towel and started drying the dishes as his sister-in-law handed them to him.

"Seems like you and Helen have hit it off pretty well," he ventured, seeking some topic of conversation.

"Nate, you need to think beyond this girl—Millie. She is not your responsibility or Ginny's, regardless of what Lavinia wanted. No one consulted either of you and it is ridiculous to…"

"It's our choice, Gert."

"But…"

"What would you have happen to Millie?" he challenged, realizing he had raised his voice when Gert took a step away from him.

"Well, there are places surely even out here, and if not…"

"And if this were your child?"

"My children have me," she snapped.

"And Millie has me and Ginny."

Gert opened her mouth to say something more, but Nate folded the dish towel and handed it to her. "And that's the end of any discussion, okay?"

He didn't wait for her reply but walked back to the front room, where Ginny was sleeping. As he covered her with an afghan, someone knocked at the front door. Nate flipped on the switch for the porch light and found Gus's mother standing on the porch.

"You'd best come," she said, as soon as Nate opened the door. "That man's house is on fire and Clara says the girl is trapped inside."

Nate stepped out onto the porch, pulling the door closed behind him, hoping Ginny hadn't wakened. Mrs. Olinger led the way across the street and into her house, where a distraught—and badly bruised—Clara paced the kitchen floor.

"I tell you the man is crazy. He came storming into the house demanding to know where Gus was. I made up a lie that his ma here had taken ill and…"

"What about Millie?" Nate demanded.

Clara started to sob. "She was still in the attic, but I swear all I said was 'upstairs.' Then he wanted to know who'd been in the attic—he'd seen the light when he went to find Gus and…"

"Clara, is Millie in danger?"

The housekeeper nodded. "I said I'd get her, but he followed me upstairs, and when I headed on to the third floor, he shoved me so hard that I fell down the stairs. He never stopped, just ran up those stairs to the third floor. I kind of blacked out I think, but only for a minute and I came as fast as I could to get Gus and…"

Gus's mother took up the story. "When she got here, I was taking out the trash. We both looked back toward the house and saw the smoke. I called the firehouse and then came to get you."

Nate didn't wait to hear more. He started running, down the street and through an alley until he reached the back of Roger's house. Firemen were spraying water at the flames that had spread to the roof, but their hose was too short to reach the high peak of the attic.

He recognized the broad back of Roger Fitzgerald, who was shouting at the fire captain and gesturing toward the house. "My stepdaughter is in there," he cried.

Nate pushed past him and began climbing a ladder the firemen had placed against the house before realizing that it would not reach the third story window. "Millie!" he shouted as he reached a small porch off one of the second story bedrooms. "Millie!"

The attic window was above him. He leaned over the bannister and shouted to the men below. "Lift that ladder so I can bring it up here." While one man handled the hose, another started to lift the ladder. It took forever, and all the while Nate was aware that Roger was holding onto the arm of the captain—the only other available source of help--and gesturing wildly toward him.

Finally, the captain shoved Roger away and ran to help hoist the ladder. Nate managed to drag it over the bannister and set it against the wall of the house, so it stretched up to the attic.

He saw movement in the window and ducked as a stuffed toy and an album of photographs flew past his head and landed near his feet. "Millie, I need you to do exactly what I say, okay?"

A choking cough was his only answer. He started up the ladder that was wet from the hose. The water was starting to freeze, making his footing treacherous. After what seemed like a lifetime, he reached the open window, pulled the neck of his undershirt up to cover his mouth and nose and tried to peer through the smoke. "Millie?"

He saw a body huddled close to the window. When she turned, she was coughing, and her arms were full of stuff.

"Drop that," he ordered.

She started toward him. "It's all Momma's things," she managed.

"You don't need that stuff to remember your mother, Millie. Put it down, okay?"

The window was too narrow for him to climb through, so he stretched out his hand, hoping the ladder would hold without slipping. She hesitated, then let go of the items she was holding and reached her arms out to him.

"Got you," he muttered, when he felt his hand connect with her arm. He pulled her forward, felt that she'd gone limp, and at the same time saw the box she'd just been standing next to burst into flame. Using his elbow and fist covered by his sleeve, he smashed the rest of the glass on the small window and broke the frame to make a larger space. Then he let go of the ladder and bent over the sill of the window from his waist as he used both hands to pull Millie up and through.

"Steady there," one of the firemen shouted, and Nate realized they had somehow made their way to the porch and were holding onto the ladder.

As Nate anchored Millie over his shoulder, one of the firemen scaled the ladder to help guide Nate down. "We got you," he kept repeating, like saying it would make it true.

The second the fireman and Nate stepped off the ladder, both firemen lifted the ladder over the side and the captain anchored it below while everyone waited for Nate to bring Millie down. All he knew was that she wasn't moving. When he looked up and saw the two firemen about to follow him down, he shouted, "Bring all that stuff she tossed out with you." If it was important to Millie, that was reason enough for him.

They hesitated, but then the captain shouted, "Just do as he asks."

By the time they reached the ground, the yard was crowded with neighbors. Some had come to help while others were just there to gawk. Blessedly, one of those people was a doctor who identified himself to the fire captain and then directed others to take Millie inside the garage, blessedly untouched by the fire. Nate tried to follow them, but he was having trouble catching his breath and after a few steps, felt his knees buckle as he dropped to the ground.

He heard the doctor barking out orders, felt himself being lifted and carried, tried to tell them to tend to Millie and leave him alone, and then he passed out.

When he came to, somebody was holding an oxygen mask over his mouth and nose to help him breathe. He looked around, saw the doctor and others and tried to get up.

"Whoa," the doctor said and rushed to his side, easing him back down.

"Millie," Nate mouthed.

"Is doing just fine," the doctor promised. "See for yourself." He stepped aside, and Nate saw her sitting at a small table nearby wrapped in a blanket. She looked over at him and he held out his hand to her.

Freeing herself of the crowd of women surrounding her, she rushed over and knelt next to him. "You're going to be okay, Nate," she croaked. "Doc Rockwell says so…" She started coughing violently.

Nate tried to sit up.

"We've got her, sir. You just relax," a man said, as tears ran down Millie's soot-covered cheeks.

There was a commotion near the door and Ginny and Gert crowded into the small room. Ginny checked on Millie first, then sat on the side of the bed and looked at Nate. "Are you trying to drive me nuts?" she demanded, the fear in her eyes far more evident than her angry words.

Nate reached up and touched his fingers to her lips. "It's all over," he repeated.

But then from outside the room, which Nate had figured out was Gus's apartment behind the house, they heard voices raised. Nate saw Millie move closer to Ginny and realized one of the voices they were hearing was Roger's.

"On what charge?" he demanded. "The girl started the fire. Children playing with matches in secret. It happens all the time."

Before either Nate or Ginny could stop her, Millie was up and out the door.

Millie

-37-

Millie was still feeling weak and shaky, but when she heard Roger's voice, something in her shifted. She needed to confront him. She needed to stand up to this man who had probably killed her mother and tried to kill her. So, when Ginny reached out to stop her, Millie brushed her hand aside and ran toward that voice she had hated from that night he first hit Momma.

Roger was talking to a man in uniform—a man Millie recognized as Sheriff Wilson, who'd come to talk to her class one time. Mr. Stoner was standing a little behind Roger, looking like he'd really prefer to be somewhere else. She could smell the remains of the fire, but for the most part it seemed to be out. She was aware of the firemen putting away their ladders and hose. Her chest felt like it was full of cement and she wasn't sure she could stand up much longer, but mostly she was focused on Roger.

"Ah, here's the little pyromaniac now," he said, pointing at her. He pulled a cigar from his breast pocket, stuck it in his mouth and then seemed to search his pockets for his lighter.

"Your lighter's up there," Millie said, jerking her head toward the attic. She took pleasure in seeing Roger hesitate before removing the cigar from his mouth and tossing it away. She turned to the sheriff. "Once it's safe to go back in there, you'll find it," she assured him.

"She lies," Roger said with a laugh. "The little thief took it. If it's up there it's because she took it there and lit the fire."

Millie moved closer, so she was practically toe-to-toe with him. "I could have died in that fire," she reminded him. "You know what you did. You set the paper in those boxes on fire and then you just walked away and locked me in for good measure. Well, I didn't die, and now everybody is going to know that you not only tried to kill me, but you murdered my mother."

There was an audible gasp from those gathered near enough to hear.

Roger glanced around, then turned to Mr. Stoner. "Al, let's go."

The gathering of neighbors blocked his way, and Mr. Stoner moved a step closer to Millie. "You had that lighter on the train earlier today, Roger." He looked as if he was trying to figure out a puzzle or math problem. "You used it to light that guy's cigar in the lounge car." He looked at Millie. "The girl couldn't have had the lighter until…"

It was like the funny papers when a light bulb is inserted above a character's head. All of a sudden, Mr. Stoner put a protective arm around Millie's shoulders. "You tried to murder a child?" he asked softly.

"Shut up," Roger hissed.

The sheriff stepped between Roger and Millie. "Roger Fitzgerald, I'm arresting you on suspicion of murder, attempted murder and arson." He nodded to another man in uniform, who produced a set of handcuffs, and to Millie's amazement and joy clamped them on Roger's fat wrists. She saw Benny Helton duck his head and smile as the deputy led Roger away.

When Mr. Stoner squeezed her shoulder, Millie spun to face him. "Did you know?" she demanded. With Roger in handcuffs, she was feeling pretty powerful.

"Now you listen to me, young lady," Mr. Stoner began, as he took a step away, "I was simply doing my job. I work for your stepfather and…"

"That man is not my stepfather," Millie snarled, as Benny and others moved in to back her up. The image of the wolf pack closing in on the elk herd suddenly came to her mind, and for maybe the first time since she'd come to

Montana, she didn't feel as if she was the weakest member of the herd. "I want Momma's will," she said, her voice a feral growl.

Ginny stepped forward, wrapped her arm around Millie and faced Mr. Stoner. "You have a choice, sir. You can continue to defend your client, or you can do the right thing."

The deputy opened the door to a car and waited for Roger to get in. "Al, just remember who pays your bills," Roger shouted as the deputy slammed the door.

"Not anymore," Mr. Stoner murmured, and turned to Sheriff Wilson. "I'll give you my statement."

The sheriff nodded and indicated the lawyer should follow him.

Millie felt Ginny's arms tighten around her. "Your mother would be so proud of you," she whispered. "What a wonderful, courageous girl you are." She looked up at Benny. "Help us get Millie and Nate back to the house, okay?"

Gert made such a fuss over Nate once Benny half-carried him into the house that Millie saw him give Ginny a look that practically begged her to rescue him.

Ginny clapped her hands to gain attention and announced, "Okay, let's all go to our corners and get some rest."

"But..." Gert protested.

"Go," Ginny repeated, but she kissed her sister's cheek. "Thank you, Gert," she whispered. Then she squeezed Helen's hand and said quietly, "And what would we have done without you and Gus riding in like the cavalry with the sheriff?"

"She's a good kid," Gus muttered. Then he straightened and glanced toward the door. "I'd best check on Momma and Clara—they'll be wanting to know what happened and that everybody's okay."

"I'll come with you," Helen said.

It looked to Millie as if maybe Helen might be as sweet on Gus as he was on her.

"Come on, Gert," Helen added. "Gus's mother makes a really terrific cup of hot cocoa. It'll help you sleep."

After they left, it was just Nate and Ginny and Millie—Nate lying on the sofa, Ginny on an ottoman pulled up next to him. She patted the spot beside her, inviting Millie to join her. Millie had never wanted anything so much, but hesitated, figuring maybe she should give Nate and Ginny some time. So, Ginny held out her hand to her. "Look at us," she said softly. "We make one fine-looking family, don't we?"

Did Ginny truly mean it? Millie knew she did when Ginny stood and held out her arms to her. "You heard me, Millie. If you're willing, Nate and I…"

Millie didn't give her time to finish that thought. Instead, she collapsed into Ginny's outstretched arms as tears of relief and happiness ran down her cheeks. She wondered if Momma might be looking down from heaven and nodding her head, happy at last that she'd made sure Millie had a real family—a mother and a father and in time a little sister or brother.

"I'm going to make you both so proud," she promised, "and never ever give you a reason to be sorry you took me in."

Nate barked out a kind of coughing laugh. "I've no doubt you'll make us proud—you already have. As for that other part? You have a way of testing the limits of even a patient fella like me."

Millie grinned at him. "You're the one who taught me."

"What?" Ginny asked.

"Survival," Nate said, and as he reached out his hand to Millie, she knelt and rested her head on his shoulder.

"Thank you," she whispered and felt him stroke her hair away from her face.

Epilogue

January 1950, Chicago

When the call came, Millie, Jeremy and the children had just returned from church. Millie had gone upstairs to finish packing. Nate had suffered a heart attack and while everyone—including Nate—kept assuring her he was fine, she felt driven to see for herself.

Downstairs, the telephone rang and she half-listened as she continued packing. Jeremy's voice was low, and she only caught a word or phrase.

"I see."

"This afternoon."

"Day after tomorrow."

"Thanks."

She heard him replace the receiver in its cradle and then there was a pause before he slowly began to climb the stairs. Millie tightened her grip on the blouse she'd been folding and clutched it to her chest.

Please, no.

"Millie?" Jeremy crossed the room and placed his hands on her shoulders. "That was Gert."

"Nate's gone." She did not have to ask.

"I'm so sorry, babe." He turned her so that he could fold her fully into his embrace. They stood that way, rocking from side to side in a sort of macabre dance, their tears wetting each other's cheeks.

"Momma?"

Millie looked over Jeremy's shoulder at their six-year-old son, Nathan. He was frowning, trying to make sense of the scene before him. His sister, Lavinia—half his age—was sitting on the floor in the hall, playing with her doll.

Clearing her throat and swiping the tears away with the back of her hand, Millie stepped away from Jeremy and smiled at their son. "Daddy and I have decided we should all go to Gardiner," she said, with a sideways glance at Jeremy to be sure he agreed.

Jeremy nodded. "I'll go call for reservations." His voice was husky.

"On the train?" Nathan's frown turned to a hopeful smile.

"Well, we can hardly walk all that way," Millie said brightly.

"Come on, Vinnia," Nathan called, already running toward the steps that led to his room. "We've got to pack a suitcase. We're going to see Grandpa."

Lavinia got to her feet and toddled after him. "And Grandma too," she reminded him.

But while Nathan loved Ginny, he had formed a special bond with Nate. Millie watched the children go, dreading having to them tell them news that she knew would break their hearts. She picked up the doll Lavinia had left abandoned in the hall and went to lay out the children's clothes for the trip to Gardiner.

Jeremy managed to secure a sleeping compartment for the four of them. They'd decided they wouldn't tell the children about Nate until the train neared Gardiner, to give them the chance to enjoy the thrill of the journey before they heard the upsetting news.

"How are you doing?" Jeremy asked after they'd settled the children for the night and slipped out to the observation car for a nightcap.

"I'm numb. I can't believe it. A world without Nate?"

With his arm around her shoulders, Jeremy pulled her closer as she stared out into the blackness of the night. She closed her eyes, recalling their wedding day, when

Nate had walked her down the aisle. At the altar, he had hesitated and then leaned in and whispered, "Jeremy's a good man, Millie. You know I wouldn't give you over to just anybody?"

She'd stifled a laugh. Nate had been the one questioning Jeremy's intentions when he'd first started coming around the summer after the fire. He'd shown up for their first real date with a ragged bouquet of wildflowers he'd picked along the way. Ginny had taken the flowers to put them in water while Nate scowled at the poor young man.

"You'll have her back before ten," he'd instructed.

"Yes, sir." Jeremy had practically saluted and Millie couldn't help comparing this suddenly nervous teenager to the school boy who had delighted in tormenting her with punches to her arm and relentless teasing just a year or two before.

At their wedding, just before turning to place her hand in Jeremy's, Nate had whispered, "You can always come home—always remember that."

Home. Millie rolled the word around in her mind as she rested her head on Jeremy's shoulder. "Honey?"

"Hm-m?" He was half asleep. It had been a long day already, with more to come.

"Have you ever thought about us moving back to Gardiner?"

He didn't move, but Millie felt a stillness sweep through his body. "Sweetheart, this isn't the time to make big decisions," he said.

"I just want to know if you've ever missed it—the small-town life we both knew."

"Yeah," he admitted. "How about you?"

"Yeah," she agreed.

When the train pulled into the station the next morning, she saw Gert and Gus waiting on the platform. As always, Gert was dressed to the nines, all in black. Despite everything she had lost, she remained determined to present herself as a woman of style and means, at least in public. She had become an icon in Gardiner, working tirelessly to raise funds for the library, fire department and other pet projects. She might have little money of her own, but she refused to let that keep her from playing the benefactor. "I just have to find donors," she explained.

Millie, on the other hand, had come into a fortune. The amount Momma left her was massive and mostly unaffected by the Depression. She was barely old enough to babysit and knew she couldn't manage something so complex. So, she turned to Nate. To her surprise, he suggested Roger's lawyer, Al Stoner.

"But he worked for…"

"He made some poor choices when it came to clients, Millie. That doesn't make him a bad man. It's a small town in an area of small towns. Folks have to learn to forgive and work together."

"Survival?" Millie had asked.

"Exactly."

Money was put aside for her college education and for that of Ginny and Nate's daughter, Madeline. Then Millie had had an idea. What if she paid for Gert's three children to attend college as well? When all was said and done, they were family, too.

When Mr. Stoner told Gert what Millie wanted to do, she was speechless—for perhaps the first time in her life. Millie knew very well that Gert didn't much care for the fact that her sister—with a baby to tend to—had decided to take Millie in, but from the day she'd learned of that generous offer, Gert had gushed over Millie as if she were one of her own children.

"Gus! Gert!" Millie waved as she stepped off the train.

They hurried forward and Gus embraced her and then shook hands with Jeremy. "Oh, my darlings," Gert cooed. She bent to hug the children. Jeremy and Millie had broken the news to them earlier that morning. Nathan seemed to understand, but, of course, Lavinia was far too young.

"Did Grandma and Grandpa come with you?" Lavinia demanded, pulling away from Gert's embrace and looking around.

"No, darling. We'll see…" She faltered, and tears filled her eyes.

"Grandpa is dead," Nathan announced, looking up at Gus for confirmation.

Gus wrapped an arm around Nathan. "Come on, buddy. I need a big strong guy like you to help me load this luggage." He picked up the suitcases and groaned. "What did you do, bring the kitchen sink?"

Nathan giggled and Millie silently blessed Gus for diverting his attention.

Lavinia started to cry. "Is Grandma dead too?"

Jeremy picked her up and walked a little away from the rest of them, consoling her and assuring her she would see Ginny very soon.

"Is she staying in town with you?" Millie asked Gert.

"No. She and Maddie insisted on returning to the cabin. Nate was still working, you know, and they refused to leave that little place, though I could never understand it."

After Roger's arrest, the owners of the concessions in the park had not only given Nate back his job but had promoted him. He and Ginny had moved back to their beloved cabin. As a baby, Madeline had shared their room while Millie had the loft to herself, but once Millie left for college, Madeline moved to the loft.

"We'll go there then," Millie said.

"Oh, my dear," Gert protested, "there's not nearly enough room for all of you. Let the children stay with me."

Millie nodded, too exhausted to argue. She turned to Gus, who had finished loading the luggage. "How's Helen?"

Once married, Helen and Gus had opened an art gallery on Main Street that featured Helen's photography as well as the work of other local artists. They lived above the shop. Helen still had her studio in the garage of the old Douglass place, and rented the house to Gert and her children. Gus supplemented their income by doing odd jobs around town.

"She's fine—minding the gallery. She'll be at the funeral home later…" He did not finish the sentence. "Shall we go?"

It seemed to Millie as if everyone was struggling to believe Nate was really gone. She kept expecting to see him coming down the street, his steps measured and sure as always, his shoulders broad and ready to take on whatever might come, and his smile slow to blossom, but once it did…

"Millie?" Jeremy took her arm. "We should go."

She allowed him to lead her to the car. He held the door for her to climb into the back seat, then herded the children in with her. Lavinia climbed onto her lap while Nathan leaned his head against her shoulder and picked at an invisible thread on his jacket. Gert sat next to her, and Jeremy climbed in front next to Gus.

They drove through town, which still wore the remnants of Christmas decorations. When they turned the corner, Millie felt a sense of calm wash over her. The old Douglass house was a showplace, thanks to Nate and Gus and the repairs and renovations they'd made over the years. A ladder leaned against the side of the house and for a moment she imagined Benny Helton up there that summer after Gert moved in. She felt a tug at her heart as she remembered Benny. He had been among the first to volunteer when war was declared in the Pacific. And he had been the first from the entire state of Montana to die on the battlefield. She realized that the only time she'd ever been inside the funeral home was when she'd come back for Benny's memorial service.

She stared out the window, thinking how much everything had changed since that terrible night when Roger had finally snapped and tried to kill her. And yet, that was the night her life had changed forever. Over the subsequent years, Ginny had shared memories of her mother as a young woman—and stories about the father Millie had never met. Nate taught her to fish and track and ski, and he believed in her ability to achieve anything she set out to accomplish. In return, she'd figured out how to be a big sister to Madeline, and despite the fourteen-year difference in ages, the two of them were closer than ever. Millie felt a special connection to Madeline on this of all days—Nate had been her father too.

She leaned forward so that her face was close to Jeremy's shoulder. "Let's get the children settled and then I want to go directly to the park."

Gert made a sound that hinted at her objection, but Gus eyed her in the rearview mirror as he said, "I think that's a good plan, don't you agree, Gert?"

Gert pursed her lips but said nothing.

They piled out of the car and the children shrieked with delight when they saw Gert's daughter, Angela waiting for them. Of all Gert's children Angela had remained in Gardiner, taking over the diner after Thelma Orson died. She'd never married, and Millie's children adored her, calling her "Auntie Angie."

It struck Millie that children were perhaps the antidote to death. They were so full of joy and life, no matter the circumstances. Angela hugged Millie and Jeremy before leading Nathan and Lavinia up the front steps and back inside, with promises of hot cocoa and cookies in need of decorating.

Gus handed Jeremy the car keys. "We've got everything under control here. You take Millie to Ginny."

They didn't talk as they passed under the Roosevelt Arch and drove on into the park. Memories flooded Millie's mind as they traveled the road she had walked the day she ran away from Roger's house. The road had been cleared and widened, making travel at least as far as Mammoth easier.

That morning on the train, she and Jeremy had dressed in layers of warm clothing—both knowing Millie would want to go to the park. For her, that was where Nate's spirit could be found.

They reached the administration building, where now Park Supervisor Dan Atwood came out to meet them. "Millie, so very sorry for your loss," he said, as he hugged her.

"It's the loss of everyone who had the privilege to know him," she replied, returning his hug.

"I've got snowshoes for you both," Dan said, sniffing back his emotions. "Come on inside and warm up with a cup of tea before you head out."

They followed Dan into the office, where Roger had struck her the first time and Nate had retaliated—and been arrested.

So many memories.

"Still take your tea with milk, Millie?" Dan asked, a twinkle in his eye.

For the first time since learning of Nate's death, she felt a bubble of laughter rise and break into a genuine smile. "No. These days I take it straight."

The three of them sat in Dan's office warming their hands on the mugs and sipping the tea. Dan cleared his throat. "Nate was so proud of you, Millie. You know that, right?"

At college, she had majored in journalism and then become an investigative reporter for a Chicago paper. A series she'd written about soldiers coming home after the war had garnered her a Pulitzer. Nate and Ginny had traveled to Chicago to celebrate the achievement. It was the only time Nate had agreed to come to the city since she and Jeremy had moved there.

"And you as well," Dan said, turning to Jeremy. "Although you must know that when you started coming around Millie, he was not a happy man. I can't count the number of conversations we had in this office about you."

Jeremy blushed. "When I went to ask his permission to propose to Millie, he gave me such a long lecture. Who knew the man could string that many words together?"

The three of them chuckled and then fell silent until Millie stood, finished the rest of her tea and set the mug on Dan's desk. "I need to see Ginny."

The two men followed her outside, where Jeremy helped her strap on the snowshoes. "Maybe you should go on your own," he said. "I'll stick around here and follow in an hour, okay? Give you and Ginny some time?"

He was the dearest man. She cupped his cheeks in her mittened hands and kissed him. "Thank you," she whispered and set off.

This was not the first time she had retraced the steps Nate had followed that night he found her half-frozen in the hotel. She and Nate had made the journey dozens of times in all seasons over the years, and every time he teased her about how she had thought about running away from him that night.

She stood at the top of the rise, looking down at the cabin, with its hedge of lodgepole pine trees and the steamed windows of the greenhouse.

Home, she thought. *Nate, I've come home.*

Running in snowshoes was not possible, but she gave it her best shot. Ginny must have seen her coming because the door opened, and she was on the porch as Millie stumbled toward the cabin.

"Madeline," Ginny called. "Your sister's here."

Millie unfastened the snowshoes and waded through deep snow for the last few steps. "Jeremy will be here in a little while," she said, not knowing what to say to this dear woman whose loss was so much more than hers could ever be. "He'll get this path shoveled."

"Never mind," Ginny said, as she took hold of Millie's hand and pulled her inside. "Madeline," she called again.

Ginny looked older. She looked exhausted—and lost--her eyes darting around as if searching for something.

Or someone, Millie thought.

"We came as soon as we could," Millie said, watching from the corner of her eye as Madeline—now a young woman as beautiful as her mother--hurried down the loft steps. Millie was sitting in Nate's chair and wondered if that would upset Madeline, so she stood and opened her arms to her sister.

Madeline stepped into the embrace and they stood that way for a long moment, tears running down their cheeks and mingling as their faces touched.

"You look great," Millie said, at a loss for something to say. "I like your hair short like that."

Madeline's hand went to her hair. "Dad says...Dad said it makes me look even more like Mom."

"Heaven forbid," Ginny said, as she stood and headed for the kitchen. "Coffee?"

"I'm fine. Ranger Dan made tea."

Ginny returned to her chair and collapsed into it. "I can't believe it," she murmured, after an uncomfortable silence had settled over the room like a fog.

"I know," Millie murmured.

Then Ginny was on her feet again. "Maddie, get your coat and hat. Your father would not want us to sit around here boo-hooing. We need to be outside—Nate would want that."

Millie had to agree.

The three of them bundled into coats and hats and scarves and mittens—as they had so many times during those long winters they'd lived in the cabin. Outside, they stood facing the sunset, their arms around each other. A light snow fell, the fat flakes sticking to the hair that stuck out from their wool caps. They glanced at each other and then in unison stuck their tongues out to catch the flakes.

Nate had done that. No matter how many times the snows fell, he would insist they go outside and catch those flakes. "It's about living," he would say when Madeline or Millie protested it was far too cold. "You should never pass up a chance to taste a bit of life."

That's the way Nate was, always teaching them something through little moments like this--lessons you'd never learn sitting in a classroom or staying inside a warm cabin on a cold winter's night. A day hadn't passed that Millie hadn't thought of how different her life might have been had Nate not found her and decided to take her home that night.

Madeline started to giggle, and Ginny and Millie joined in. Soon their laughter echoed off the trees and hills around them.

"Hey!" Someone was shouting at them. They turned as one to the sound and saw Jeremy standing at the top of the rise. "Everything okay?" he shouted.

Ginny tightened her hold on her two girls. "It will be," she said softly.

Survival, Millie thought she heard the wind whisper as it moved through the trees.

BOOK CLUB DISCUSSION GUIDE

1. The title—THE WINTERKEEPER—would indicate it is Nate's story, but is it?

2. Millie makes some brave—some would say foolish—choices. What in her background makes her act the way she does?

3. What lessons might pre-teens reading this story take from it?

4. Nate is facing his own life-changing moment when he finds Millie and jeopardizes his future—and Ginny's—by not telling. How do his decisions regarding Millie drive the story?

5. Ginny is being pulled in several directions at once—her loyalty to Nate, her sister and her friendship with Millie's mother—not to mention her responsibility for the baby she's carrying—being tested. How do you think she does juggling these different demands?

6. It is 1933 and the Depression has gone on now for three long years. What role does the time and political environment play in the story to limit the choices each character has?

7. If this story were set in current times, how might that change what happens to each of the main characters?

AUTHOR'S NOTE: Yellowstne winterkeepers were hired by individual park concessionaires, not the park service (since it wasn't created until 1916). They were hired primarily to shovel snow from the roofs of hotels and stores and keep an eye on the concessionaire properties inside the park. There is documentation of winterkeepers hired by concessionaires as early as 1880. In his book, *Snowshoes, Coaches, and Cross Country Skis: A Brief History of Yellowstone Winters*, author Jeff Henry talks of an 1887 winter expedition of 13 men who explored Yellowstone by cross country skis, and took shelter with several different winter keepers at Norris and Old Faithful. James Roake, winterkeeper at Old Faithful in 1887 lived there with his wife and 4 children (ages 4-14). Most of the park was linked via telephone in 1887, so winterkeepers were able to keep in communication with one another and could get in touch with people outside of the park in emergency. Several of them were married and lived with their families inside the park.

I hope you enjoyed THE WINTERKEEPER and that you will be in touch by going to my website at www.booksbyanna.com to let me know.

Other Books by Anna Schmidt:

- *Cowboys and Harvey Girls series*
- *Last Chance Cowboys series*
- *Peacemaker series*
- *Women of Pinecraft series*

Visit Anna:
- *www.booksbyanna.com*
- *@annaschmidt70 (Twitter)*
- *On GoodReads*

Leave a review at:
https://amzn.to/2HCzbQF

Made in the USA
Columbia, SC
08 March 2020